Praise for *Purgatory Road*

"Parker, unlike lesser suspense writers, succeeds in making the reader feel the tragedy."

—Publishers Weekly, starred review

"Parker's dark debut thriller will grip suspense aficionados from the first page."

—Library Journal, starred review

"Seamlessly melds elements of thriller, suspense, and the supernatural to create a scorcher."

—Killer Nashville

"This is a skillfully written, gripping thriller, well supported by the author's fine eye for setting and ear for dialogue."

—Booklist

"Not for the faint of heart, *Purgatory Road* is a compelling story that suspense fans are sure to love."

—BookPage

COLDWATER

Also by Samuel Parker

Purgatory Road

COLD WATER

SAMUEL PARKER

Revell

a division of Baker Publishing Group
Grand Rapids, Michigan

© 2018 by Samuel Parker

Published by Revell
a division of Baker Publishing Group
P.O. Box 6287, Grand Rapids, MI 49516-6287
www.revellbooks.com

Printed in the United States of America

Library of Congress Cataloging-in-Publication Data
Names: Parker, Samuel, 1974– author.
Title: Coldwater / Samuel Parker.
Description: Grand Rapids, MI : Revell, a division of Baker Publishing Group,
    [2018]
Identifiers: LCCN 2017038473| ISBN 9780800727345 (softcover) | ISBN
    9780800734800 (print on demand)
Subjects: LCSH: City and town life—Fiction. | Ex-convicts—Fiction. | Revenge—
    Fiction. | GSAFD: Suspense fiction. | Christian fiction.
Classification: LCC PS3616.A7464 C65 2018 | DDC 813/.6—dc23
LC record available at https://lccn.loc.gov/2017038473

18 19 20 21 22 23 24   7 6 5 4 3 2 1

For Kris and Kim,
this story is not about us.
And as always, for my wife, Elizabeth,
who makes this all possible.

Midway upon the journey of our life
   I found myself within a forest dark,
   For the straightforward pathway had been lost.

Ah me! how hard a thing it is to say
   What was this forest savage, rough, and stern,
   Which in the very thought renews the fear.
                              —Dante, *Inferno*

ONE

THE DAY WAS BORN IN DARKNESS.

Michael opened his eyes and saw nothing.

Blackness.

The motes in his eyes drifted across the void.

His mouth was sealed with what felt like tape. Michael tried to lift himself and felt the hard knock of wood against his forehead. A light sprinkle of sand fell on his face, but he was blind to its source, he could only feel it as it dusted his lashes, scratching at his pupils. He raised his head slowly again until he felt the board press against his skin. He lay back down. His shoulders ached, his back. He tried to move his hands up to his eyes to rub the grit out of them but found they were bound together. He started breathing faster, nostrils flaring in the dark.

He was as a newborn cast out into the vacuum of space.

He could feel his heart beat faster as his mind raced to keep up with this discovery of himself. Michael could feel his nerves begin to fire in all his limbs as electric panic coursed through his body. He lifted his head again and hit the boards, a few inches above him.

And again.

Banging his head against the darkness with the dirt washing his face.

He tugged at his arms. They were bound at the wrist and the tape dug into him with each movement. His feet were fastened together at the ankles as he tried to kick at the darkness. His knees found the roof of his coffin and sent a spark of pain up his thighs. The motion caused more dirt to fall into his open eyes. They felt thoroughly encrusted with grime.

Michael tried to force breath out of his mouth, but the tape's seal held. His nostrils felt too small to supply the air he needed as he kicked around in his confined cell. Sweat started to form on his body as he lurched back and forth.

Suddenly, he stilled. His mind slowly calming, moving from the rapid chaos of panic to the quiet, disembodied trance of a hopeless man.

Breathe, he thought.

Just breathe.

The sound of his lungs echoed in his head as he worked to slow himself down, his breathing easing to long, deliberate exhales. He closed his eyes to shut out the blackness and felt the sand in his eyelids grind his corneas with fire.

Just breathe.

Michael could feel his pulse dissipate from the thunderous bass drum to a softer beat. His mind began to clear and assess his situation. Flailing around was not an option. If he wanted it all to end, as he had wished many times, then he could just go on doing what he was doing until the air ran out or the sand from above buried him in an hourglass of his own making. But his thoughts focused on hope, as illogical as it was to do so, and he willed his body to soften, to cooperate with his mind.

He focused on his hands. One by one he touched fingertip to fingertip, thumb to thumb, index to index, until he was assured they were all there. They were. For some reason this brought him a sense of comfort.

He tried to bring his hands to his face and failed several times. The box wouldn't allow him to move his elbows from his sides, and when he kept them tucked in, his hands would press against the ceiling before he could bring them up to his chest.

Breathe.

Slowly and methodically, he started to rotate his wrists back and forth, attempting to loosen the binding. It felt like duct tape. It was impossible for him to guess how many times it might have been wrapped around his wrists. He concentrated on his breathing and the rhythmic turns of his hands.

Inhale, twist. Exhale, twist.

The hairs on his arms pulled with each turn until Michael was assured that none were left. He told himself he had all the time in the world, or at the least, all the time he had left, to get his hands free.

He kept twisting his wrists until the skin burned. In the dark, he felt as if it had rubbed down to the bone. The dirt sifting from above him got under the tape, and though it worked as an antidote to the adhesive, it also added to the grinding down of flesh he felt with each twist.

Eventually he loosened the tape enough to turn his hands and grab onto each wrist. The tape had rolled in spots, and he could feel the stickiness of it mixed with warm fluid. It felt like raw skin and blood. In this position, and keeping his elbows in, he was able to force his hands up to his face, where he instantly grabbed the strip across his mouth and pulled it free.

Like a skin diver resurfacing from a deep descent, Michael gulped in the stale, moldy air around him. The dirty and confined area flooded his senses, but he did not care at the moment. With his mouth free, he bit into the binding at his wrists, yanking and pulling with his teeth at tape and skin. His hands came free with ripping fire and he screamed.

Now unbound, Michael was able to feel around his confinement. He was, as he had figured, in a box. He could feel the rough-hewn pine all around him. The cheapness of the wood and the fact that it was still holding up meant that he was not buried too deep. He assumed that too much earth would have come crashing in already. True or not, it added weight to a sliver of hope.

Michael had never been buried alive, but his mind offered up the blueprint of escape as if it had been programmed with the script for survival. Up. Up was the way to freedom. Scratch, claw upward. He had to get to the surface quickly—that or he would suffocate or be crushed before he knew it.

In the dark, he beat against the boards until his hands shot white-hot pains up his forearms. The dirt dropped onto his face as one of the boards cracked, filling his mouth and absorbing the air from his lungs. He spewed out the earth as he beat and dug and scraped upward.

The ground came down heavy around him, threatening to replace the wooden coffin with an earthen one. His fingers gripped the soil and pulled.

He was a rhythmic engine of adrenaline, pushing up against the world, and then shoving the incoming dirt down to the end of the box. Over and over again until the lid started to give more and more.

As the dirt flowed in, Michael worked to push it to the corners of the box. It was damp and clumpy but not tightly packed, two things incredibly in his favor. He worked furiously, his muscles screaming. His pulse pounding in his ears, stifled by the packed ground.

Then he felt it. His hand punched through to the cool air of the living world. With one last colossal effort, he got his feet under him and drove up through the loosening soil, breaking out to his waist into the majestic air of night.

Michael pulled himself out of the grave.

His whole body screamed for oxygen and the open air embraced his constricted muscles. He lay on the ground and looked skyward, but his scratched and swollen eyes were packed in a gritty embalmer's salve, obscuring his vision into a watery blur. His breath formed small wisps of vapor in the dark and then dissipated.

He was in a forest. He dragged himself away from the entrance of his tomb and braced himself against a tree. This was the closest to death that he had ever been, but he knew it would not end here. They would not let this rest. They would never let it rest until he was buried for good.

TWO

WHEN HE STAGGERED TO HIS FEET after freeing his legs, the smell of earth and mold permeated his senses, the chill of early autumn passing through him like a phantom breeze. The moon was out tonight, and it illuminated the woods with a menace, a black-and-white world on the verge of preparing to sleep through the upcoming winter, itself to be buried by the cold indifference of Mother Nature.

His eyes burned with the scratched rubbing of his lids still caked with dirt as he peered into the darkness. It was impossible to get his bearings. A blind man in a maze. All he could smell was the grave. But he listened to the quiet of the woods. Faintly he could hear running water in the distance. He took a step toward the sound, using the tree as a crutch and holding out one arm to break a fall that was all but assured. The noise of his steps masked the water.

Step.

Quiet.

Listen.

Repeat.

His body was wrecked. The men who had jumped him had pushed chemicals into his cells and then tenderized the muscles. He could feel his clothing rub against the bruises on his chest and back with each movement. His legs throbbed as if the sinews were wrapped too tightly around the bone. His hands were numb from the tape that had cut off his circulation. One finger felt dislocated, an issue that, with a tug and a shriek of agony, he quickly remedied.

Each step was a torturous effort, a willing of the mind to force the body forward.

Step.

Quiet.

Listen.

Repeat.

Soon the consistent sound of the river guided his steps, and he made his way forward with arms outstretched, knocking branches out of his way, stumbling on exposed roots that lay hidden underfoot. Michael blindly felt the ground slope toward the water but soon lost all sense of balance and fell. He rolled down the embankment, adding bruises to his already beaten body, until he came to rest on the rocks next to the river. He got to his hands and knees and crawled to the water.

His throat was bone-dry and the cool water shocked his system. The burning thirst overcame the repugnant smell of the river, and after a few gulps, he took a deep breath and plunged his face into the depths.

The coldness of the creek stung his senses, but he held himself under, flushing the earth from his eyes. The sensation of no pain in his sockets brought him back to the surface and he collapsed.

With his blurred vision slightly improved, his head resting on stone and sand, Michael peered out across the river, the moonlight slashing a gouge in the black water.

A puzzle piece locked into place in his brain, a sense of reassurance that he was closer to knowing where on earth he was. There was only one major river near Coldwater, a river named after the town—or vice versa—and Michael knew this must be it. From what he could tell, however, it was a portion that he was not familiar with.

He hadn't ventured out to the river much in his life anyway, but he knew enough to get some sense of direction. He was on the northern bank, judging from the slow current. The river cut against the upper part of the county and eventually made its way down south through South Falls, a good sixty miles away by road. Upriver, its source was hidden in the reptilian ridges of the north woods. He knew of several crossings, all of which would keep him away from Coldwater, but he wasn't quite sure which one he would come to first. Upriver would be the right course to take. He knew that, and it settled in his mind as the only correct option.

But for now, exhaustion was getting the best of him.

He crawled back to the embankment and found a hollow that fit his body decently enough. The night was cool but not frigid, and as he closed his eyes and listened to the flow of the river, he slept the sleep of a dead man, a dead man resurrected to a dark night.

THREE

THE TWO MEN DROVE OUT from Coldwater that morning in silence, like the quiet of two men going to work, content to allow each other to wake up and process the day without the aggravation of conversation. The truck motored north up the county road several miles and then headed east on gravel, and the gravel turned to dirt, and the dirt slowly gave way to a two-track heading into the woods. A developer had attempted to plot out a subdivision in the area but gave up when the market told him that city folks didn't want to live this far in the sticks.

Coldwater was sixty miles from the nearest "metropolis." City, really. Sixty miles from where a family could buy groceries was the more proper way to say it.

The old Ford pushed on through the woods until the two-track finally gave up its ghost and terminated in a large clearing. The truck came to a stop. The passenger, who was half slumped in the seat, spoke first.

"Go on, Kyle, check it out so we can get out of here."

"Why me?"

"Well, I sure ain't going to do it!"

"Why don't we both go?"

"Come on. You know I got this bum leg in the mornings. Just walk up there, check it out, and we can head back."

Kyle hesitated, staring into the woods. A tremor of fear slowly crept into his face as he white-knuckled the steering wheel.

"Here, take this," James said, handing over a long hunting knife.

"What good is that going to do?"

"You serious? He's tied up . . . underground. How much more protection you need?"

Kyle stepped out of the truck, forcing his body to move as his nerves were getting the best of him. He almost tripped over one of the ruts in the mud made by the vehicles the night before. They were all over the clearing. He was braver last night, when there were so many of them, but now, on his own, his courage was long gone.

He stood by the truck.

"Get going!" James yelled from the cab. "You're the one that wanted to come here. Now go check it out."

"Now that we're here . . . I don't know."

"Just do it! Otherwise you'll be bugging me all day to drive back out here. Go check it out, see that he's still buried, so we can go home."

"This is stupid."

"It is stupid, but you ain't going to leave me alone until you see it with your own eyes."

Kyle wiped a sweaty hand on his jeans. "I didn't sleep at all last night."

"I knew Haywood never should have let you come along."

"What does that mean?"

"It means exactly what I said. You were all gung ho yes-

18

terday, but now you're giving me an anxiety attack. Don't make me get out of this truck and drag you up there. 'Cause when you see he's still underground, I'll be mad at you for wasting my time."

"Okay, okay . . . calm down."

"Just go already."

Kyle closed the truck door and walked up the trail into the woods. About a quarter mile up, he saw the small clearing in the trees, saw the disturbed dirt. He inched his way closer, slowly. The site scared him. He was startled by sounds coming from every side of him. The birds, the insects, the sound of the swaying trees in the light wind. He approached the clearing.

He saw the spot where they had buried Michael. Saw the earth pushed aside and sunk down into the crater, saw the drag marks from the hole and the footprints that led off deeper into the woods. In one quick second, his mind had processed the whole scene. His nightmare had come true, his guilt had been telling him all night that his fear was real.

Kyle turned and ran as if his life depended on it. He would have screamed, but his voice was lost, lost in the chaos. He could see the truck through the leaves. He ran, harder and harder, until he made the clearing. Jumping in the truck, he slammed it into drive, spun around, and floored it back to the county road. James was almost ejected from his seat.

"What are you doing?" James shouted.

Kyle was mute. His face was drained of color and he was shaking uncontrollably.

"Kyle . . . Kyle!"

Kyle looked over at James. And with a ragged breath said, "He got out!"

FOUR

MICHAEL HAD BEEN AWAKENED by the sound of a truck pulling into the woods, its exhaust system ruined years before. It belched smoke as it pulled in close to his location and stopped. He had heard the door of the truck open and shut and then saw movement through the trees. The man stalked the woods with the jittery movements of a spooked rabbit.

Michael was too far from his burial site to get a good look at the man who had walked into the clearing, but not too far to sense the ominous feeling the man brought with him. He watched as the figure had walked up to the clearing, saw the empty grave, turned tail and ran.

He heard the truck fire up and speed out of the woods, the dying, choking cough of its engine disappearing quickly as the forest returned to its unmolested state of quietness.

The mysterious stranger must have been part of the group that brought him out here yesterday. Judging by the man's skittish behavior, Michael knew it wasn't their leader. The panic with which the man ran from the site when he realized Michael was no longer buried proved that he must have been one of Haywood's weaker minions.

Michael arose from his secluded spot on the riverbank,

walked up the slope to the clearing, and looked down at the hole in the ground.

He had come so close to dying. Closer than he ever had before.

Yes, this was the closest he had come. By no right should he be standing now over his grave.

The man had come out to check the status of their previous night's work. It would be naive to believe that the men who had done this to him would rest on their laurels and leave him to nature. They would be back, most definitely now that they would know he was no longer buried in the earth.

Michael looked down the path that led to where the truck had been parked. He slowly made his way toward the parking area, taking his time and readying himself to run back if another vehicle materialized. One never did.

He walked into the opening and let the morning light hit his skin. Its warming effects energized him and brought his attention to the soreness of his face. Looking around, he saw ruts crisscrossed in the mud in every direction. It would have taken an expert tracker to figure out how many vehicles had made so many tracks, but it appeared as if the entire community of Coldwater had ventured out to witness his burial. An entire community complicit in the deed.

He turned and walked back into the forest, back toward the river.

The man who had ventured out here would head down to Coldwater and come back with the others. Others with more fortitude.

They would search the woods for him.

They would not stop until they found him. Michael knew this instinctively. Men who would go to such lengths to bury a man so far from civilization would go to great lengths to make sure he stayed there.

Back at the relative safety of the riverbank, Michael weighed his options. Downstream was the easier path but most likely led to people, and people . . . well, he had no use for them anymore. He'd be running back into the embrace of murderers. Upstream would take him toward the north woods. With the cold fall air drifting in day by day, he wasn't sure what would await him in that direction, but it would give him time to figure out where he was, and the downstream current supplied a quick escape route, should he run into anyone.

Michael waded in up to his waist and started trudging upstream. The dogs, because they most assuredly would bring dogs, would have trouble following him if he used the river. The water was bitter cold, but he braved it as he walked, the sun on his shoulders, and ice on his legs, and the water flowing about him as if he were a minor inconvenience on its journey to the south.

FIVE

KYLE DROVE THE TRUCK into Coldwater with the same reckless abandon as he did in leaving the woods. The silence he and James shared on the way out to the grave site was repeated on the way back to town as he thought through the ramifications of their discovery. In his mind he traced the level of his own complicity in the actions from the night before, his conscience ebbing and flowing between responsibility and absolution.

"We have to tell Haywood," James said with a low growl. His eyes were fixed forward in deep concentration. On good days, his voice was like a bag of gravel. Now it sounded like a rock tumbler.

"Of course we do," Kyle said. "I mean, it's his show after all."

"Sure is."

"He's the one who dragged us all out there, right? I mean, it was all him!"

"Now just hold on. Don't get that idea in your head. And definitely don't say that in front of Haywood. He'd move to bury you out there next."

"I knew we shouldn't have gone out there last night. Should have just stayed home."

"Too late now," James said.

"What do you mean?"

"Too late. You are part of this. Me too." James looked out the window onto the quiet main street of Coldwater. "We're all part of it."

Kyle turned east at the sole stoplight, drove one block, which was the width of the town, and pulled up to Haywood's residence.

It was a two-story Victorian with a wraparound porch, better suited for a country house than one just off Main Street, but the house had stood well before the single stoplight was installed and a handful of people decided to stay put and set down roots. As the truck came in the driveway and parked, Haywood stepped out of the front door and stood on the porch, the screen door flapping behind him. Kyle and James approached the house, anxiety dripping off them like sweat.

"What's going on, boys?"

"We got a problem," Kyle said.

"What kind of problem?"

"Well, you see, me and James went up to the . . . I mean . . . we drove up where we all, you know—"

"We drove up to Springer's Grove," James interjected, "because Kyle here was driving me nuts with his paranoid delusions. I drove up with him so he could see that Michael was still buried. Bad news . . ."

"Go on."

"He got out," James said.

"What do you mean, he got out?"

Kyle found his words again. "Just that. I walked up the trail and the . . . the . . . grave . . . was dug up."

"Dug up?"

"Well, not so much dug up, but dug out. He dug himself out. I don't know how."

"You see him?"

"No."

Haywood wiped his forehead and looked at Kyle and James. The man's penetrating stare piercing through them, his mind someplace else, processing the news and creating a game plan.

"Alright," Haywood said. "It's better than not knowing he's loose."

Kyle could feel the tension release from his neck, like the times when he was a child and his father's punishment for a stupid deed was unexpectedly lenient.

"I want you two to go and gather up the others," Haywood said. "Let's meet up at Springer's in an hour. I'll get Murphy and his dog. Michael couldn't have got very far."

"Sure thing," James said.

"I-I think I've d-done . . . ," Kyle stammered. "I mean, I have some things I have to do with Tami today . . ."

"Get in the truck, Kyle." James grabbed his companion's arm and spun him back to the vehicle.

The two of them got in the cab and Kyle drove out of Haywood's driveway much slower than when he had arrived. He pulled away reluctantly, becoming less eager to be a part of this situation with each passing minute.

In the rearview mirror he could see Haywood staring after them until he made the turn at the stoplight. This was not the morning he had planned, but he had known—deep down inside he had known—that the events of the night before would haunt him. He just wasn't expecting the ghosts to come calling so soon.

SIX

THE MEN WHO HAD DONE THIS to Michael had taken extra precautions and had planned out a method of execution with the utmost attention.

Michael stopped into Gilly's Pub twice a week. The pub was as old as the town and had taken up roots on the corner that housed the stoplight. The entrance to Gilly's was through a glass door, down a long dark hallway adorned with cheap beer mirrors. In the back, the hallway exited to a large room with a wooden bar on one side. Several tables and booths filled the space. There was a small doorway that led to a semi-private room where the more uppity townsfolk held court.

The night before, Michael had walked down the dark hallway and stood at the end of the bar. He would order the same thing each time—a whiskey sour, just one—and drink it quickly before heading back down the hallway and out into the street. This he did in an effort to establish a sense of normalcy, a way to connect, to be part of the American fabric, to do what all men do. The drink took a long time to discover. He had not acquired the taste for alcohol when all men do, when they sneak it out of their dad's cabinet before

SAMUEL PARKER

heading off to the high school football game. He had missed that part of life.

The bartender would see Michael and nod, prep the drink, and carry it over. Never a word spoken between them once the formula was right.

This night, however, the drink was ready for him. Rather than being suspicious, Michael had taken it as a gesture of intimacy. He leaned against the bar and drank the mixture in a long, smooth motion. The warmth coated his throat and instantly filtered into his head. The taste was mildly off, but all too often that could be attributed to the pub's ancient soda guns and the fact that they mostly spit out flat streams. He finished the drink and pushed away from the bar.

The wall in front of him went in and out of focus before settling back to normal. His legs felt heavy and his arms loose, as if all the blood was pooling in his feet, leaving his upper half hollowed out and empty. Michael swooned and looked at the bartender, whose back was to him. He was playing at cleaning some glassware, but Michael knew that he was deliberately being shunned. His eyes went to the back of the pub, to the doorway of the private room, and he saw Haywood standing with several men behind him.

"What did you do?" Michael asked, his words slurring together, his mouth and tongue no longer working together but each trying to manipulate sound in its own unique fashion. An energy inside him began to course with rage, and then, just as quickly, evaporated, the drug he had ingested putting the inner demon to sleep.

Haywood just stood there, coming in and out of focus, his arms crossed.

Michael turned toward the front door. The darkness was

creeping in and the long hallway to the outside world was twisting and turning before him like an expanding kaleidoscope of demented shapes. He tried to move his foot. It felt like a brick as it slid across the floor. The tunnel before him extended to black singularity and the world vanished.

Michael didn't feel the floor come up to meet his face when he fell.

He didn't feel the blows of Haywood and his men as they pounced on his body.

He didn't feel a thing.

Until he had awoken in the ground.

■ ■ ■

Stories, the good ones that people remember, are a string of coincidences tied together until the improbable becomes true. How else could Achilles die from getting shot in the heel, or Chaucer happen to fall in with a crowd of interesting people? It is the unusual, not the ordinary, that gets retold. Ordinary is forgotten, dismissed, unnoticed. Ordinary is out of sight, out of mind. Michael was not ordinary.

His childhood, his move back to Coldwater, all of it was illuminated like a marquee for all to see. The tale was so horrifyingly different from what the people of the town experienced in their own humdrum lives. It's why he caught people's gazes when he walked into town, his face hidden under the hood of his ratty coat, hands tucked into the pockets.

They noticed.

They always noticed. If Coldwater had been a large city, wives would have clung tighter to their husband's arms and mothers would have scooped up their children when he passed. But Coldwater was small, and its townspeople drove past him on the road, their windows rolled up, their scowls showing behind glass.

He was a leper in their minds, devoid of the disease.

It was no surprise really that they had come for him. It was no surprise that the town wanted him dead, gone, erased from sight. What surprised him was that it had taken them so long. The fear-riddled population had actually summoned up the courage to act rather than continue to hide behind whispers and stares.

When he had moved back to the property that he grew up on after being away for so many years, he knew he was not welcome. Haywood, the town's sole backbone, had point-blank told him so. But there was no place left for Michael to go. He had cast his future aside so callously that when the state's prison system had released him, there was nothing to do but go back to Coldwater, to the house that he left when he was just a kid, abandoned and forgotten.

Though he had given the state his youth as they had demanded, the town would not be content that justice had been served. His younger years now gone, the town, and especially Haywood, made it known that his older years should have been forfeit too.

And so they scowled at him, insulted at his audacity to populate the same patch of earth they called home.

The outcast.

The scourge of Coldwater.

To the residents of the town, Michael was a constant reminder that evil was real and lurking in the dark.

It made no difference that he was now an adult, a man whose childhood self was such a distant shadow as to be but a wisp of breath on the river behind him. He would be forever damned. Damned by his past actions and damned by the unforgiving memory of the town that sang hymns on Sunday and sharpened their knives on Monday.

It was justice for him to be here at this time. Justice without mercy, for he knew better than anyone that mercy was earned, never given, and no act of contrition would ever pay the fee required.

Michael continued trudging upstream, the current of the world pushing him down and away like the water that flowed against him.

SEVEN

THE MEN GATHERED at the clearing at Springer's Grove with less enthusiasm than the previous night. They were ordinary men now, not vigilantes, not a gang of desperadoes. They were simply men, men who hardly would have been thought capable of such a brutal act as drugging a man in a bar, dragging him out to the wilderness, and piling the earth on top of him.

There were six of them, paired together by fate since elementary school seating assignments.

James and Kyle.

Frank and Earl.

Clinton and Davis.

Several of them moved slowly, their bodies bearing the same bruises they had inflicted on Michael. If any of them had compared scars and stories, they would have realized that each mark on their body corresponded to the location and severity of the punches they had landed on their victim the night before. Frank stepped out of his truck, sporting a black eye and squinting as if the sunshine was driving a migraine through his skull. Davis moved as if his ribs hurt.

The men now stood silently and gave questioning looks to each other. They knew Michael was out of the grave, but none of them walked up the trail to see the site for themselves. Instead they waited for Haywood's arrival and kept their own counsel.

Haywood's car pulled into the clearing, and he stepped out confidently, animating the men out of their dull congregation. Behind him, Murphy arrived in an old Dodge with his even older dog, Clyde, in the passenger seat.

"So you've all heard, I'm sure," Haywood said.

The men nodded.

Haywood walked past them and on down the trail. The group followed his lead, and when they all got to the open pit, they formed a circle around it and waited for Haywood to speak.

"As you can see, gentlemen, we have ourselves a situation. Now, some of you may start questioning what it was we did last night, whether it was right or wrong. Whether we sinned and are now reaping what we have sown. I'm going to ask you all to put away those thoughts. You can have those thoughts when you are tucked away in your beds at night. You can have those thoughts when you are old and gray. But for now, I need you all clearheaded and with me. You hear what I'm saying?"

With slight movements and inarticulate grunts, the men consented.

"Alright. Now, obviously we aren't experienced killers. If we were, we wouldn't be here right now. We'd be getting back to normal life and Michael would be yesterday's business. But we aren't. No one here is to blame. No one."

Haywood looked around the circle, making sure everyone understood him. The last thing he needed was for these guys to break and start slinging blame on him. He knew they would eventually, when the guilt of murder crept up on them, but today he needed them. After inspecting each of the men's faces, he continued.

"We have no idea how long he's been out. Spread out and start looking for anything. Anything at all that might point us in the right direction."

The men divided up into their respective pairs and spread out into the woods. Kyle and James pointed themselves toward the clearing where the trucks were parked and gave mild effort in looking as if they were searching for clues. Frank and Earl headed south for the river. Haywood was with Murphy, who had his dog on the leash before him. The dog was as old and obese as Murphy, and even if the dog was able to pick up a scent, which Haywood doubted it was still capable of doing, it was unlikely the animal would last more than a hundred yards on a slow trot before it would be forced to lie down and take a nap to recover. Clinton and Davis, walking west, mumbled to each other about this and that.

■ ■ ■

"You scared, Frank?"

"Aren't you?"

"Uh-huh," Earl said. "You think he's close by?"

"No. And if he was, he'd hear you coming a mile away."

Earl was making a point to step on every twig and leaf he could find as the two came up to the bank of the river.

"Last thing I want to do is sneak up on him," Earl said.

"I hear you."

■ ■ ■

"You okay, Murph?" Haywood asked.

"Yeah, just old," Murphy said, the sweat already pouring down his withered dome.

"You think Clyde is picking up anything?"

"Hard to tell. I'm not sure if he can much smell anything anymore."

"Yeah, well, he's still better than us, I'm sure."

The mutt looked up at its owner with the sad eyes of a dog yearning to go back home to its couch where it could sleep the rest of the day.

"Even if he picks up a trail, I'm not sure what happens next," Murphy said.

"What do you mean?"

"I mean, what are you going to do when you find him? When you find Michael?"

"Just worry about the dog, Murph," Haywood said.

"Alright."

EIGHT

MICHAEL WAS TEN YEARS OLD *when he realized that the world wanted him dead and gone. He had not yet grown enough to fit in the courthouse chair that he was forced to sit in during his trial, and he had not grown enough to fit the judgment that was passed down on him, but it was voiced by both the judge and the newspapers that he would never grow out of being the monster they thought he was. At ten years of age, the world had already measured his full potential and concluded that there was absolutely no hope that the boy from Coldwater would ever contribute to a just and civil society.*

He was led out of the courthouse, loaded in a van, and taken downstate to one of the supermax penitentiaries. When Michael arrived, the warden had no idea what to do with him. The man was used to dealing with the worst psychopaths in the state who were dropped off at his door, but looking down on a young boy who was scared out of his mind left him baffled.

How was he going to keep this kid safe from a zoo of predators and killers, a kid who himself was, as the reporters described him, a killer?

Michael was led by a large guard down the detention block

to a door near the guard station. The thin window over the lock was too high for Michael to peer through, but soon the door was opened and Michael saw into the cell. There was a bed, a metal toilet, and a desk. The guard ushered him in, and Michael walked in and sat on the bed.

"This is your place. Guards are just over there. Anybody mess with you, just start yelling."

"Okay."

"Okay," the guard said, as he reluctantly turned and walked toward the cell door, seemingly unsure if he was doing the right thing by leaving a kid in here. The guard had kids at home Michael's age, and he couldn't help imagining their own little selves locked in this cell. But he did his duty, stepped out, and locked the door.

The catcalls started almost immediately. The sycophants and lunatics, the pedophiles and terminally incarcerated, yelling obscenities, threats, and promises at the child behind cell door number 20. Their voices bled through the walls, calling for Michael, offering friendship of a kind that was anything but.

He pulled his feet up onto the bed and curled up in the corner like a baby snuggling against its mother. He put the pillow over his head and began to cry silently, afraid that if he wailed, the voices would hear him and come in even larger numbers.

And he wondered if the world was right in wanting him gone.

All he ever wanted was to be noticed. To be valued. And in this cell he realized that he had gotten what he wanted in the worst twisted and vile way. He was now the center of attention to an army of the deranged.

NINE

JACKSON'S PARTY STORE was located on Townline Road, just south of the river, surrounded by forest and not much else. Outsiders would think it an unusual spot for a business. But to the locals, it was a vital resource for their beer and lottery tickets. Michael had followed the river northeast for several hours until he started to recognize the surroundings and knew he was close to the store. Despite running for his life, he felt his stomach growl with hunger pains that soon started to consume him more than the discomfort of the bruises on his face and body. Plus, he knew he needed some provisions if he was going to have any luck at outlasting his pursuers.

Jackson's was run by Old Man Jackson, and from what all the people in Coldwater knew, Old Man Jackson had always been old. He had been sitting behind the counter of the dilapidated store, ringing up people's purchases since the beginning of time. His eyesight had grown bad, his change-making skills had slowed, and his memory had deteriorated. All of these things Michael saw as to his advantage. He did not want to risk being seen, but he also knew he could not risk running for days without food. Even the nasty food offered at Jackson's.

Michael made his way through the woods, leaving the river behind him. He felt nervous, as if he was leaving his safety blanket behind, but he ventured out regardless.

He came up to Townline Road and crouched in the ditch across from the store. He could see one car in the parking lot. He waited.

He pulled off his right boot and felt under the insole. It was still there. A ten-dollar bill, stained and drowned in river water and sweat. His hiding spot for valuable things. A lesson learned in prison was now the only thing that could offer aid to the hunger pains in his belly.

Soon, a woman and a small child came out, got into the vehicle, and left the parking lot, heading south toward town. The road was empty. Michael gathered himself, crossed the stretch of asphalt, and ducked into the store.

The chime on the door jingled in the still air like a coffin bell in an abandoned cemetery. Its tingling subsided and was replaced by the low volume of a radio set to a news station. From his peripheral vision, Michael could see Old Man Jackson leaning over a newspaper by the register.

Michael turned right and hurried toward the coolers lined up against the back wall. He grabbed a couple liters of water, his dry mouth begging him for a sip. He grabbed some random packages of nuts and granola from the adjoining aisle. The barest of resources, but they would keep him going.

He caught his reflection in a Bud Light mirror hanging on the wall and stared at a stranger's features from behind a mask. He looked awful. The bruising on his face was much worse than he anticipated. His long hair was clumped and sweaty, his skin a Monet of color. He had the appearance of a crazed man looking through the axe-busted shards of a bathroom door. Michael turned from his image and walked to the counter.

Old Man Jackson was no longer there.

He stepped past the counter and inched toward the doorway to the back room. He could hear Jackson talking nervously.

He was on the phone.

"I tell you, he's here."

Michael could not make out the muffled voice responding on the phone's earpiece.

"He just walked in. I know it's him. Unless there's another person you all tried to beat up last night."

More inaudible chatter.

"How am I supposed to keep him here? I'm not part of this," Old Man Jackson said with whispered urgency. "Okay, okay. Just get here already. Hurry."

He hung up the phone.

Michael darted away from the door and hid next to the closest cooler near the register. He could hear Jackson fumbling around the back room, the sound of several small yet weighted items fall onto the tile floor, a distinct pump of a shotgun.

■ ■ ■

Old Man Jackson emerged from the back room, weapon in hand. He felt even older all of a sudden, if that were possible, and he moved like a man aware of his own frailty. The gun was old, one that had not been used since he had gone by the name of Little Boy Jackson. The shotgun felt unusually heavy for his withered arms.

"Michael? Is that you? Michael?"

No answer. Jackson took another step. "Michael?"

He tried to stop the tremolo in his voice . . . fear mixed with old age. "Now, Michael, don't do anything foolish. Haywood will be here in a couple minutes and he will get this whole thing sorted out. Until then . . . just—"

There was a flash of movement from his left. Michael appeared like an apparition and grabbed the shotgun, while an invisible hand pushed Jackson up against the wall.

Jackson grabbed for his chest. The shock poured over him like water, and he gasped for air. Most days the pace of the store was too much for his frail condition. A gunfight was enough to put him in his grave. The pain in his chest spread, down his arm, into his throat. He gaped at Michael, tried desperately to speak.

"Mich . . . Mi . . ."

Michael stared at him as if he were a specimen under glass. Transfixed.

Jackson slumped to the floor, his legs splayed before him. "Michael . . . ple . . . please . . . help me," he begged. His eyes wincing with the crashing waves of pain. He was dying while Michael just watched.

Michael stepped back, the shotgun in his hand. Jackson watched him grab supplies off the counter and stuff them into various pockets. He looked back at the old man.

"Haywood's coming . . . ," Michael said as he turned toward the door, "he'll get this sorted out."

TEN

HE HAD BEEN IN PRISON for only a couple weeks when he started to understand the scales of cosmic justice on which he had been placed. The guards did their best at keeping him secure and separate from all the other inmates, but the system was not designed for such arrangements. The warden had even considered locking him in solitary, but the thought of that singed his conscience as utterly inhumane. Eventually something would happen. The warden knew it. The guards knew it. The inmates, licking their chops at their cell windows, knew it.

A pool had gone up, betting on who would get to the kid first.

As it happened, one of the inmates found the opportunity.

One day Michael was sitting at a table eating his lunch, food slopped on a plastic tray with extreme prejudice. He was alone in the room but for the two guards leaning on the far wall, talking to each other. As usual, he ate alone, after the other inmates had dined and been ushered back to their cells. When he was done, he stood and walked over to dump his tray into the trash can that was by the door to the kitchen. On this day, it wasn't there. He peered through the *door and saw that it was inside the room next to the sink, so he walked in as naively as the child he was.*

As soon as he scraped his tray and set it in the sink, he turned to leave. The door swung shut in front of him and he saw the devil incarnate standing before him. The man was the convict from directly across the cell block. Michael did not know his name, only his face with its long unkempt beard and balding forehead that he always had pressed up against the glass. The man's orange jumpsuit was the same as Michael's, only infinitely larger to cover his massive body.

"Hey, boy . . . looks like it's just you and me."

Michael could hear the guards from outside running up to the door, their fists banging on the metal.

"Michael! Michael!" they shouted as they tried to bring the door down, but the convict had barred it.

The man started unzipping his jumpsuit and walking toward the child. "I don't think they are going to get here in time, do you? And time, boy, is all I have. You should know that. I ain't ever getting out of here. Never. So there ain't no reason to suspect that I . . . I ain't going to do what I want to do."

Michael looked around the room for anything to protect himself, but there was nothing. It was prison, there would not be anything at hand. And if there had been, the convicts would have already swiped them up and carried them off to their cells to fashion whatever weapons they could. He grabbed the trash can and pulled it in front of him in an effort at defense, but the inmate pushed it aside and it spilled to the floor.

The guards pounded on the door and Michael could see it start to flex on its hinges.

It was then that Michael first felt it.

A sense of heaviness began in his gut, wrapping up around his spine, into his neck, as if he was embraced by a many-armed shadow squeezing him tighter and tighter. Time slowed down, and as the pressure increased, a wave of nausea built up inside him. But what he started to feel more and more was a sense of rage, not from his own mind, but rage flowing from another place, another thing. Something foreign. It was as if he were standing behind a raging beast ready to gore whatever was in front of it.

The convict took another step and Michael felt the rage pour out of him instantly of its own accord. Hit by an unseen force, the convict stopped and a look of absolute panic washed over him. His eyes shifted past Michael as if he was peering into the abyss, over the event horizon of all things dark. The man clasped his chest and fell to the floor, clawing at Michael, who wilted in the corner at the sight in front of him.

With the guards pounding on the door, the inmate rolled on the ground, clutching at his heart as blood started spurting from his mouth. His eyes rolled back and a scream echoed through the deep chasm of his chest. Finally the door gave way and the guards rushed in to find the inmate dead on the floor and Michael huddled in the corner, his head buried in his arms.

One guard grabbed the boy and pulled him out of the room and got him back to his cell.

"What happened?"

"I . . . I don't know," Michael said.

"You don't know?"

"He was trying to hurt me."

"Did he?"

"No . . . he wanted to."

"You stop him?" the guard pressed.

"No."

"No?"

"It wasn't me. I don't know what happened."

"Uh-huh."

The guard closed the cell door and went back to assist his partner.

It didn't take long for word to spread through the cell block about what had happened. The story began to take on ridiculous dimensions, as all stories will when no one has a clue what actually occurred. But as the tale began to grow, the betting pool slowly dissolved as inmates took their names off the list. The allure of the boy gradually morphed into fear. What had happened in that room? Only the homicidal could wager a clue, and none of them wanted to find out for themselves.

ELEVEN

HAYWOOD ARRIVED FROM SPRINGER'S GROVE with the other men in tow. They pulled into Old Man Jackson's store far away from the front door, not knowing for certain what lay on the other side.

"Alright, boys," he said, adjusting his belt as he stood down from his truck. The men from the other vehicle nodded at him and stood ready to listen. "I'm not sure what we are going to find. I haven't been able to get Jackson back on the phone. Let's not all bunch up at the door. Alright? But let's not take our time either. You all with me?"

The men nodded again like a row of bobbleheads.

"Okay."

The group headed for the entrance. With a flick of his eyes, Haywood got Clinton to open the door and the big man disappeared inside. Haywood followed, as did the others. They spread out quickly down the aisles, ducking and scooting haphazardly, several of them imitating what they had seen military teams do on TV. They moved awkwardly, but were soon placed all around the store.

It was quiet, save for the whirring of an oscillating fan in the back room.

Davis was the first to spot the store owner's feet from

behind the counter. He motioned to Haywood and pointed. Haywood followed Davis's silent commands and saw the boots protruding around the half wall.

"Jackson!" he forced in a whisper. "Jackson!"

There was no response.

With his eyes and a quick nod of his head, Haywood silently commanded Davis to check on the old man. He did so quickly and quietly. Davis felt for a pulse, removed his hand, and shook his head at Haywood.

"Is he shot?"

"No, not that I can tell."

"Anybody in the back room?"

Davis moved around on his squatted legs and peered into the back. It seemed to take him forever, and the others were busting at the seams, expecting someone to jump out and attack. But it never happened. Davis looked back and motioned that the back room was empty.

The men in the store started to relax. It was apparent that Michael was gone. But the sight of a dead man in the corner unnerved them. Almost in unison, they realized how unarmed they were, and though they slowly came out of their crouches and fighting stances, subconsciously they positioned themselves behind one another, not wanting to be the one to receive a bullet to the chest by a well-concealed gunman.

Haywood pulled out his cell phone and called for an ambulance.

"Awful way to go," Earl whispered.

"Sure is," Frank said.

Haywood completed the call and put the phone back in his pocket. He rose from his position and walked over to Davis.

The others came up behind him and each caught a glimpse of Old Man Jackson.

For most of them, this was the first time they had ever seen a dead body. The stillness of it all was the most unsettling. No tremors, no rising or falling rib cage, the animating force of life departed with all remnants of its existence.

"We got some serious trouble, boys," Haywood said, more to himself than to the men standing around him. "Better go home and get your guns."

They all nodded and headed out of the store. Haywood was set on waiting alone for the ambulance to arrive. He knelt down in front of Old Man Jackson, took off his hat, and wiped his brow.

"Sorry, old-timer," he said in an exhaled eulogy. "I'll make sure Michael pays for this."

Haywood put his hat back on, stood, and headed out to the parking lot, preferring to keep his own company rather than that of a dead man.

TWELVE

HAYWOOD WATCHED THE PARAMEDICS load up Old Man Jackson into the back of the ambulance. It had been an hour since he and his men had discovered the body, but it took that long for the county sheriff to arrive. Haywood made no mention of Michael to the officer. For all intents and purposes, it was a scene of an old man simply giving up the ghost at his appointed time. The sheriff left the parking lot behind the ambulance as escort down to South Falls.

Haywood stood alone again.

The fact that it took so long for authorities to arrive was one of the graces that Haywood found in Coldwater. It was a village where a person could be left alone, unhindered by overruling bureaucracy and authority. A man could burn a brush pile in his yard without getting ticketed, check out the max horsepower of his car on a back road, howl at the moon at night if that was his pleasure, and not worry about a policeman showing up at his door. The joke was, you could get a pizza delivered before police would respond to a 911 call, and that was how most residents preferred it. Sure, there were always issues between neighbors, but disagreements were settled over a beer at Gilly's.

Haywood was seen by most people as the mediator of the town. He had spent most of his life here, except for the four years he was downstate at the university. His family had money the same mysterious way that rich people in small towns seem to have it. When he came back to Coldwater, he took over his father's machine shop. His ability to manage a business, coupled with the fact that he was boss to several of the townsfolks, lent to him the air of an arbiter.

He was not the law in the village, some backwoods Boss Hogg looking to strip-mine Coldwater, but he saw it as his obligation to keep the peace where he could. His neighbors often followed his lead and direction, assuming he knew best.

Now, standing outside of Jackson's, looking down the road that was edged by the creeping forest, he grew small inside. Michael was out there, lurking or running, he did not know. His decision the night before had begun to haunt him. Standing in those same woods, the men laying Michael in the pine box, the dirt shoveled into the grave by the glow of a half-dozen flashlights. He could feel it creeping in . . . slowly at first, tickling its way through his stomach into his throat. Guilt. The guilt of burying a man alive.

They had been too decent to shoot Michael. The suggestion was circulated several times, but no one came forward offering to pull the trigger. Perhaps Haywood should have done it. Perhaps, as unspoken leader of Coldwater, he should have taken up the call and executed Michael. Been done with it. But no, he knew—deep down inside, he knew—that he was not capable of doing it. He could not shoot a man in cold blood. So the men decided to leave Michael to fate, and now fate had released him back into the world.

Haywood could feel the forest eyeing him like a jury of angry trees.

He felt exposed in the parking lot, so he collected himself and got into his truck to await his men's return.

Guilt was a horrible thing to bear, but fear was just as bad. Before last night, he and his neighbors suffered the latter. Now they had to shoulder both.

THIRTEEN

KYLE WATCHED AS JAMES got out of the truck and walked inside his trailer. His own thoughts came to keep him company.

How did it get to this point?

He wasn't a policeman, a vigilante, a hired thug. He was just Kyle, nothing more and nothing less.

Kyle's whole life had been spent in the area of Coldwater. He had never thought of leaving, and no one in the town ever gave the idea of him leaving much consideration either. Kyle was the epitome of a Coldwater native: born, raised, and more than likely going to die within the village limit, the wider world none the wiser that he had ever graced it with his presence.

He was several years younger than Michael, had heard the stories of him through his years in school, but never knew him. Michael was a myth and a boogeyman, a tale spun up from truth and folklore. When Michael had moved back to Coldwater, Kyle had responded like the rest of the town, with a morbid curiosity and the firm resolve to keep his distance.

Now here he was waiting in his truck while James grabbed his guns to go in search of the guy.

Why had he left his house last night? Why had he gone

with everyone out into the woods and buried Michael in the ground?

The guilt of the deed mixed with Kyle's own self-awareness that he was a sucker when it came to James and Haywood telling him what to do. When Haywood had hatched his plan, James was gung ho to execute it as quickly as possible. Kyle knew he didn't stand a chance of persuading them to leave Michael alone. He also knew that he didn't stand a chance of not getting sucked up into the mess either. He was part of the group, even though he always felt like a weaker member.

And Frank and Earl were in on it, so that had helped his conscience at the time.

But now, sitting alone in the truck with his thoughts, the enormity of what he had participated in came crashing in and crushing his mind like molten lead. His fingers ached, and he realized he was clutching the steering wheel so tight, his hands had turned to vices. His palms sweating against the vinyl.

He hadn't been able to sleep last night, not after he got home. All that ran through his head was the thought of a live body trapped under earth, of his complicity in the act. That sooner or later someone would pick him up on the street and put him behind bars for the rest of his life.

He was no killer, he was no judge. What business had he had out there in the woods?

When James had arrived at his house last night and told him to get in the truck, he did so. He always did. But most of the time it was to go check bait piles, run up to Gilly's for a beer, or head to the city for some car parts. He hadn't thought at all about climbing in. But when they arrived at Gilly's and he realized that this was the night Haywood was going to set it all in motion, he had said nothing. When he heard Haywood talk about the danger the town was facing due to Michael, he had said nothing. When he watched from the back room as Michael took his poisoned drink and slumped to the floor of the bar, he had said nothing.

The only thing he could tell himself to soothe his soul was that at least he didn't join in with James and the others in roughing up the limp body of their victim. His hands were at least clean in that regard.

But when that pine box was lowered into the ground and the dirt began to pile up, he had kept his mouth shut.

Now he wanted to scream.

He wanted to go back to that very moment when he had heard James honking the horn and he got off his couch. That mindless moment, that moment of action that was spurred by no conscious thought. That would always be the moment in time that all others would now be defined against.

James came out of his trailer, a rifle in each hand and a backpack full of random supplies. He placed them in the bed of the truck and opened the driver's door.

"Move over," James said.

"What?"

"I'm driving."

Kyle scooted over to the passenger side of the bench and put his seatbelt on. He said nothing.

They pulled out and headed north.

"What's spooking you?" James asked.

"Nothing."

"Nothing? You look like you're going to puke or something."

"I'm fine."

"Whatever."

Kyle could see the glint of bloodlust in James's eyes. He had seen it before, back in high school days before a football game, or before James would fight someone outside of Gilly's, which happened more often than it should have. He had that look now as he pressed the pedal down. But for Kyle, his mind was not on the road ahead.

He was thinking of that one moment.

If he had just stayed on the couch, he could have gone on living in blind ignorance, forever content to be a nobody in a no-name town till the end of his days.

How many more bookmarks in time were in store for him in the hours ahead?

FOURTEEN

BACK AT JACKSON'S STORE, all the men congregated again in the parking lot, except for Murphy, who had taken Clyde home to sleep on the couch, content to let younger men chase the wicked. Haywood watched as they had all arrived, like a general surveying his makeshift army.

The six stood together in a semicircle facing their leader, except for Davis, who leaned against the building and inserted another cigarette between his lips.

"Alright. Michael has to be heading north," Haywood said. "Most likely he will follow the river up and stay off the roads. Now, I need a couple of you to head over to the Post Road Bridge and keep a lookout for him. Keep in touch by text and let us know if you see anything."

Haywood held his tongue for a moment as he thought about the situation they were in. The guys allowed him time to reflect.

"Stay up on the bridge. You should be covered pretty well from up top. There's a chance he is armed now."

"Yeah, Old Man Jackson had an old shotgun in the back room," Kyle said, "probably the first ever made."

"That thing still work?" Earl asked.

"Who knows? But the gun is gone," Haywood said. "We

have to assume that Michael has it. Staying up on the bridge should give you the ability to spot him but keep you safe from any potshots he might take."

"I don't much like the idea of sitting up high if he is armed," Clinton said, his deep voice punctuating the conversation like a bass drum.

"Safer than being down in the woods with him," Earl said.

The men all nodded in agreement, Davis stood back, enjoying his smoke, apparently content to do whatever they all decided.

"You really think he'd start shooting at us? You know, if he had Jackson's gun?" Kyle asked.

"Wouldn't you?" Clinton boomed. "I know I would."

"I'd shoot you first, Kyle," James said.

"Ain't funny," Kyle said.

"Take it easy, guys," Haywood said. "More than likely, he's going to lay low and just try and get away. Either follow the river or head up to the north woods. He's not going back to Coldwater. That would be a stupid move. And he's probably not going to double back to Springer's Grove. That leaves those two options."

"Makes sense," Clinton said. "I'll take the bridge."

"Us too," Frank said.

Clinton and Davis, then Frank and Earl loaded up into their trucks and kicked up a rooster tail of rocks as they pulled out of the parking lot.

Haywood turned to James. "Now, the bridge is upriver about five miles. No way he's made it that far yet. I want you to go up to Countyline Road and drive back and forth between here and the bridge. Keep a watch for him, and let the people up there know we are looking for someone."

"What do we tell them?" James asked.

Haywood thought about it. He couldn't send James and Kyle door to door asking, *Would you mind keeping a lookout for this guy that we buried in the woods last night? It seems he got out . . . probably pretty mad about it.* "Just tell them that we got word from the authorities in South Falls that an inmate broke out of jail, and they are asking for people to be alert. Just say you are doing a public service."

James nodded. He turned and walked to Kyle's truck and resumed his spot in the usurped driver's seat. Kyle stood as if balancing between two worlds.

"Something on your mind?" Haywood asked.

"No," Kyle said.

"You sure? You look like you're about ready to explode."

Kyle wavered but said nothing. He kept looking between Haywood and James.

"Kyle! Get in the truck," James yelled over the engine noise.

Kyle's shoulders dropped as he walked to the truck and took his place in the passenger seat. Haywood watched as the vehicle disappeared north into the forest.

With each passing moment the sense of impending doom clouded over him. They had to find Michael before he ranged out of their orbit. If Haywood had just manned up the night before, had taken decisive action, put a bullet in Michael's head, and buried him, then this odyssey would have been over and done with. Now, the longer he was on the loose, the harder it would be to keep this group focused.

Clinton and Davis were solid. Frank and Earl, not so much. James would keep Kyle in line, but this could not go on too much longer. He needed to end it. And as he stood in Old Man Jackson's vacant parking lot, Haywood knew that it was on his shoulders alone to bring everything to a conclusion. It would be up to him to kill Michael. He couldn't bring himself to do it last night, but he was growing more and more confident that he could do it the next chance he got.

FIFTEEN

TWO TRUCKS IDLED ON OPPOSITE ENDS of Post Road Bridge. Clinton stood next to the open door of his truck, rifle leaned up against the cement wall of the bridge, looking down on the Coldwater River. Davis sat on the bumper, smoke from his cigarette drifting over the railing, floating southwest in the air, mimicking the current in the water below.

"You really think he killed Old Man Jackson?" Davis asked, his breath held with a deep toke.

"Hard to say. For all we know, Jackson died five years ago and nobody could tell the difference," Clinton said.

Davis grunted half-heartedly. "I'll give you that. But even so, I don't think he did. I know I wouldn't have killed the old man. If I was trying to hide, I wouldn't leave a body out for show. I would have at least put it where no one could find it."

"Unless you forgot"—Clinton's deep voice was slow and steady as he scanned the riverbank for movement—"we're not exactly experts at hiding bodies. Maybe Michael isn't either."

■ ■ ■

Earl paced back and forth in front of Frank's truck on the south end of the bridge. His eyes darting from tree to tree on the embankment below. With every sound he would flinch a little, expecting a shotgun blast to come racing up at him.

"You need to calm down a little bit, you're going to give yourself a heart attack," Frank said. He was half seated in the driver's seat, peering over the wall.

"Calm? How can I be calm right now?"

"I'm just saying. You look like you about ready to jump out of your own skin."

"This has gotten out of hand. We never should have did what we did. You know what's going to happen to us?"

"Ain't nothing going to happen to us."

"No? What do you think is going to happen?" Earl asked. "All Michael has to do is call the cops and that's it. Finished. Over."

"He had a chance to, at Old Man Jackson's. If he was even there," Frank said.

"Yeah? Well, how about this then . . . if he had the chance to call, and didn't, then that means he's going to come after us, deal with us himself."

"I never thought about that."

Earl stopped his pacing to look his friend in the eye. A million thoughts raced through his mind, his synaptic nerves all firing at once, and he struggled to settle his brain.

"This morning," he said, "when I woke up, my biggest fear was the police rolling into the drive. You know, lights flashing and the SWAT teams, like on TV. But now, I don't think I'll ever be able to get to sleep, not knowing that Michael's roaming around out here. I'm starting to think going to jail would be better . . . better than waiting for Michael to show up."

"We ain't going to jail, man. And Michael ain't going to show up and kill us all. So stop it. Just stop."

"How you know?"

"You just have to trust Haywood," Frank said.

"You trust him?" Earl asked.

"I think we have no choice at this point."

■ ■ ■

Davis stood up, stomped his cigarette out with his boot, and slung his rifle up to his shoulder. He leaned against the bridge rail and looked through his scope downriver.

"You think you could shoot him?" he asked.

"Don't know," Clinton said, his eyes fixated on the woods.

"It's a good thing James ain't here. He'd be ready to off him in a heartbeat."

Clinton nodded. He was a big man, and people always thought him a mean giant, but everyone knew that James was the domesticated psychopath. He was glad that he wasn't up on the bridge with them now.

"Yeah. James seems a little bit excited about this whole affair," Clinton said.

"But if Michael shows up here? What do you think is going to happen?"

"It's up to Michael at that point."

"What you mean?"

"We point our guns at him and tell him to stay put until Haywood gets here," Clinton said.

Davis eased up from his firing position. "And if he don't stay put?"

"Well, I guess we'll cross that bridge when we get there."

"Take a look around, man," Davis said as he stuffed another Winston into his mouth. "We already crossed that bridge."

■ ■ ■

"He's like a chimney over there," Earl said, his stress eating away at him as he gouged a path in the asphalt. His eyes began to ache from straining his vision at distant objects. "Davis might as well just be letting off smoke signals."

"Come on, man. It's just Davis," Frank said.

The sun began to edge toward the western horizon.

"How long we supposed to wait up here?"

"As long as it takes."

Earl rubbed his palms on his shirt. No matter how hard he tried, the sweat seemed to pour out of them. His head pounded from the anxiety of it all. He looked at Frank, and though his friend seemed relaxed, he knew him enough to tell that he was just as nervous about the whole situation. That was the one thing cool about Frank, he let Earl be the vocalized panic for both of them. He resumed his pacing.

The river passed below them with an easy current, drifting away without a care in the world.

"You remember when we were out fishing last weekend?" Earl said. "The river looks different now. I don't know if it ever will look the same again. If you had asked me then what we'd be doing today . . . this sure wouldn't have been the answer. I wish we could go back, redo this whole thing. But we can't. I envy that water. Always flowing in the way it should go, never jumping its course for no reason."

"Dang, Earl. I didn't know you were a poet," Frank said, a sly smile over his face.

"Shut it," Earl said.

SIXTEEN

MICHAEL SAT IN THE TREE LINE on the side of Countyline Road. He looked to both horizons and saw an empty stretch of pavement. Across the road was the front wall of the north woods and the beginning of an endless expanse of wilderness. The city of Coldwater behind him, a labyrinth of nature before. The people who lived in the north were stretched out and isolated, the kind of people who preferred to be left alone, not bothered. If there was any place left on earth that a man like Michael could disappear to, it was there, just across Countyline Road.

Following the river had been a rash and thoughtless decision. It cut a clear path through the rugged country, but it also gave any pursuer a road map to where he would be headed. He had managed to make it to Old Man Jackson's without incident, but when he came upon the Post Road Bridge, his luck had run out.

From the shadow of the embankment, he had seen men on top of the bridge. A truck on each end, heads moving back and forth, peering over the sides. Michael had counted four, but there could have been more. For all he knew, there were men down by the river searching the banks.

He had doubled back as far as he dared, forded the river, and cut a trail north.

And now he found himself on the dividing line between the last bastion of civilization and the northern wilderness, Countyline Road. Though it was only two lanes, it seemed an overwhelming gauntlet to run. The tree line provided a sense of comfort, an embryonic shell from which to peer out into the open. The road before him would be like walking naked into the world. Nightfall was approaching quickly and he could wait until then to cross, but each minute delayed meant more time for his pursuers to catch up with him.

Michael calculated the distance across the road.

It was about thirty yards.

He looked in both directions again.

Any car that appeared on either horizon would see him just as soon as they crested the hills overlooking this small valley where he found himself. He would be the fish in the barrel. There would be no warning. Each moment was as safe and as dangerous as the next.

Michael marked his crossing in his mind—away from the tree line, up the ditch, across the road, into the brush on the other side. He mapped it out, peering for anything that might trip him up, slow his progress. Once he had his route committed, he listened as hard as he could for the sound of a vehicle approaching. He heard nothing.

Gathering himself up, he made a dash for the crossing.

■ ■ ■

From his seat, Kyle gazed out the side window at the passing trees. They loomed ominous in their depth. In his mind's eye he envisioned Michael by every tree, Old Man Jackson's shotgun raised and ready to fire at the truck as it moved down the road. He counted each breath and tried to anticipate what the flash from the barrel would look like from the hanging leaves, the sound of the shot hitting the truck, whether or not the shell would pass through the metal and into him. If he would have any conscious thought between the blast and when his body would erupt in a fountain of gore.

His shirt was drenched with sweat, even though the cool evening air blew in through his open window.

James drove the truck down Countyline Road slowly, deliberately, seemingly reveling in the slow creep down the blacktop. They had been hunting in these woods all their lives, but this was a different hunt altogether, and while Kyle was quaking in his seat at the mere idea of the man lurking in the woods, James appeared as pumped up as any other time in his life. To him this was an adrenaline rush. This was sport. Kyle wondered if James was a man who wanted to be evil all his life and was suddenly given a free pass to do so.

The truck inched down the road and crested a small hill that opened up on a gully. The asphalt sloped down before rising up to a distant ridge.

James's eyes widened as he stared through the windshield off into the horizon. A sinister smirk crossed his face.

Up ahead, a shadow of a man ran across the road, stopped momentarily at the center line, and then took off into the woods on the other side.

"There he is!" James yelled as he punched the gas.

■ ■ ■

It was if stepping on the road's centerline had caused the truck to materialize on the western ridge. Michael could see it crest the hill and he stopped midstride, looked at the mechanical beast, then his reflexes took over. He sprinted across the blacktop, tripping over his feet and stumbling to safety in the opposing ditch. He clawed up the far bank and cut into the woods. Branches hit his face, grabbing at his cheeks and eyes, tearing at his skin to leave streaks of blood, but he pushed on. With each step into the blackness, he could hear the truck's engine growling closer as it raced down the road to his location.

His mind was firing on all cylinders and his eyes darted for a solution.

Michael looked into the forest. Though the trees were thick, he could see clearly through old forest for about a hundred yards. He would never disappear in time.

The engine in the distance dropped another gear, and the roar changed tone but then increased in ferocity to a new height, as if the devil himself was going full bore down Countyline Road. There could be no doubt that they had seen him. There could be no doubt that the occupants in the truck were hunting for him.

They would never stop hunting for him.

It was with this realization that Michael could feel the tension in his stomach start to form, snaking up his spine. The same feeling that had crept over him many times in his life, that had crept over him earlier at Old Man Jackson's when the shotgun was pointed at his face.

The same feeling he first experienced in the prison kitchen as a young boy when he knew that danger was imminent.

All he had to do was step out on the road and watch the destruction unfold. This silent protector of his, the killing shadow, the curse that hung around his soul since he was ten years old, would protect him. He would be safe, but at what expense?

That is not what he wanted.

He wanted to be left alone.

His only hope was to hide himself as best he could, and that's what he did. Nestled down in the nettles and the leaves, Michael waited for his pursuers to arrive.

■ ■ ■

"Slow down, James! What are you doing!"

The truck roared down the road, chewing up pavement at a faster and faster rate.

"I saw him . . . I saw that son-of-a—"

"Haywood said to wait! What are you doing? Slow down!" Kyle yelled, his foot pressing into the floorboard in a futile attempt to apply the brakes of the truck. But James kept the accelerator down, racing toward the fugitive's trail. He was whipped into a frenzy, a vigilante. Bloodlust.

The fear arose in Kyle double-time.

"Slow down!"

James was lost in his own world. His gaze was fixed on the point in the road where he saw Michael disappear into the woods. His foot on the gas, oblivious to how fast the truck was going or how hard the engine was squealing in agony. He paid no more attention to Kyle in the passenger seat, his ears deaf to the yelling. He was possessed, transfixed on the point in the road and the rush of speed.

The truck arrived at the spot, but before James could slow down, the vehicle's back end pushed out to the side, fishtailing in an uncontrollable swerve. James stared at his static fists on the wheel, his expression locked in terrifying wonder as the machine was no longer under his control. The momentum carried the vehicle over on its side and onto its top, rolling several times. Kyle could feel the glass shatter across his face, the roof crumbling down against his head. The seat belt gouging into his chest and waist as the truck rolled and rolled . . . finally landing in the ditch upside down. James was gone. Thrown out at some point without a sound.

Kyle was stuck in the seat. The smell of gasoline fumes and mud flooded his senses. The pain was overwhelming in every part of his body. He reached for the buckle and unsnapped it, falling onto the roof as he did so, his body crumpling like a rag doll.

His door was gone, ripped off during the crash, and he managed to drag himself out into the ditch. He couldn't move his legs. He couldn't tell if they were broken or if it was his back. His vision was blurred and the earth was spinning uncontrollably, but he fought his way up the bank until his head rested on the side of the road.

He could see James's lifeless body lying on the asphalt. Kyle's mind couldn't process the sight. With as much strength as he could he tried to call out to his friend.

"James . . . James . . ." The sound was more a bubbling of thick liquid than words.

Then Kyle saw *him*.

The shadow he had seen crossing Countyline Road.

The man they had buried in Springer's Grove.

Michael stepped onto the road, between the wrecked truck and James's body.

■ ■ ■

Michael watched the whole crash unfold before him from the false safety of the tree line on the north side of the road. He watched the truck accelerate, swerve, and roll as if in slow motion. The driver had been jettisoned at the first roll and was crushed by the vehicle as it careened into the ditch. He heard the whimpering sounds of the passenger as the man inside the cab struggled out of the wreck.

Michael knew that the only safe course was to start running, but he felt compelled to investigate the carnage. He still needed supplies—all he could scrounge—and he figured that any car coming down the road would be more interested in the accident than the shadow slinking back into the woods. It was worth the risk.

He stepped onto the road. To his right lay the driver. Motionless. His life gone as quickly as the truck's abrupt deceleration. He turned toward the heap of twisted metal simmering in the ditch. He could see the passenger lying halfway on the road, the man's head on the asphalt. Blood covered most of his face and was pooling from his mouth, but his eyes were wide open, the whites visible in the lessening evening light. The man stared in shock. He was trying to speak, single sounds, calling for his companion, but the noise was unrecognizable.

Michael walked toward him. The man on the ground was unarmed, and even if he had a gun on him, it appeared that he was so messed up that he wouldn't have the ability to raise it and fire.

Michael stepped around him, went down in the ditch, and searched the upside-down truck. He found a variety of things on the ceiling-now-turned-floor of the cab. He found a backpack and dumped out its contents: a lighter, two water bottles, a half pack of cigarettes, and a couple candies. There wasn't much but litter.

Leaving the truck, he walked up the ditch and stepped over the bleeding man, squatted down and looked him in the face. The man moved involuntarily, his body shaking uncontrollably.

Michael reached over and pulled the wallet out of the man's back pocket and thumbed through it until he found an ID.

"Kyle Moore."

The name seemed familiar, but he could not place it with certainty. Michael opened one of the water bottles and poured a little bit into the man's mouth. Kyle took some and spit it out, along with the blood that had pooled in his cheek. He tried to mouth some words, struggling to get the noise out.

"Pl . . . please . . . hel . . . help me."

"Why should I . . . Kyle?" Michael said, flipping the driver's license off into the ditch. He stared down at the mess of humanity before him, feeling a duality in his thoughts. There was a certain amount of satisfaction in seeing justice meted out in so quick a fashion, but seeing carnage up close, he would be lying if he didn't feel sympathy for the poor soul.

Kyle kept uttering his request as if Michael had said nothing.

"Pl . . . hel . . . help me."

SEVENTEEN

FEAR IS THE DEMARCATION between light and dark.

It is future's shadow, hidden in mist.

Michael could not remember a time in life when he did not feel the encroaching arms of fear embracing him. It was there since he was a boy, when he had crossed from one world to the next. It abided in him as if he carried an absorbed twin in his cells which whispered despair. Softly. Subtly.

But now, standing on the road looking down at Kyle, he saw what fear looked like in its rawest form.

Kyle was afraid.

His fear controlled the muscles in his face, contorting them into a childlike visage of macabre wonderment. The pain and anticipation of what lay at the end of each breath. The hope that there would be one more, the agony that there were thousands left.

Kyle could no longer talk. His eyes communicated the fear of a man dying alone on a country road. Michael could feel the fear coursing through Kyle's broken body. The fear of how long it would take to get to the end, the fear of wanting to both live and die and not knowing which was worse. But mostly, Michael could feel the fear of loneliness, the sense that Kyle was terrified to be left alone to suffer in isolation on a back country road, no one to comfort him in what could well be his last minutes alive.

Michael poured another stream of water over Kyle's mouth, but it fell through his lips and onto the ground.

"I hope you understand," Michael said, "that none of this needed to happen. It was you boys who came hunting me. It was you boys who jumped me and stuck me in the ground."

Kyle's eyes stayed fixed down the road.

"To be left alone. That's all I tried to do. I didn't mess with you all. Kept my distance. We could have gone on like that till the end."

Michael stood erect and Kyle's eyes followed him.

"You all could be sitting in the back of Gilly's right now. Me, minding my business. You all minding yours. But it's never going to be like that again, is it? No, none of this had to happen."

Michael looked back and forth down Countyline Road. The night was setting in. He wasn't sure how much traffic came this way once night fell.

"Hopefully someone will come along shortly and call an ambulance."

Kyle closed his eyes and coughed, which appeared to cause him excruciating pain.

"There's nothing I can do for you, Kyle."

Michael gathered what supplies he had salvaged, stepped down into the ditch, and walked north into the woods. He stopped, turned, and spoke to Kyle's back as if performing a eulogy.

"It was you boys . . . didn't need to be this way."

He repeated this to himself as he ventured into the wild unknown, each utterance working to absolve his conscience from the guilt that attempted to find a place to take root in his heart.

EIGHTEEN

ADRENALINE MIXED into Haywood's blood to create demon octane, making him unable to sit still or take confidence in what his eyes were telling him. He would find himself in his truck, running down dirt roads through the north woods, a spotlight affixed to his door shining into the recesses of the forest in hopes of catching a reflection. He did this until the clock hit midnight, then drove home. But once home, his nerves would not let him settle down and he was back in the truck heading north again.

Haywood would not rest again today.

He probed his conscience but found no trace of guilt. The trees passed by and the washboard dirt roads worked the vehicle's suspension, but nothing about the actions of the previous days shook his resolve. He was in the right. There was no question.

The other men might be at home second-guessing their actions, but not Haywood. He even envisioned some future court case with him in the defendant's chair, arguing to the judge that he was justified in all his actions.

The state was the one who chose to expose Haywood and his community to this sickness. There was no rehabilitating someone like Michael, someone who could commit a cold-blooded act like he did. It made no difference how young he had been. To his core, Michael was an unredeemable psychopath. The only right course of action was to have him locked up for the rest of his life, since the death penalty was no longer an option. Now Haywood and his town would have to live with the PC bureaucrat idiots and their overly sensitive inclinations.

If the law wouldn't keep them safe, then Haywood would step up and protect them.

No, it wasn't guilt propelling Haywood forward. It was disappointment.

Disappointment with himself. He should have manned up and killed Michael himself. Burying him was a coward's route. Somewhere inside him, he still wanted a force outside himself to resolve the situation. He wanted nature to step in where the law had failed. But nature had failed him as well.

And Haywood felt convicted that he had failed himself.

Strong action requires strong will. He should have taken Michael out to Springer's Grove, put him in the pit, and put a bullet in the back of his head. Swift, commanding action. He was, if nothing else, a man of action. Or was he?

He had lived his life thinking that he was, but when it came to the moment, what might become the defining moment of his life, he had taken the easy way out. He had walked all the way to the edge and merely peeked into the abyss rather than ruling the precipice.

Here and now, in the truck in the north woods, he committed himself to never faltering again.

His rifle was on the passenger seat, and if Michael were to show himself, Haywood would take action without the slightest reservation.

He drove through the night, his adrenaline keeping him awake, crisscrossing the north woods.

Haywood's thoughts drifted to another tale. The prologue to this whole ordeal. Another friend who met a cruel end alone in the forest away from town. Haywood's best friend.

John Morrison had been found in the woods several miles outside of Coldwater, propped up against a tree, as if he was watching the morning sun break through the forest. It was Haywood who found him. Morrison hadn't been seen at Gilly's Pub, the bar he owned in town, for several days, and though it wasn't uncommon for the men of Coldwater to disappear and then return as if nothing had ever happened, it was unusual for Morrison to be away when there was good drinking to be had with his buddies.

Morrison's truck had been spotted on a turnout near Old State Road. This had caught Haywood's ear, since he knew John usually hunted west of town. Old State Road ran north and south, as far east of Coldwater as you could go while still being in the county. It was odd for him to be out there. It was sparsely populated, mostly junk forest and swamp. A few houses, one of them Michael's, though that thought wouldn't cross Haywood's mind until after he found his friend.

Haywood drove out and found the turnout after a few back-and-forth runs down the road. He pulled in behind Morrison's truck and investigated. The driver's door of his friend's pickup was closed, but not latched, and he pulled it open without having to engage the handle. There was nothing peculiar sitting in view on the bench seat except for the half-full coffee mug in the cupholder. Haywood dipped his finger in it; it was ice cold. The early-morning dew still coated the vehicle, even though it was almost noon. Nettles from the pines that lined the turnout had fallen on the hood. The truck had been sitting for a while.

"Morse!" Haywood yelled. "Morse!"

He walked into the woods, following the natural contour of the forest floor. There wasn't a defined path, but it wasn't that hard going. He kept calling out, but the world was empty, his echo zigzagging through the trees. He kept the truck in sight and called out in all directions. Nothing.

Walking farther, he saw a small flicker of light on the ground. He stopped and moved back a little and let the sun hit the object again. It was a shell casing. He turned to get a bead on where the truck was behind him and plotted a straight line deeper into the woods.

Not more than a hundred yards farther, he found him. From a distance, Haywood could see only two feet stretched out on opposite sides of a tree. Just a man enjoying quiet time in the woods.

"Morse! What are you doing out here?" Haywood said as he approached. "Everyone in town is wondering where you've . . ."

His words escaped him as he came around the tree.

There, sitting on the ground, was his friend.

Dead.

In his graying hands lay his shotgun, the barrel of which appeared as if it had blown apart and fragmented. His face was marked with powder burns, at least the parts that were not blown off.

Haywood doubled over and fought the urge to retch out his breakfast. There was no use shaking or attempting to revive Morrison. He was gone, propped up and placed here like a sign.

Haywood pulled out his cell phone but could not get a signal. The walk back to the truck was done in a daze, but when he arrived, he called for an ambulance and then called James to gather up the boys and get out there. The image was too much to bear alone.

And now, as he drove and drove, his mind mixed together the separate scenes of dead townsfolk being loaded into ambulances—Morrison, Old Man Jackson, James. If it hadn't been for Clinton taking the long way home from Post Road Bridge, Kyle most assuredly would have been the fourth.

The sun started to crest the eastern horizon when he turned south. He returned home and showered, filled his veins with coffee, and set himself for another day of pursuit. But before he did, he had a stop to make down in South Falls. He had to talk to the last man who saw Michael alive, and he had to talk to the man while there was still breath in his body.

Kyle was still alive but didn't look long for this world when they had carted him off to South Falls, and he might just have some piece of information that would end this whole debacle quick and easy.

NINETEEN

SIXTY MILES DOWNRIVER FROM COLDWATER, in the city of South Falls, a woman walked into the Gun Club, signed in for a lane, was admitted to the back room, and prepared herself one last time. She put the case on the ledge in front of her and unlocked it. Inside was a standard Glock pistol, the likes of which resided in countless nightstands across America.

She adjusted her ear protection, slid the magazine into the weapon, and aimed downrange.

She felt the recoil in her wrist, but that had become second nature. She fired one shot at the target. She ejected the magazine and cleared the chamber of the next round.

One shot.

That's all she wanted. Just one.

The weapon secured, she pushed the button that would bring the target up to her.

She had spent many hours over the course of years at this range. Firing and firing until her skill with the pistol was as good as it could possibly get. She wasn't a marksman and never planned to be one. She wasn't training to be an assassin, a one-woman army. She was practicing for a solitary moment in time. A moment she felt had come.

Today was nothing more than a reassurance. Verification that she was ready. The next bullet out of the gun would be the one that would bring justice to her and to her family. The next shot would be the one that counted.

As the target came forward, she imagined that the silhouette was a real person, approaching through an alleyway, a wooded trail, the middle of the street. The next time she held the gun aloft, it would be directed at a living, breathing person, and the bullet would have to find its mark and end the story.

One shot. It had to be one shot.

She had never seen what a bullet could do to a body. Paper targets were one thing, flesh and bone something else altogether. She knew herself enough to understand that when her eyes witnessed the exploding face of her target, her will might falter. She might not have the nerve or wherewithal to pull the trigger again. She had no idea the thoughts that would possess her the second after she squeezed the trigger.

The act would transform her into a different creature. But transform her into what? She had thought long and hard on this. Would the woman who was so determined to fire the first shot still be there if a second shot was needed?

It was a mystery that she would not solve until the moment arrived.

By then it would be too late to prepare if she evolved into a coward. If the horror she unleashed rendered her incapable of finishing the business she was setting out to do.

And so, every weekend for the past six weeks, she came to the firing range and fired one shot. The target came and stopped in front of her. A hole dead center on the head of the outline. The same exactitude as the past six Fridays.

She was ready.

Locking the case back up, she headed out of the range, put the case under her driver's seat, and pulled out of the parking lot. The midday traffic was light, and in fifteen minutes she had navigated out of the city grid of South Falls and was heading north.

North to the woods and backcountry roads. North to the isolated village of Coldwater.

North to the place where the man who had destroyed her family now resided.

The man who would receive the fruits of her practice, and the lead of her pistol.

TWENTY

THE SOFT GROWL OF A SMALL DOG was Michael's alarm clock the first day in the north woods. The light coming through the trees was obscured by foliage, but Michael's internal clock told him it was midday.

He cleared his eyes and saw, not more than ten feet from his head, the shape of a Labrador puppy. The dog was staring at him, its teeth bared minimally, as if it was testing out its new defense mechanisms. Michael didn't move but simply stared at the animal. From the ridge over top of him, Michael could hear the voice of a boy calling out.

"Otis! Here, Otis!"

The dog's ears perked up, but its teeth remained exposed. He heard its name called again. This time the dog sat on its haunches but kept vigil over the man lying in the undergrowth.

"Otis! What are you doing, you dumb dog! Get up here!"

The dog looked up the ridge and then back down to Michael. It was a standoff. Michael considered getting up and quickly moving on, but he thought the dog might be naive enough to chase him. The voice lashed out again.

"Now! Otis! Come!"

With no response, the boy ventured down the ridge.

Michael tried to sink more into the hillside, but there was nowhere to go. He didn't want to scare the boy. He decided to wait to make his presence known, hoping that his current posture would be less traumatic.

The boy slid down the hill and reached for the dog's collar. Otis bared his teeth again, and the boy followed the gaze of his pet to the face of the vagabond in the leaves. He jumped back, frightened, almost losing his balance and tumbling down the hill out of sheer surprise, but the grasp on the dog collar kept him from doing so. Michael didn't rise. No use scaring the boy even more. He spoke in a slow, clear voice.

"Sorry. I'm not going to hurt you."

The boy got his feet under him and positioned himself behind the dog, using Otis as a shield, a stance that energized the pup, though the dog would be short work for any man intent on harming the kid.

"That's a good dog you have there. He's very brave."

"He's vicious too!" the boy blurted, puffing himself up much like a cobra but without the venom.

"I bet he is. You mind if I sit up? The cold from the ground has seeped into my bones and it's killing me."

"Let me see your hands first."

Michael pegged him for nine or ten years old, but he couldn't be certain. What did it matter to show his hands? If his intention was to strangle the boy, he didn't need the element of surprise to do so. Michael obliged slowly, in feigned subservience to his captor. "See? Empty."

"Alright, but move slow, otherwise I'll sic Otis on you."

The dog cocked his head like he was asking his owner if he was serious.

Michael nodded and easily pushed himself up. His joints

82

ached with stiffness and he did what he could to stretch them out. He felt like the Tin Man of Oz after a long rainstorm. As he rose to his full height, the boy became uneasy and nervous in his position. Michael posed an imperious figure. His bruised face added to the horror, leaves hanging from his hair, his clothes mired with mud and sweat and blood.

"What now?" Michael asked.

The boy seemed perplexed. His stance said he wanted to run, but there was no place to go. The way uphill, back to the ridge path, was essentially blocked. Below him, the hill descended sharply into a tangle of briars and thornbushes. Either route looked hazardous, and he would have to pull his yapping dog with him. Michael could see scenarios play out on the boy's face, each one seeming bleaker and bleaker.

"Well, until you decide, know that I am not going to hurt you. There's nothing I can say that'll convince you of that, but maybe we can come to an agreement. If you keep your attack dog off me, I won't hurt you. Deal?"

The boy thought about it. "Deal," he whispered with total lack of confidence.

"Alright."

They faced each other for what seemed like an eternity. Otis finally gave up his attempt at ferocity and changed his snarling to panting, his red tongue hanging out the side of his half-smiling mouth.

"So, Otis. Good name. You got a name?"

"Will."

"Good name too."

"What about you?"

"Michael."

The boy nodded. "You been out here long?"

"A while."

"You homeless?"

"At the moment it would appear that I am."

"You got food?"

"I got a little."

The boy reached into the pocket of his pants and pulled out a granola bar. It was violently smashed in its wrapper by its travels in such tight quarters. Will examined the bar and then tossed it to Michael, who caught it midair with efficiency of motion.

"You sure, Will? I don't want to take your lunch."

"It's just a snack. I tell my mom I don't like them, but she keeps buying them anyway."

"Well, I sure do appreciate it."

Will nodded again. He shuffled on his feet. "Well, I best get home."

"No problem, Will. Again, thank you for the snack."

Will grabbed Otis by the collar and half dragged him uphill to the top of the ridge, never taking his eyes off the mysterious man. Michael followed the boy's movement as well. He watched as the tension in the boy's body relaxed once he knew he was out of Michael's orbit. Michael waved a parting salute.

"You know," the boy yelled down, "I have a fort on the other side of the hill here. It's hidden from the trail, but if you're homeless, you can use it if you like."

"I would appreciate that."

"Look for the triple-forked tree along the ridge and then turn left, down the hill. It's a hollow under the bank. I have a tarp in there. You could use that if you want."

"Thank you."

"Only thing, I got some toys in there. Don't take them, otherwise I'd have to sic Otis on you."

Michael raised his hand in solemn oath. "On my honor, I won't touch them."

The boy nodded, and just as quickly disappeared from view.

85

TWENTY-ONE

HAYWOOD STROLLED into South Falls Hospital with acute determination. Clinton and the boys had come upon the accident not long after it happened. James was dead, but after finding Kyle unconscious but alive, they had searched the scene for anything the county cops would find questionable, and then called it in. Haywood arrived as the ambulance was loading Kyle up for transport.

"Busy day for you guys," he told the paramedics.

"You could say that. What's going on up here?" the trooper asked, lifting his eyes from the notepad he was using while interviewing one of Haywood's posse.

"Just bad luck, I guess. Are you able to tell what happened?"

"Speeding. Looks like the driver lost control and rolled it."

"Is he okay?"

"Driver is deceased. The passenger looks close to it himself."

Thankfully, that was the extent of the inquiry.

Haywood was there now, making sure the story stayed simple. Kyle had a mouth on him at the most calm of times. Who knew what he would say when he fully came to his senses, and Haywood wanted to make sure he heard it before the police did . . . wanted to make sure this mess didn't get even more out of control.

The prognosis was bad. Kyle's back was broken. Most likely never walk again. His face was torn and bruised, and for a minute he looked like Morrison, albeit in a bed rather than sitting next to a tree out in the woods. Seeing Kyle like this and with Old Man Jackson and James dead all on the same day, the suspicion that had driven him to bury Michael now formed a steel resolve. Michael was a killer, as dangerous as Haywood had believed him to be when he heard that he had been released from prison and moved back to town.

Old Man Jackson had been a recluse, but James had been one of his boys just as much as Morrison had been. Brothers of a hick town since childhood. It was James who had convinced the others even more so than Haywood to go along with the plan. To back Haywood. Now with him dead, the others would most likely scatter off like cowards. Kyle being the most likely candidate to turn tail first.

Haywood grabbed a chair and pulled it over close to the bed. The squeal of the legs against the tile woke Kyle from his morphine-induced slumber.

"So what happened up there?"

Kyle slowly and painfully reiterated the events to Haywood—how they saw Michael in the distance crossing the road, how James went manic and sped after him like a lunatic.

"And he lost control?"

"It was more than that. It's like we were picked up and thrown."

"What do you mean?"

"I mean, it was like it was all in slow motion, but it wasn't. We was driving straight for him and then it was like we was pushed sideways. I can still see James's hands on the wheel. Knuckled down at 10 and 2. He didn't swerve or nothing. The truck just started spinning and then rolling. I can see James being thrown out his window, the bottom of his boots and the rotating sky and ground. He was there, then he was gone. It's like still pictures."

"They say he died instantly."

"I hope so," Kyle said.

"What else?"

"Then I remember pulling myself up to the road. I couldn't feel my legs, but it didn't hurt. I was lying there and I saw him come up."

"Michael?"

"Yeah. He knelt down next to me. I could see his mouth moving but couldn't hear anything. Then he got up and ran off."

Haywood exhaled slowly. He stared at Kyle with an intensity as if he was probing his mind for any more facts that he was holding back, but the man's swollen and bloodshot eyes hid nothing.

"Cops come in here yet?" Haywood asked.

"No."

"Don't tell them that last part."

"About Michael?"

"Yes."

Kyle strained to keep conscious. "What we did was wrong," he whispered.

"What's that?"

"What we did was wrong."

"What we did was necessary. It was the right thing to do. We just . . . we just didn't do it right."

"Right? James is dead! My legs! I can't move my legs! How is this right?"

Kyle's monitors started to beep wildly as his heart rate increased. Haywood tried to calm him down and was moderately successful.

"We had no business burying him up in those woods."

"What should we have done, Kyle? Could you have shot him? Could you have pulled the trigger yourself? Huh? He was dangerous. He *is* dangerous. After Morrison, we couldn't just wait for him to kill again. You think Jackson, Morrison . . . you think those were accidents? You think James being dead is an accident?"

"It's justice."

"No, it's not justice. Michael is a killer. He brings death with him. Morrison. Think of Morrison. It's all Michael's fault. I know that. I know it deep down in my bones. He is dangerous. Dangerous to all of us."

"Morrison." Kyle grunted. "If it hadn't been for him —"

"Watch yourself, Kyle."

"He was riding Michael from the start. You and him. If you guys had just left him alone. If Morrison hadn't gone out in those woods. Antagonizing him, punking on him—"

"Morrison didn't deserve what happened to him," Haywood said. "I can't believe you would even think so."

"And now he's out! He's out and he knows what each of us did to him. You think he was dangerous before? You created a monster now. Why did we ever listen to you? We trusted you. James trusted you!"

This time Kyle noticed his monitors, groaning in despair, and managed to calm himself. He looked back at Haywood, who sat deeply contemplating the situation.

"I'm scared, man," Kyle said.

"Me too, Kyle. Me too."

"We can't tell anyone, I know that. I know you think I'm going to say something to the cops, but I ain't. What would I say? That we buried a man alive because we think he killed Morrison? If it's not jail, they'll straitjacket me. But I'm more scared of what's coming. He's going to come for us, Haywood. He's not going to stop. He's going to come for all of us."

"He headed up to the north woods."

"He ain't going to stay away. You can count on that. I mean, would you?"

Haywood stood, patted Kyle's shoulder softly, and started to make his exit. "I saw Tami out in the hall," he said. "Hopefully she can help ease your mind."

"What would she come up here for?"

"To see you. To make sure you're okay."

"Might as well tell her to go back to Coldwater. I can't walk. Can't walk, I can't work. You think she's going to stick around? No, she's probably already making other plans." Kyle began to weep quietly at the enormity of his injuries and what his life would be like. "I've lost everything, Haywood. Everything . . . I've lost everything."

Haywood made his way out of the hospital room, down the hall, and outside.

"No, we haven't lost everything yet. Not by a long shot," he said to himself. "There's so much more we could lose."

TWENTY-TWO

MELISSA STOPPED HER CAR before the village sign designating Coldwater. Her heart felt heavy and the butterflies flew deep. When her fingers began to scream in agony, she realized that she had been clenching the wheel. The town on the map that she had studied all these years had been but a lifeless dot on a page. Here, before her now, was the real thing. The place where it had all started for her. She had not been back since she was taken in by her aunt to live down in South Falls.

Her aunt never brought her to visit.

Her aunt never let her speak of it.

Coldwater was a word never uttered in the house.

The green sign on the village limit simply read COLDWATER POP. 436. There was another sign mockingly hanging underneath it that read WHERE WE TAKE CARE OF EACH OTHER.

The slogan made her stomach turn.

Coldwater had done everything but taken care of their own.

The drive up north took about an hour. North of South Falls, the two-lane road became more and more barren and wooded. Coldwater was the last little outpost before the forest won out and became the abode of hunters and those

91

who wished never to be found. In her mind it was the home of hillbillies and illiterates. Of people who never did know the meaning of caring for each other, much less themselves.

This was where she was born, and her memories were snapshots at best. Before Michael had destroyed everything.

Melissa put the car in drive and eased back onto the black-top. As she drove into town, the whole place became part of her disgust for the past. An accomplice to the one who had taken away her childhood, her life, her God-given right to normalcy.

Now she was back, a grown woman, but with all the anger and determination built up since childhood focused and sharpened.

Her knowledge of Main Street came from the peering eyes of Google and the countless hours she spent staring at street-view images it had recorded.

She pulled her car into the town's sole restaurant, a diner, which sat on the far side of a parking lot opposite Gilly's Pub. Behind both establishments sat the dilapidated Cold-water Motor Lodge, which was as old as the town. She would be checking in later. The place looked more rundown and backwoods than the two-dimensional pictures allowed, but she was still determined to spend several days here.

She got out of the car and went inside the diner. As she did so, memories came rushing back like the wind on a high desert plateau.

The place hadn't changed since her childhood, and she couldn't help but remember sitting at the counter with her father, many years ago, when he brought her here for ice cream. She couldn't remember how old she had been then, but she could still feel the melting ice cream as it smothered her face and dripped from her fingers onto the countertop. It wasn't a stretch to believe that the mess was still on the linoleum, crusted and rotted, never cleaned up.

She felt her knees buckle at the thought.

It seemed like forever ago, and yesterday.

And then the sensation was gone.

Melissa walked over to one of the booths and sat down, the duct-taped vinyl cushion straining to keep itself together. She looked around at the faces of the few people finishing up their lunches.

She wanted to be noticed yet also remain invisible. Wanted to ask anyone who would look at her where Michael might be, while at the same time not wanting to draw attention to her designs.

Three old men got up from a table, grabbed their hats, and started to leave. The first one to pass her smiled with his eyes like all old men who realize that their mouths only bring repulsion to young women. The two trailing geezers followed as fast as their arthritic limbs could carry them. As they walked past her, she heard pieces of their conversation.

"Jackson was old, died of a heart attack."

"Same day as the accident with James and Kyle? Just odd."

"Things always happen in threes."

"What?"

"Threes. Just the way it is. Tragedy happens in threes."

Melissa watched as the old-timers walked out the door, got in their vehicle, and headed out to escape into the wilderness.

Old folk mythology, she thought. Very soon, there would be a fourth.

TWENTY-THREE

THE FORT THAT THE BOY DESCRIBED, and where Michael now sat, was little more than a small cave in the bank of the ridge with its low opening facing north. It was an almost invisible location from the path on top of the ridge as the overhang to the entrance sloped over like a porch roof and was covered in moss, scrub, and a few shallow-rooted poplar trees. Inside, Michael saw that Will had troweled into the walls a tiny ledge that he had then used to hold odds and ends of childhood memorabilia. Most of the toys looked as if they had seen hard times, none of them seemed firsthand by any degree, but they were on display as if they were pride of possession. The dugout was cramped, and Michael found himself knocking over some of the toys by the simple act of turning around. He did his best to put things right.

As the afternoon wore on, Michael heard movement in the woods and the sound of a dog barking. Will and Otis were making their way down the path again. Michael stayed in the cave and waited, not knowing if the boy was alone or had brought someone with him.

Otis was the first to arrive. He stood several feet from the entrance and stared at Michael. He wasn't growling this time, but he looked none too happy to see the interloper occupying this space. Will appeared right after and stood behind Otis.

"I see you found it."

"I did, thank you."

"It will be better than staying where you were. It's supposed to rain tonight. Ma didn't want me coming back out due to the storm that is coming, but I told her I'd be right back. I figured you'd be hungry so I brought you something."

Will unzipped his backpack and pulled out a paper bag. Inside was an assortment of edible items, a collection that only a ten-year-old would think suitable for a meal. Michael took the bag.

"I also brought you this." Will tossed over a blanket, old and ratted, but still solid and usable. "It was in the bottom of my closet. I doubt anyone will miss it. It's been in there for as long as I can remember. Supposed to get cold too."

"Will, this is all more than I would have ever expected."

"Ain't nothing. Us adventurers have to stick together."

"Adventurers?"

"Yeah. Me and Otis come out in these woods all the time, exploring and adventuring. I can see you're like us. I'd hope if ever I get stuck on an adventure, someone would help me out. It's dangerous work."

"It's also dangerous befriending strangers, Will. I want to thank you for your bravery."

The boy rocked on his heels a bit, letting the compliment sink in. Though he was doing his best to act like a fearless adult, being called brave forced a half smile to cross his lips and made him look like the young boy he was.

"Sure. Well, I gotta get back. Come on, Otis!" and with that, Will made for the path. Otis, however, sat looking at

Michael and the provisions that his master had left behind. He had a questioning look in his eyes, as if he was telling Michael to be careful around the boy. Eventually the dog moved on after Will, and Michael was alone again.

He dug through the bag and pulled out some of the rations and ate a bit. Afterward he found the tarp that Will said was in the dugout and worked on propping it over the entrance to keep out whatever rain might come down. He wrapped himself in the blanket and crawled into the hovel in the hill . . . to the musty smell of earth, the chirping of crickets, and his thoughts about the vigilantes of Coldwater.

TWENTY-FOUR

THE WAITRESS STEPPED OVER TO TAKE MELISSA'S ORDER.

"I'm Lila," the woman said. "What can I get you?"

Melissa jolted out of her daydream of observing the old men leaving and looked up.

"How's the club sandwich?"

"Disgusting."

"Sounds fine," Melissa said, playing along.

"Coffee?"

"Sure."

The waitress sauntered off and slapped the paper order onto the sill. The chef grabbed it and disappeared into the kitchen.

The bits of conversation that she picked up from the old-timers still echoed through her head. Something happened very recently in Coldwater. The names were foreign but the talk of death was familiar. Death and Coldwater, two sides of the same coin. Two things forever entwined.

Maybe this wasn't the weekend that her plan would come into action. Part of her was frustrated, and part of her, a tiny part that Melissa refused to acknowledge, was slightly relieved.

She was not a practiced expert on the art of assassination.

Most of what she knew, or thought she knew, was cobbled together from books and film. She never overestimated herself. She knew this was dark business, but she was confident in her intelligence, which had always served her well in life. It's why she had planned, and planned, and then planned some more.

She thought she was ready, on the drive up she most assuredly was. But for a moment she could feel doubt creep in around the edges.

The waitress returned with the food, set it on the table, and asked if there was anything else needed.

"I'm good, thanks," Melissa said.

"Alright."

The woman turned and walked back to the kitchen.

As she ate, Melissa's mind turned over the words of the old locals.

"Jackson was old, died of a heart attack."

"Same day as the accident with James and Kyle? Just odd."

"Things always happen in threes."

Coldwater was off the news grid. There wasn't usually anything in the South Falls paper about the goings-on up here. The only newswire was the gossip of the townspeople. Lila came back to the table with a coffeepot in hand, refilled Melissa's cup, and was about to head back.

"Excuse me," Melissa said.

"Yes?"

"Can I ask you something?"

"Sure thing."

"Those men who just left. I heard them talking about an accident? Something recent?"

"Yeah. A lot happened yesterday. More than Coldwater is used to, that's for sure."

"What happened?"

"You mind if I sit down?" Lila asked.

"Please."

Lila set down the coffeepot on the next table and sat down across from Melissa. She pulled a packet of cigarettes from her bra, tapped one out, and stuck it in her mouth. She went to put the pack away, stopped, and then offered one to Melissa, who declined. The waitress lit it and blew the smoke over her shoulder.

Lila told Melissa about Mr. Jackson, the old geezer who owned a small store north of town who was found dead in his shop. Apparently from a heart attack. Then, not more than a couple hours later, a rollover accident had killed a man and sent another to the hospital down in South Falls. Nobody knew if he was going to make it.

"Local guys?" Melissa asked.

"Yeah. James and Kyle. They say James died instantly. Was thrown from the vehicle. Kyle got mangled. Nobody is sure how long he had been laying up there before the ambulance arrived."

Lila related the story with the casual familiarity of simple townfolks. She spoke as if Melissa was on a first-name basis with all of them. She blew another cloud over her shoulder. The smoke clung in the air like a dying hand slowly submerging beneath water.

"Lila! This ain't Gilly's. Put that thing out!" the chef said, shaking a spatula in his right hand.

"Just be thankful I agreed to cover for Tami, or you'd be out here bussing tables!" Lila hollered back.

She reached over and flicked the butt of the cigarette into the coffeepot. Melissa nudged her own cup away from her in response to what she saw.

"Did you know them? The guys in the car accident?" Melissa asked.

"Yeah, everyone did. Ain't too many going to miss James. But Kyle was a good guy. Is a good guy. He's dating the waitress here, Tami. That's why she ain't here. She's down in South Falls. She ain't taking it so well."

These "accidents" were an interesting cog in the wheel. With the people seemingly on high alert, it would seem that her plan for this weekend was definitely off. One more local dead and the southern authorities would absolutely be up here questioning everyone they could find. Melissa's heart began to sink.

"It only took a day for the conspiracy theories to start," Lila continued.

"What do you mean?" Melissa asked.

"Two deaths, possibly three, in one day? In Coldwater? People think we have a serial killer on the loose. I never saw Gilly's so dead on a Friday night. People stayed at home. You know these people are scared when they just decide to drink at home."

"They think someone caused these accidents?"

Lila chuckled. "They already think they know who caused these accidents."

"Who?"

"This guy who lives outside of town. Ex-con. Murdered someone a long time ago and got released from prison just last year. He's our resident boogeyman. Anytime anything goes wrong in town, it's his fault." Lila pulled out another cigarette and lit it. "Already heard as much. Old-timers think he is stalking around cursing the town. I mean, Mr. Jones walked out of Gilly's a week ago, saw he had a flat tire, and was convinced that Michael Sullivan had come into town and slashed his tires."

Michael Sullivan.

At the sound of the name, Melissa's heart stopped. She was thankful that Lila was too lost in her talking and smoking to notice the twitch that she felt in her eye at hearing the name.

"Last winter, John Morrison, the owner of Gilly's, was killed out hunting in the woods. It seemed that his gun backfired. Killed him quickly. Well, the folks around here know the truth. They'll tell you. It was Michael.

"I'm sorry," Lila said. "Here I am rattling on and on. You probably think I'm too much, don't you? It's not often there is a new person to talk to."

Melissa adjusted herself in her seat, trying to think of something to say to this particularly odd woman across from her. She decided to come at this straight on.

"So this guy Michael, you said he lives outside of town?" Melissa asked.

"Yeah, moved back to his parents' property after he got out of prison."

"Live out there by himself?"

"I couldn't tell you," Lila said, her eyes starting to register an uneasy feeling.

"Do you think he's dangerous? Do you think he did these things?"

At the question, the vivacious waitress suddenly lost her voice. She appeared like she had realized all of a sudden that she was late for an important meeting but couldn't find her keys.

"I'm sorry . . . I . . . I really should get back to work."

Melissa looked around at the empty diner. "Wait, please. Did I say something to bother you?"

"No, no. You're fine, really. It's just . . . well, it's just . . . no, I don't know much about him."

Lila got up, grabbed her coffeepot, and headed to the kitchen. She stopped, put her chin to her chest, and took a deep breath. She slowly turned and walked back over to the booth, her inability to hold her tongue surrendering her to confession.

"It's a small town, and people say things. I don't know what's true or not. Some people, well, they got this bad vibe about him. Others say horrible things, things that anybody in their right mind knows is ridiculous. But most are not happy he came back. They think he should have been locked up forever. I know he was just a boy when he did what he did, but still."

Lila reached for a replacement cigarette, but then reconsidered. "They think that he is responsible for Morrison. And what happened to James and Kyle. Like I said, it's a small town. Small-town people. Small-town minds. Some of the stories are so made up it's laughable. Some, well, they don't leave you laughing. But you will find that most people are scared of him, even the mere mention of him gives people the chills."

"And you, Lila? Are you scared of him?"

Lila thought about it for a minute. "Yeah, I believe I am. It's hard not to be. I haven't seen him for a while now. But I usually see him coming into town, walking, hood up to where you couldn't see his face. Always gave me the creeps a little bit. I can see why people tell stories. It's easy to attach stories to loners, I guess."

Lila walked away, this time for good.

Melissa sat in the booth a little while longer. She reached for her coffee cup, remembered how they made it here, and put it back down. She got up, threw some money on the table to cover her meal, and walked outside.

She thought about it. It had been years since her childhood in Coldwater. It seemed like a different lifetime. But the feeling that always accompanied any thought of those years, thoughts of her childhood in the woods, were thoughts of fear.

And anger.

A slow-burning anger that began in the pit of her stomach and grew to an all-consuming boil until she felt too tight in her own skin. The people in Coldwater had every right to fear Michael. Sure, they had created folklore around him as all small towns will for people like him. But though the tales they invented could have been far flung, the resulting fear they created was justified, even if in a roundabout way.

And it was why her own fear and anger were justified.

It was why her trip back to Coldwater was justified.

It was why the plan she brought with her was justified.

Melissa had lived it, the fear that these backwoods people speculated about. She had been witness to the destructiveness of Michael's actions. How they had burned down her childhood and spread the ashes to the wind. Her doubt receded, and she was doubly determined to move forward with her plan.

TWENTY-FIVE

THE REST OF THE POSSE had gathered at Gilly's that Saturday afternoon. The daylight snaked down the long hallway from the glass door facing Main Street. They sat around the table in the back room, nursing their beers and occasionally glancing at each other. This was the first day back into the routine that they had perfected over many years. In just two days their mundane lives had been forfeited for ones none of them could have described the week before. Several seats around the large circular table were empty.

James wouldn't be coming back.

Kyle, if he ever made it back, would arrive in his own chair, and leave in it as well.

They sat waiting for someone to start the conversation. Clinton, after taking a calculated sip, broke the silence.

"Anyone seen Haywood?" His voice was deep and solid. If their group had a member made out of granite, it was Clinton.

The others shook their heads.

"Heard he was going down to South Falls to check on Kyle," Davis replied.

"Probably making sure he keeps his mouth shut," Earl said.

"What does that mean?" Frank said.

"Haywood wouldn't do anything to Kyle," Clinton said.

"You sure about that?" Earl said. "You don't think he would do to us what he made us do with Michael? Shoot, man. I mean, he was the mastermind behind all this, am I right?"

"Now Earl, we all went up there of our own free will," Clinton said.

"Did we?" Frank shot back. "Do you think if it wasn't for Haywood that we would have buried . . ." The volume of his own voice caused Frank to check himself. He leaned closer to the others. ". . . you know . . . done what we done?"

"He's right," Earl said. "This is all Haywood's doing. We should go to the cops and tell them what happened. What happened to James and Kyle. What happened to Old Man Jackson."

"And what did happen to them, Earl?" asked Haywood, who now stood by the open doorway that separated the back room from the bar. They hadn't noticed his arrival. He slowly walked over and sat down in James's forever-unoccupied seat. He looked around at the boys who now tried to bury their eyes in their own beers.

"You boys think this is my fault, what happened to James and Kyle?"

The men said nothing.

Haywood reached over to the pitcher, raised it to his mouth, and took a sip. He then looked each man in the face, slowly making his way around the table.

"I miss James just as much as anybody. Kyle, now I'm just crushed about Kyle, but he's going to make it. And he's going to need us once he gets out of the hospital.

"Now you all are sitting here wondering about what we

did. You're probably wondering how this mess came down on us, what we could have done differently that would have changed our current situation. Believe me, I've been thinking about it the whole time. What we should have done. But what we should have done is something that none of us were willing and capable of doing. That's the problem."

"What we should have done is left the man alone," Clinton said. "He was minding his own business—"

"Now you know that ain't true," Haywood responded. "You think Morrison just drove out into the woods, sat next to a tree, and blew his face off?"

"No," Earl said, "the problem is that we let you convince us it was Michael who did all that. James and Kyle would be sitting here right now drinking with us if you hadn't forced us to drug Michael and drag him up . . ."

"I didn't force anyone, and don't you all forget it. You're grown men. You did what you wanted. So you should ask yourself why you all chose to go along. I'll tell you why: because deep down inside you know I'm right. You knew that Michael was dangerous. You've known it all along. When they found Morse out in the woods and people asked how that could have happened, whose face popped up into your mind? I'll tell you. Michael's. And do you know why that is? Because somewhere in those thick heads of yours you know what evil looks like. You've seen it."

"What happened to Morrison was an accident," Earl said.

"It was no accident. When Michael moved back to town, while you all went on with your lives, I've been waiting . . . waiting for that maniac to start killing at random. And then it happened and I knew we had to do something about it."

"So why didn't you just call the cops, man?" Davis said,

his exasperation at the long speech evident. He was a man of few words, the countersilence to Clinton's deep baritone. The conversation was obviously annoying him.

"Why do you think? It took all I had to convince you guys that something had to be done, and you've known me all your lives. What do you think the cops would have done?"

"Put you in a straitjacket, I reckon," Frank said with a nervous laugh.

"You're probably right," Haywood said, a thin smirk on his face in an attempt to ease the tension out of the group. "So, rather than harping on each other, we need to start thinking about what we are going to do now. He may be gone, but he's not gone forever. I bet he'll be back. And I bet when he comes back, he ain't going to come back quietly."

TWENTY-SIX

THE GLOCK ALWAYS FELT HEAVY TO HER, its grip just a bit oversized for her slender fingers. Melissa sat on the bed of her room in the Coldwater Motor Lodge, the lights from the parking lot shining through the window like a scene from a David Lynch movie, light reflecting off the barrel of the gun.

Night had descended on the town, and before there was a thought, the day was coming to an end.

She sat in silence, looking at the weapon.

In the gun she saw the tool of justice. The instrument that would bring order back to her life.

Melissa had never visited her brother after he went to prison. She was too young to remember the trial, the sentence, the short celebrity status that the event had given Michael. But even as a little girl she knew that he was the reason for the disintegration of her childhood and family.

After Michael went to prison, her mom escaped into another world, locked inside her own mind. She would drift in and out of the house, sometimes being gone for days, and then wander back in quietly, never saying a word. In fact, if Melissa thought hard enough, she wasn't sure if her mom ever spoke again after the event. She had become a shell of a person, her heart ripped out, and all that was left was a walking cadaver.

Her father lasted as long as he could, but was never well to begin with. He died not long after, and soon Melissa was left to the care of her zombie mom. Melissa's aunt stepped in and took her to live with her in South Falls. She was ordered never to talk about her brother, never to ask about him, to shut off that piece of her past as if it had never existed.

But it had existed.

And through her life, Melissa was fixated on her brother.

It wasn't a white-hot fixation, but a low, underlying anger that seemed to be embedded in the cells of her skin. Rage was a passion, this was so much more cerebral, long lasting. Over time Melissa wanted Michael to pay dearly for the chaos he had caused, the family he destroyed, the childhood he had robbed from her. Having him locked away pacified that need for retribution for the longest time.

But then he was released and she felt the feelings of anger intensify.

How could justice be served so quickly with her father dead and her mom blown to the four winds, insane and wandering the earth. It was up to Melissa to bring order back to the cosmos. It was up to her to make sure justice was served up in its entirety, not delivered half-heartedly and with a level of disinterest as the state had done.

She had come to Coldwater to kill her brother.

As she looked across the room, she caught her reflection in the mirror above the sink in the corner. Her hair covering half her face, the gun in her hands, her arms on her crossed legs. She had all the appearance of a casual assassin. But she knew that she wasn't. There was one thing holding her back. Holding her back from finding Michael and killing him. That one thing was herself.

Her anger still had holes in it where fear crept in. She didn't know if it was fear of getting caught, fear of killing another person, or fear of coming to learn that she liked the experience. Knowledge of what it felt like to take another person's life still escaped her. It was on the other side of a door, a door with only one handle, and it led to a room that, once entered, she would never be able to leave; the door would close behind her and there would be no way to exit. It was a room that her brother had entered when he was a boy. In killing him, she would take his place. Once she had the knowledge of what it was like to kill someone, she would never be able to unlearn it.

But she was not like him. Michael had acted out of selfishness, out of hatred. He had done what he did out of pure contempt with no remorse. She was justified. She was righteous. She was good.

Wasn't she? Her motivation, the reason she was here to kill Michael, would absolve her of all guilt, of all judgment. She was completing justice, was she not? All she wanted was to set things right. She owed it not only to herself but to the family that Michael had destroyed.

She laid the gun down on the bed, stretched out her legs, grabbed one of the bullets that was lying on the comforter beside her, and rolled it through her fingers.

Such a small thing. Such a world-shattering thing. The bullet was the key to the room. It just needed to find its lock.

And as she gazed at the bullet between her fingers, she wondered if she was capable of opening the door.

TWENTY-SEVEN

LILA STEPPED FROM BEHIND THE BAR AT GILLY'S—her normal night gig now that the diner was closed—grabbed Earl's arm, and led him to the corner of the room. The music was playing loudly and the cacophony of voices mixed in the air with beer fumes and cigarette smoke to blanket their conversation in a haze of solitude.

"I need to know something," Lila said.

"Anything," Earl said, his heart rate elevating just as it always did when he was close to her.

"There was this woman, I've never seen her before. She was over at the diner and was asking questions."

"Questions about what?"

"Questions about the accident, about Old Man Jackson."

"Who isn't talking about that?"

Lila looked over her shoulder, nervous eyes scanning the bar. "There's more."

"More what?" Earl asked. His mind was half on her words, and half on the perfume he could smell coming off her. She was rough, no doubt about that, but there was also beauty locked in there somewhere. Earl was brought back to the here and now when Lila smacked him upside the shoulder.

"You hear what I said?"

"What?"

"She was talking about Michael. Asking questions," she said. She startled and looked around, then lowered her voice to a whisper. "But it was more than questions, you know. She was asking where he was, what people thought of him."

"What you tell her?"

"Not much. She asked if I had seen him lately."

Earl opened his eyes wide and concentrated on every word coming out of Lila's mouth. All of a sudden he felt exposed, like a giant light was being turned on and the actions of the past days were coming into view. Lila noticed.

"What's wrong?" she asked.

"Nothing."

"Don't 'nothing' me, Earl."

"It's nothing . . . really."

"You know something . . . I can tell."

"I don't know anything, and if I did, which I don't, why would I tell you?"

"You're the worst liar in town." She glared at him and he quivered under her stare. She took a step back and really looked at him.

"Were you here on Thursday?"

"Maybe," he said.

"Glenn told me there was an incident here. Said that Michael came in, and that a bunch of guys took care of him."

Earl fidgeted. "Yeah, you could say that."

"What you do, Earl?"

"Nothing, I told you."

"Earl!"

"Like Glenn said, we took care of him. Haywood, Frank, all of us."

"James and Kyle too?" she asked.

Earl looked at her dead in the eyes. He nodded. Lila gasped and put her hand over her mouth.

"What did you boys do?"

"I told you," Earl said, "nothing. Now quit grilling me about this and leave it rest. If you want to know so bad, talk to Haywood. It's his show."

"And this woman, the one who is suddenly interested in where Michael is, who is she?"

"I don't know, but we need to find out. Haywood is going to want to know."

TWENTY-EIGHT

HAYWOOD WAS BECOMING more and more unhinged as the days went on—at least that was the perception of Frank and Earl as they stood on his porch the next morning and knocked on his door. Haywood opened it with the chain still attached, his body hidden behind the frame so as to avoid being shot through the door. Even when he saw it was just Frank and Earl, his eyes fluttered to the driveway and road before letting them in.

Last night at Gilly's, Haywood told them to be at his house first thing in the morning, which wasn't hard since none of them had had a good night's sleep after they took Michael out into the woods. Each one of them had been tormented in the silence of the dark by their own conscience. Earl had made it a habit of checking each window and lock of his own house every fifteen minutes, a routine that had become so habitual that even when he did drift off into dreamland, his body would wake him and send him on the circuit again.

It was fear. Plain and simple.

Fear of what they had done. Fear of being found out. Fear of the sleeping dog they had awoken and buried in the woods, of their own ghosts of guilt haunting them in the night.

Haywood appeared before the two men the worse for

wear. Over four days, his fear had morphed into an obsessive compulsion. He looked as if he had been standing up all night, pacing back and forth, fueled by a bottomless cup of coffee and a mind that was running faster than any words could express.

On the table in the dining room was a map of the surrounding area. Haywood had marked it up with a black Sharpie with symbols and signs that resembled the frantic scratches of a child. The men had all lived in the area their whole lives, but looking at Haywood's markings on the map transformed the familiar into a world unknown to them.

There was a circle around the location of Michael's house, an X where they had taken him to Springer's Grove, a line following the river over to Old Man Jackson's store. The place where James and Kyle had flipped the truck was marked too. Both Frank and Earl studied the map. They saw several lines starting randomly on the north of the map, slinking down and terminating at different locations. One of those locations, Frank noticed, was his house. Earl saw the same thing for his house. Haywood's also.

Haywood had mapped out the paths Michael might take to launch his offensive.

"What . . . what is all this?" Earl stuttered, pointing to different marks on the map.

"These are where he might be," Haywood said.

"You really think so?" Frank asked.

"Absolutely," Haywood said. "And don't act all surprised. You think he's just going to run off and stay gone? Would you?"

Frank and Earl were silent.

"You know I'm right. I know you've been looking over

your shoulders the past couple days, worried that he is going to sneak up on you."

Frank looked at Earl and the two men's eyes held a silent conversation. Haywood was absolutely right. They thought about that one step over the line of everything normal and knew it had proven to be a line that they could never go back over. They were on the other side until the end and they hated it. Hated that they had gone along with Haywood's madness. Hated that they had not seen the evil they were doing when they took Michael away. Haywood had convinced them so soundly as to the righteousness of their action, how they were protecting their families, their children, their community. But now, they slowly started hating themselves for what they had done. Even more so, they began to hate Haywood for dragging them all into the pit with him.

"I think it's time we call the police," Frank said. "This is out of hand . . . we can't be doing this . . ."

"You want to call them? Really? Here . . . then do it!" Haywood said and tossed his cell phone at him. "And while you're at it, tell them you would like extra pillows in your cell. What about you, Earl? Any requests you might have?"

Frank and Earl stared at each other.

"You think prison would be better than this? Don't get me wrong, that's where we are going if you call them up. All they will have to do is find Michael and he will tell them what we did. And who do you think they are going to believe? Kyle won't be able to keep his mouth shut, and neither will you, Earl—you'll start crying as soon as they start questioning you."

"Now come on, Haywood," Earl shot back.

"I'm telling you guys, we are in this to the end. Ain't no turning back."

"Now, how come Michael just doesn't go to the police himself?" Frank asked. "For all we know, we're as good as cooked as it is."

"Because he's in the same fix we are in."

"You still believe that?"

"I know it."

■ ■ ■

Haywood knew more than any of them what was coming. He knew that Michael would destroy them all, and not with the quietness of calling the authorities. Haywood's mind thought of every horrible way that Michael would end their lives. Seeing Kyle broken in the hospital was visible proof of what kind of future these men could look forward to.

This could only end one way, and now Haywood knew it was either them or Michael.

Haywood stood up, ran his hand over his forehead as if he were attempting to pull out some piece of reasoning stuck in his frontal lobe. He was tired of having this conversation with these guys. It had been a conversation that he had been repeating over and over, and no matter how hard he pushed, he knew that no one would believe him with absolute certainty. The fact that the boys went along with him the night they drugged Michael wasn't due to their convictions in what he had told them. No. They went along because they believed in him, had known him their whole lives, had probably been beat down to the point of exhaustion by Haywood's relentless storytelling.

Morrison in the woods? Michael.

And now James, Old Man Jackson? Michael.

But Frank, Earl, Clinton, Kyle . . . maybe even Davis—they were not true believers. Haywood had been able to stoke their fear, had been able to connect enough of the dots to show them how dangerous the ex-con was. He had persuaded them, he knew, and thus he would always have to keep persuading them until the very end.

"Okay, let's assume that he isn't going to the cops," Frank said. "What makes you sure he isn't going to just keep running? You know, get as far from here as possible?"

"Because, he's not a man of means. He's going to have to come back. Where else is he going to go? I doubt he's got a stack of money to set him up someplace else."

"It's not like Coldwater is the only place he can be a bum in."

"No, he'll come back," Haywood said. He rubbed his temples again. The guys would just never understand. "Michael isn't some innocent man running scared. He just isn't going to leave and not look back. The sooner you all remember that, the better off we all are."

Frank and Earl reluctantly conceded the point.

"Most likely he's going to return to his house. It's the only place he knows. I suggest you guys go up there and stake it out."

"Whoa now," Earl said, "what happens if he's there? That's a long way from town. If he is as dangerous as you say he is, I sure don't want to be the one to run across him, especially out in the sticks."

"Just drive up there and see if you notice anything, that's all I'm asking. Give me a call if anything looks out of the ordinary."

"And what are you going to be doing while we're off searching for the lunatic?"

"I'm going to go up past Countyline Road with Clinton and Davis. Ask if anyone has seen anything. See if they've noticed anyone or anything out of the ordinary."

All three took one last look at the map and then parted ways.

Frank and Earl climbed into their truck and headed out of town toward Michael's cabin. Haywood, to pick up Clinton and Davis and head up to the north woods.

TWENTY-NINE

*I*T WAS A LONG TIME *before the warden discerned the pattern of sickness in Cell Block D, and when he did, he kicked himself for not seeing the pattern sooner. It was plain as day, after all—he just wasn't expecting it.*

Michael. The boy prisoner.

The death of the inmate in the kitchen not more than a month into the boy's sentence was seen as coincidence. The man had had a massive heart attack, luckily for Michael, and fell dead before he could violate the boy. It was written up and dismissed as such. The prison created its own mythology, but the warden was a man of reason and was convinced by the coroner's report.

What followed suit for the next year was viewed in much the same way. It took the maintenance crew one visit in his office, asking the most benign of questions, to awaken his mind to the possibility.

After the crew left, the warden spent the next week looking over past incident reports in the cell block. They all had one common denominator. Michael.

The first incident involved the convict in the cell adjoining the boy's. His name was Malcolm Johnson. He was in for armed robbery and arrived about three months after the boy. Malcolm was quiet for the first several weeks of his stay, apparently content to serve his time and not bother anyone. Then he kept asking to see the doctor. There were several visits recorded, all the same thing. Headaches.

The warden looked at the time stamps of the paperwork. The visits to the doctor increased over a week's time, the doctor giving ibuprofen and sending Malcolm back to his cell.

It was a Tuesday when the guards saw Malcolm on his bed, his body seizing uncontrollably, blood pouring from his nose and ears.

The medical staff removed him and carted him to the hospital.

There was no diagnosis from the hospital in the file.

Malcolm returned to the jail but to a different cell, eventually transferred to another prison downstate. The warden got on the phone and called the prison that Malcolm was sent to.

"What can I help you with?" his colleague asked.

"Malcolm Johnson, can you look up your records of him?"

"Sure. What are you looking for?"

"I'm wondering if he's had any medical problems you're treating him for."

After a short wait, the other voice returned on the line.

"Nothing here. Clean bill of health. No problems."

"Thanks."

"That all?"

"Yes."

Six months later, another inmate had started vomiting uncontrollably. He was screaming of visions and panic attacks. The warden attributed it to a nervous breakdown and had the inmate moved to the infirmary and eventually moved to Cell Block B. He looked at the record and saw that he too *had been in the cell next to the boy, moving in after Malcolm had been transferred. The warden looked at the rest of the inmate's file. The man had been released on parole last year, no further medical or conduct incidents in his history.*

There were many such stories. When the guards started getting ill a while back, the warden had called in a crew to check for environmental hazards such as mold or rodents. Their analysis came up clean. Laying out the reports, illness spread out through the cell block in concentric circles of severity. Michael's cell was the epicenter.

And he was as healthy as any boy could be.

The maintenance crew had been doing work outside when they noticed that the grass spreading out from the wall of the cell block was dead. Not just yellowing from the sun, but dead as dead could be. The dead patch went from the wall under a fence topped with razor wire, a location of the grounds not used for anything. How long it had been dead was anyone's guess, but the maintenance team wanted to know how the warden wanted it fixed before the weather started to wash the soil away and compromise the fence.

When the warden walked out to investigate, he saw a sign that opened his mind to the unimaginable. The dead earth sprouted from the wall right under Michael's cell.

The boy was slowing killing Cell Block D.

THIRTY

IT WAS AS IF A POISON RAIN had fallen through the night, blanketing the world in a creeping fog of mourning. Michael awoke to sunlight filtering through the tarp at the dugout's entrance. He felt damp from the moisture in the air, and his joints felt the arthritic ache of an uncomfortable night's sleep, his third now. And though the earthen hideout was damp, it was drier than the open hillside he had slept on the previous night, and just a little more spacious than the pine box he had been buried in.

His head pounded and his skin felt constricted against his frame. Running his fingers through his greasy hair, he could feel the particles of grave dirt dance beneath his hand. Michael smelled of earth and wilderness. He moved the tarp to crawl outside and stretch his legs.

Outside the forest was wilting. The green brush and undergrowth that had met his arrival on the western ridge had started to fade to brown, the plants bowing prostrate in a weeping gesture. They were dying. The mere presence of the man in the cave had sucked their desire to live. Keeping low off the ridge, Michael walked down and away from the shelter and into the green.

The past days seemed like a dream. A cycle of dying, waking, and then dying again.

He had always been alone. It was his lot. His just reward. He knew that in the very fiber of his being.

He emptied his bladder by a tree and then headed back to the camp. The morning air hung heavy and the creatures of the forest were welcoming the early light that drifted through the canopy and onto the forest floor. The air was cooler than natural, like the basement of the world opened up in summer. Michael walked up past the dugout to the top of the ridge, the air warming on his ascent.

The backbone of the ridge wandered east and west in a meandering course, disappearing on both ends into the forest. He could have been hundreds of miles from Coldwater or right next door, it was impossible to see through the overgrowth. The path of the ridge was little more than trampled weeds and foliage, the kind of path made in equal parts by weather and the feet of a small boy and his dog. This was wild land.

Michael looked down from his perch to where he had spent the night. It was invisible from this point of view except for the slowly browning circle in the valley. Soon the small area in front of the dugout would die out, exposing a curiosity in the woods that would attract the attention of anyone who passed by.

The dying off always pointed him out.

He made his way back down the hill and into the cave.

He couldn't stay here long, but he wanted to, all the same. The boy made him want to halt his running. It had been a long time since someone had talked to him, had come upon him and not seen the baggage that he carried with him, but had instead seen something of value. Something worth engaging with.

Will was young and naive. He had not experienced the world enough to know that he should avoid some people, people the world had written off and consigned to oblivion, people he shouldn't even talk to. He hadn't learned this yet, but he would, and his boyish curiosity would fade and die like the ever-enlarging circle of death surrounding the cave that Michael lay down in.

It pained Michael to think about that as it brought him back to his own childhood, wasted and dead before it had even started. In Will he saw the same potential that he had thrown away so carelessly. He wanted to latch onto it, to observe it, to participate in it as if by some method of osmosis he could experience the adventure of naive youth one more time, now that he knew how precious it was.

But to stay would be selfish.

His time to dream had passed.

And in staying he would bring harm to a boy who still saw the world with endless fascination.

Michael had already done that once before. He would do everything in his power to never let it happen again.

THIRTY-ONE

MELISSA DROVE EAST out of Coldwater. Her thoughts drifted through the winding wooded roads. It had been forever since she had lived here, but her hands directed the car, instinctively guiding her to a dark destination. The area looked familiar but strange. The passage of time altering her childhood memory into a distorted present. She drove on until she came to a dirt road that branched north. She slowed and turned onto it.

The trees hung over in a blanketed canopy, a leafy tunnel extending out before her. When she was young, there was but one house on this access road. Now several two-tracks jetted off on either side every so often—hunting trails.

And then she arrived.

The woods dropped away, revealing a plot of ground that was scorched of everything save for a few weeds struggling against the dirt. Nestled back several hundred feet was a house. Her house. Her childhood home.

She sat in her car on the road for a while. Purpose had driven her out here, but now she was stopped with a sense of dread that left her feeling nauseated and doubtful. Was she ready to do this? Was she ready to put a bullet in Michael?

Melissa turned the wheel and pulled into the yard. She

stopped the car, reached under the seat and grabbed the Glock, opened the door, and stepped out.

Looking around, she saw the hard-packed earth circling the house in concentric rings of decay until the woods slowly found their starting point. At the epicenter of the circle was the house. The remains of the house she remembered.

Motes drifted in sunlight as she stepped up to the porch. The front door was slightly open and hanging off one of the hinges. It looked half rotten, the handle and lock long since disappeared. She looked in, and a small animal, squirrel or something similar, scurried farther into the house and out of sight.

"Hello?" she said, her voice echoing in the vacant building.

Melissa placed a foot across the threshold, cautiously, as if unsure of the strength of the floor beneath her feet. The silence was overwhelming. She observed the scene behind outstretched arms, the gun before her.

The room she'd entered was in shambles. What little adornment the house once had now lay scattered on the floor. A wall sconce, a mirror now broken in several large pieces. The table was pushed over toward the sink in an impossible-to-be-useful position, its sole chair knocked off its legs. The years had taken a bat to the abode and wracked its bones.

She walked deeper into the house, her own faded memories racing before her. The living area was simple. A worn couch sat next to the wall under the window but now looked to be used as a rat's nest rather than a seat. A coffee table with a chewed leg and rain-stained surface sat before it.

Melissa turned and walked into the hall that led to the bedrooms, the Glock held in trembling hands. She tried the first door, but it wouldn't open. It was her old room, a room that she had shared with her brother, the memory of it circulating in her mind in single-frame snapshots. She more felt than visualized the memory of the house.

She put some weight behind her effort, but it wouldn't budge. The handle of the door was new, its pristine brass coating standing out like a beacon in a trash pile. The handle had a keyhole suited for an exterior door. It was locked. She searched the top of the frame for a key, but found none.

Turning down the hall, Melissa walked to the back bedrooms. In one of them there was just a bed with more tattered books stacked up along the far wall. The roof above the bed had fallen away, and the weather had done its work to rot the gypsum on the walls.

Across the hall, behind a panel door that leaned against the doorframe, was her parents' old room.

Melissa returned to the living area. She slowly took a last look around. Her eyes passed over the grimy window, and she paused, then dismissed a stray thought of scrubbing off the grunge to look outside.

If she had done so, she would have noticed a truck parked out on the road, its occupants watching, waiting for her to come out.

■ ■ ■

"Haywood, that woman Lila was talking about, I think she's at the house," Frank said into his cell phone.

A voice on the other end responded.

"And another thing," he said, "when was the last time you were out here at Michael's?"

More chatter.

128

"Has this place always looked like this . . . like, dead? It's like someone let off napalm or something. It's just—"

"Odd?" Earl piped in.

"Yeah, odd," Frank said into the phone.

Frank looked at Earl as he received his instructions.

"Okay," Frank said, then hung up the phone and placed it in his visor.

"What he say?" Earl asked.

"He said to sit tight, see what she does."

"Sit tight? What, we stalking her now too? Jeez, man, this just keeps getting worse. What happens if she sees us?"

"Nothing. We're not doing anything wrong. We're on a public road. Every right to be here."

"Oh, okay." Earl scowled. "Just two dudes sitting in a truck watching a woman walk around . . . ain't nothing weird about that, Your Honor."

"Would you stop it! Haywood is right. We need to know who she is. We don't know where Michael is, and suddenly she shows up looking through his things? It can't be a co-incidence. Chances are she's here to help him. And if that's the case, where she is, he could be also."

"Which means best to stay away from her," Earl said.

"Wrong. You know where she is, you know where he is. Better than finding him in your house in the middle of the night, am I right?" Frank asked.

"I guess so."

"Right. So just relax."

"Okay, genius, what if he's in there with her right now?" Earl asked.

Frank thought for a minute. Earl wasn't dumb all the time.

He put the truck in gear and drove to a more secluded

part of the road but still kept the house in sight. He turned the truck around, feeling a little more at ease to be facing toward Coldwater than pointed away from the main road back to town.

"How long do we wait?" Earl asked.

"As long as it takes, I guess."

"What he say about all this dead earth surrounding Michael's house?"

"Said he seen it before."

"And?"

"Just said it's proof that Michael's very presence is a cancer."

Earl shook his head and looked out the window. "We never should have done this."

"I know," Frank said.

"Never should have listened to Haywood."

"I know."

"So why are we still?"

Frank sat silently and looked out the windshield. Nope, Earl wasn't dumb all the time.

THIRTY-TWO

S O HOW LONG YOU BEEN ADVENTURING?"
Michael came out of his daze and returned to the conversation in progress. Will and Otis had come that morning bearing more gifts, more snacks that would rot the teeth of the strongest jaw, but Michael's stomach was in no position to argue. They sat in the dirt in front of the dugout entrance. Otis spent his time chasing shadows in the dying underbrush.

"For a while, I guess."

"You live out in these woods?"

"No, not really."

"Where you from?"

"Coldwater. Was. Am."

"Why'd you leave?"

"Well, you could say that it was time I got out. Go adventuring."

"You going back?"

"I haven't decided yet. I guess I'm still thinking about it. There's nothing good going to come from me going back."

"Can I tell you something?" Will asked.

"Sure."

"I always like going home. Don't tell my mom that, but

131

I'm always ready to head back. Otis, now he could stay out here forever, but me, I always feel a sense of relief when I get home."

"Nothing wrong with that. The world is a scary place."

"You got that right."

"You're a wise boy, Will."

"Thanks."

■ ■ ■

They sat quietly again. The conversation had flowed back and forth between silence and idle talk. Michael's thoughts drifted to the events of his capture, his mind analyzing every detail, trying to identify faces in the dark haze of a drug-fueled memory. There were seven of them that night at Gilly's. Each one staring at him as the room spun into darkness. Each one silently watching as the poison coursed through his veins.

The two men on the road he knew. James and Kyle. They had been faces in his world but not part of it. Kyle was younger by several years. He would see him in Coldwater whenever he dared to venture into town, and he recalled his boyhood face from the school yard all those years ago. His thoughts of James were similar. Loud, large, cocky. They were all superficial caricatures he'd created. He knew no one in Coldwater intimately.

The wind blew and the rustling of dead leaves filled the silence. The clearing of dead plants was creeping ever wider by the hour. A perfect dead radius around the cave.

Michael knew that he could not stay here long. Soon the creeping would spread up the ridge and expose his hideout. Then there would be no reason to stay in the cramped quarters. This dying would follow him as it always did and he would have to move on. But move on where?

He was enjoying these odd get-togethers with Will and Otis. Even the dog had seemed to come around and tolerate his existence. Not entirely, but he would at least sit across from him and not growl.

He looked over at Will and watched him throw another piece of candy into his mouth. The boy caught his gaze and smiled back, his teeth covered in chocolate. Then Michael saw it.

From the boy's left nostril, a small bead of blood started to run down toward his lip in a slow serpentine crawl. It pooled slightly and then ran into the boy's mouth. The salty taste surprised the boy, and he wiped his nose with his sleeve. The sight of blood on his cuff startled him.

"Uh-oh!" Will exclaimed.

Michael stood up, an icy shock filling his limbs. The thought that he was slowly poisoning Will convicted him to the quick. "I think it's time you got going now."

"Just a bloody nose."

"No. You need to leave."

The boy's face twisted in a look of confusion. "But I just got out here," he said.

"Will! Go!"

"But . . . but . . ." Will's voice was a mix of surprise and hurt. The blood running from his nose added to the portrait of confusion and gore.

"Will. It's for your own good. Please!"

Otis returned from the brush, alert. He started barking at Michael.

"Okay, okay. Sorry."

"There's nothing to be sorry for, Will. You just need to get home. You need to get that taken care of."

"It's no big deal, I've had bloody noses before."

Not like this, he hadn't. Desperation clawed at Michael. "Just trust me . . . please."

"Okay." The boy swiped his nose, packed up his bag, and called for the dog, who ran up to him and seemed eager to push him up the ridge. Will stopped at the top and turned back, the look of childlike eagerness stabbed Michael's heart. "See you later?"

Michael nodded a disingenuous assent and watched the boy climb up to the path and disappear over the hill. He pushed aside his roiling emotions and went into the dugout to gather up his things.

It was time to go.

THIRTY-THREE

THERE ARE STILL PLACES on this earth where you can get lost. Michael was happy to be in such a place as he headed east through the woods. Apart from the occasional two-track or overgrown snowmobile trail, he was alone in a vast wilderness.

He was going to miss Will and Otis. It wasn't often that he talked to anyone, and now, after the attack, he was sure that those moments would become even rarer. But he knew that he couldn't stay in the dugout nor could he stay in their company. For the moment, he'd let himself be fooled by his desire for companionship, even if it was the naive ramblings of a ten-year-old boy. But when he saw the effects that his presence was having on the encampment and the blood starting to drip from Will's nose, he knew that he had fooled himself long enough.

He was a wanderer. Cursed to be alone.

He knew this, but he was also human and humans forget. Humans wish. Humans desire company.

Now, trudging through the forest, he wanted the opposite. He wanted to vanish. If he couldn't break bread with Will, he didn't want to see anybody. Even Otis with his puppy growl.

Michael knew he couldn't stay out here forever. The nights

would be growing longer and colder. He had to get back to his cabin and at the very least get supplies that would help him on a more determined trek away from Coldwater. By his estimation, heading east would bring him to State Road 42, which he could follow south and get back to familiar territory. He knew the general area he was in, having come north from Old Man Jackson's, but the north woods was still pristine, even on its outer edges. The boundary road acted as a barrier to further encroachment by Coldwater residents. It's where the world terminated. It's where James and Kyle had terminated.

He was off the grid. And while he was off the grid, he was safe from his pursuers in Coldwater, but he wasn't safe from the elements. He had to get home eventually.

Though he'd spent his early years in the area, he didn't really know it that well, just the cursory knowledge one would get from casual observation. Since his return last year, his hunting and fishing took place within easy distance from his cabin, and any supply runs into Coldwater were done hiking down Old State Road, or even to Jackson's store if he was up on the river. The north woods were as mysterious to him as they'd been in his youth.

Michael kept walking, his breath mixing with the crunching leaves underfoot and the call of birds in the canopy overhead. After an hour or two, the wind brought to him an odd odor that stung his senses and stopped him in his tracks. It was an unnatural aroma, not of the forest, but manufactured in the stew pot of hell and damnation.

Michael looked around, fearful that he had walked into a camp or someone's property. He saw nothing. Stooping down and covering his face to fight off the stench, he moved forward

136

until he could see the trees start to clear. Far ahead he saw an old trailer. Next to it was a metal garage with its door open and a faint mist of smoke pouring out of the interior. There was nobody around.

Deep in the woods someone had staked a claim and was brewing up something vile.

Michael crouched behind a tree and observed. He saw a woman come out of the trailer, walk across the clearing to the door of the garage. She stood there for a minute and then slowly made her way back. Her gait was unsteady, like she was drunk on the fumes belching from the outbuilding into the clearing. She disappeared back into the trailer and the metal door slammed behind her.

From the garage a large man in overalls stepped out. He had a mask of some sort over his face to protect him from the stench, and gloves up to his elbows. The man stood staring at the trailer and then disappeared into his dark laboratory.

As it slowly dawned on Michael what he had stumbled into, he felt a boot step onto his back, pushing him hard against the ground, and the barrel of a gun press against the back of his head.

"Have you seen enough?" a voice said.

THIRTY-FOUR

MELISSA STEPPED out of the decrepit house and back onto the dead soil. She looked out onto the landscape and let the current state of her childhood home overwrite her memory of it. Desolate. Quiet. It was a burned-out remembrance. She turned away from her car and walked to the back of the house. She noticed a fire pit in the back with charred ash in it. It hadn't been used recently. Farther back in the trees, she saw the remains of a deer hanging from a tree. It appeared that it had been dressed, but wild animals had rendered it grotesque. It was little more than a bone ornament now. There was an assortment of old junk and rusting metal scattered around the house.

Dead.

Everything dead.

Farther around the back, she saw an old battered Aljoa trailer, its two wheels flat, its seafoam coloring stained. She raised her gun and walked toward it.

Her footsteps seemed louder than they had ever been.

She reached for the trailer door. It was unlocked.

She stepped in and saw that the inside was lived-in but clean. It was as if she had stepped through the looking glass, the interior not matching the slow decay outside. There was a small stove and icebox. In the back, the bed took up half the trailer but had not been slept in. The comforter was a solid color, cheap but fairly new. This must be where Michael lived. The house was all but falling down, but here, hidden away in a tin can, is where he spent his nights.

A space that would drive a normal person to insanity, but perfect for a person who had been conditioned to a prison cell.

What kind of life was this? She thought about how good she had it when her aunt had come and taken her away from this place. Even on those odd nights before her father died and when her mother would drift back home, it felt lonely. It was never a house of love after Michael had destroyed it. Just coldness. Three people living in the same confined space.

Her mother hadn't bothered to come out of the house when she left. Hadn't even ventured out of the bedroom that day. Melissa couldn't recall the last time she'd seen her mother's face, and now she couldn't remember her face at all. When she thought of her, she could see only her silhouette, her face blurred, deleted from her memory.

There was nothing here now.

Her eyes glanced around the trailer, looking for nothing in particular, when a reflection caught her eye. Hanging from a lanyard on a nail over the stove was a key. A bright, newly fashioned key. She picked it up and examined it, then put it in her pocket.

Melissa turned and stepped back out into the parched yard.

She walked around to the front of the house, up to the porch, through the kitchen, and stopped in front of the locked door to her old room. She pulled the key out and slid it into the door handle. It fit perfectly.

She took a deep breath, as if she was about to expose a part of her life that she had kept buried from all prying eyes. This was the room that she had shared with her brother, where she had played with her dolls and had set up tea parties with imaginary friends. The room that held her last remaining happy childhood memories of her life here. Once she opened the door, she doubted she would be able to recall them again. They would be replaced by a cadaver of wilted recollection.

She gripped the handle and opened the door.

What she saw inside threatened to derail her plans entirely, and destroy the construct of the monster she had come to slay.

THIRTY-FIVE

THROUGH THE NORTH WOODS the SUV drove the dirt roads slowly, the men inside scanning the countryside for any other living creature. But the air was still, the sunlight struggling to break the canopy, and the forest was gray and dark and morbid.

Clinton was behind the wheel, Haywood in the passenger seat. Davis was in the back, his hand out the open window nursing the latest in his endless chain of cigarettes.

They had stopped at several trailers and cabins that morning, but most were deserted or boarded up for the fall. They had caught one old-timer who was packing up his car to head south, but the man said he hadn't seen anyone, and yes, he would mind very much if they searched around his property.

How far could Michael have traveled from the scene of James and Kyle's accident?

It was hard to tell. Haywood thought it could be ten miles tops, but he didn't know how much the fear of deadly pursuit could add to that number. Plus, Michael was used to walking, walking in and out of Coldwater, so he might be more capable of putting miles behind him than the average man.

The men drove north until they came to a crossroad.

"Ain't no way he made it this far," Clinton said.

141

Haywood pointed to the right. "Turn here, let's just see what's down here."

They drove east.

The first mile brought nothing but the endless continuance of trees. A private drive gouged its way through the scrub, and Clinton turned onto it. A trailer sat back about a quarter mile from the road. They pulled in.

A man was putting a duffle bag into the trunk of a beat-up car, while a woman sat on the steps, her arms cradling a small boy. Her hand was holding a rag and dabbing at the kid's face. Haywood noticed the blood. The boy was bleeding, and by the looks of it, severely. A small dog was lying next to the woman's feet. The man stood straight and watched as Clinton parked the vehicle.

"Can I help you?" the man said.

"Everything alright?" Haywood asked, pointing to the boy.

"Taking him down to South Falls. Not sure what he got into. Won't stop bleeding. Was his nose, now it's coming out his ears too."

The woman rocked the child, oblivious to the newcomers to her house.

"Conscious?"

"Yeah."

"Well, I won't get in your way. Just wanted to ask if you seen anyone cross through here today."

The man shut the trunk and the noise echoed through the forest. "Ain't no one ever cross through here. Not until you all."

"A man broke out of South Falls jail, we were just doing our part looking out for folks," Haywood said. "They said he was headed north. We thought we would check on some of the summer cabins out here."

"You guys police?"

Haywood didn't answer. His eyes darted around the property, searching for any clue. He was becoming more and more desperate as the day went on and his mind started playing tricks on him. Several times he had sworn that he saw Michael in *this* ditch or behind *that* tree. But to no avail. As his eyes wandered, they fell on the boy, whose bloodied face was now turned to him, staring at him as if he had a piece of knowledge he was holding so tight that it was filling him to near bursting.

"Maybe your boy seen something?"

"My boy needs a doctor."

Haywood approached the woman. "Can you speak, son?" he asked.

"Get away from him!" the man yelled, but Clinton stepped up with a look in his dark eyes that convinced the man to take it down a notch.

The boy looked at Haywood and nodded his head.

"You see a man around here? A stranger?"

The boy nodded again.

"He do this to you?"

"No," the boy whispered.

The woman looked at her husband with a desperate gaze.

"Where'd you see him?"

The boy lifted his arm and pointed away from the trailer, toward a trail that led off east into the blackened forest.

"How long ago?"

"This morning."

The boy's father now directed his rising anger to the unknown man in the wilderness. "I'll kill him . . . I'll kill him," he mumbled, his fists clenching at his sides.

The woman looked back down to her son and started crying.

Haywood turned back to the man. "You need to get your boy down to the hospital. We'll find him. Believe me, we'll find him."

"And what are you going to do to him?"

"Best if I didn't tell you."

The man gathered his wife and son and got them in the car. Before he got in himself, he looked back to Haywood, Clinton, and Davis, who were standing in the drive, watching him leave.

"I don't need to know what you guys have planned," the man said, "but whatever it is, feel free to make it twice as bad."

Haywood nodded and watched the car as it turned onto the road and disappeared. He looked down the trail and started walking, not knowing what they would find.

THIRTY-SIX

MELISSA STOOD AT THE DOOR and peered into the bedroom. The light filtered in from the window and illuminated the space, giving it a glow that was absent in the rest of the house.

The walls were freshly painted in a pale blue color, accented by white trim and floorboards. The wood floor had been washed clean but still showed signs of age. On opposite walls there were twin beds, made with military precision, each with a solid color comforter. She walked over and sat down on the one below the window, the place she used to sleep. The bed was not her original, for it must have rotted out like the rest of the house furnishings, but it stood in place of it. A monument to a time long past. She lay down and gazed up at the window, a faint memory of moonlight passing through glass in a toddler's eyes.

She sat back up and stared over to the other bed. It was precisely where her brother had slept. In her mind's eye she could envision him sitting there, playing with Hot Wheels cars, driving them over the foot of the bed in mock races.

The room had been restored to a reflection of its past. The paint, the cleaning, the placement of objects on the walls, they were all done by an unskilled but purposeful hand. A museum of the past. A memorial.

Melissa thought about Michael. Had he restored this room as a trophy for past sins or as a penance? An effort to bring back into being something that he had destroyed?

A memorial to a family shattered beyond repair?

Family.

Was Michael still family? The idea came to Melissa as an epiphany. For most of her life Michael had been the focal point of all her rage, anger, and spite. He hadn't been flesh and blood, merely an idea. But now, he'd suddenly become real. Flesh and blood. But more so. Her flesh and blood. Flesh and blood that had reconstructed this room and was living as a pauper, isolated from the world.

What was this feeling mushrooming inside her?

Empathy?

Empathy for the person who selfishly destroyed her family?

But if she were unable to empathize for family, what did that make her?

The days of her childhood had blended together, and Melissa could not recall the last time that she had slept in this spot. Her head began to swim with conflicting emotions until a haunting feeling of nostalgia started forming in her gut.

She shot up from the bed, ran to the hallway, and out the front door.

She could not open herself up to sentimentality.

The room was but a mere imitation of a past life. That time was long gone. It had been violently taken from her, and she had come to Coldwater to execute the justice owed her. Romanticizing her youth did nothing toward accomplishing that goal.

Melissa walked back to her car and opened the door. She reached down and placed the gun under the seat. She got in, started it up, and pulled back onto the dirt road. In her rearview mirror she saw a flash of light, sunlight on metal, and saw a truck parked back in the brush. She stopped the car and stared. It hadn't been there when she pulled in. Suddenly her nerves coursed with vibrant energy as she realized how incredibly alone she was out here in the boondocks.

She could see two shadows sitting in the cab.

Reaching under her front seat, she pulled the pistol out and held it on her lap, her eyes on the vehicle lurking behind her. She put her foot on the gas and crept down the road. The truck didn't appear to move at first, but after she had gone a bit, it pulled onto the dirt and started following her.

Melissa slid the gun under her left leg, put both hands on the wheel, and slammed on the accelerator.

THIRTY-SEVEN

HAYWOOD LED THE WAY DOWN THE TRAIL, Clinton behind him with a rifle he'd grabbed from the back of the SUV, Davis following, similarly armed. The ferns were parted by the repeated trampling of a boy's feet, but the men made their way easy enough. The dog next to the trailer had raised its head and watched the men go, then lowered it back to the ground, its motivation to run into the woods sapped from its body by some unseen force.

The trail led in for roughly a quarter mile, then rose up the spine of a ridge. To the south, the lowlands were dry, save for a few scattered marshes that reflected the sun from their dying pools. North, the woods ran on and on, the trees so dense that Haywood could not see the road they had been on when they pulled up to the family's trailer.

Haywood's eyes were fixed forward, Clinton and Davis scoured the sides in a lackadaisical fashion, the thought of actually finding Michael never a serious concern in their minds.

The ridge leveled off and the men kept walking.

The air was like a mausoleum, still and heavy and ancient. The woods felt prehistoric, the men walking back in time as they walked farther in.

"Hey," Davis said, breaking the silence, "that might be something." He pointed down the ridge to a clearing.

Haywood doubled back and saw what Davis was pointing at. It was a vast dead patch surrounded by green.

Davis rubbed his eyes with his sleeve, the smoke from his cigarette sitting over his head. "That thing growing?" He shook his head. "Nah. I'm seeing things."

Without hesitation, Haywood made his way down the ridge. A dugout and the remnants of a small campfire came into view once he had descended the hill. He moved the tarp and looked inside.

"What you see?" Clinton asked.

"Campsite," Haywood said. "Not old. There's a hole in the hill here."

"You see anything?"

"No. Looks more like a kid's fort. Probably that sick boy's."

Haywood stood straight and looked around. The dying off he recognized. He had seen it before. The edging out of life from an epicenter. It was just like Michael's house. He had been here, but he needed something more tangible. Some physical proof. Haywood trusted his gut more than anything, but he knew Clinton and Davis and the boys were getting ready to bail.

He walked around the site while Clinton and Davis stood perched on the ridge.

There was nothing.

He went back to the dugout and peered inside. It was dark and the smell of earth filled his senses. There were small toys scattered about and the dirt floor was packed down like smooth rock. He crawled inside and lay down on his back, his eyes on the low-hanging ceiling above him, the weight

of the ridge suspended over his body. As his eyes adjusted to
the low light, he saw the dirt above him, the small roots that
stuck out of the walls and ceiling. Bits of rock and stone and
mud coming into view. And something else.

Above his head was writing.

The dirt had been carved by someone's finger.

A word.

As his eyes focused, the message became clear.

Haywood.

A cold chill ran through Haywood's body as he looked at
his name scrawled with a killer's hand. He couldn't get out
of the dugout fast enough.

Haywood scooted himself out of the dugout, stood, and
brushed himself off. "He was here!"

Clinton and Davis looked down.

"You sure?" Clinton said.

"Yes." Haywood scurried up the ridge and thought about
what to do.

"You think that's why the boy is sick?"

"Look around," Haywood said. "Wherever Michael goes,
death goes with him. The dying plants, the sick boy, Kyle,
James, Old Man Jackson . . ."

Davis lit another cigarette. "You mean like voodoo or
something? That what you saying?"

"What if that's what I'm saying?"

"Then I think you might be crazy," Clinton said.

"I used to doubt it too. But now, now I don't. You all didn't
believe me when I told you Michael was evil. Not fully. But
look down there. Look at what's happened over the past couple
days. If you had gone out to Michael's place, you'd see the same
thing. Everything within a hundred feet of his house, just dead."

"Hold on a minute. Clinton, you buying this?" Davis asked.

"Call Frank and Earl," Haywood said, "ask them what they saw out there. See if it matches what your own eyes are telling you."

Clinton put his hand up to calm his friend and addressed Haywood. "You actually believe that Michael is running around cursing everyone, like out of some movie? That's a pretty big thing to swallow, Haywood."

"It's just like Morrison," Haywood said, more to himself as he looked around to see if he could spot a clue as to where Michael ran off to. He walked past the men and headed toward the trailer and the SUV, leaving Clinton and Davis looking at each other.

■ ■ ■

"You believe all that?" Davis asked, flicking the butt of the cigarette down the ridge. It landed in the dead void, a small wisp of smoke rising.

"Doesn't matter. Haywood does. It makes sense to him."

"Okay," Davis said, firing up another smoke, "as stupid as that notion is, tell me this: why are we messing with him then? If Michael is some black-magic, source-of-all-evil demon seed, why are we out here chasing him? Why in the world would we have messed with him in the first place?"

"It's a bit too late to ask that now, I guess," Clinton said.

"You boys coming?" Haywood yelled from down the trail.

"Yeah, we're coming," Clinton said and headed back to the car.

Davis looked out through the woods.

"Yeah," he said to himself as he spit on the ground. "We're coming."

THIRTY-EIGHT

MICHAEL SAT IN THE DIRT, his hands tied behind his back and his legs tied under him. The man with the shotgun stood beside him. The person he had seen through the trees in the metal garage was still tucked away in the shadows.

"You a cop?"

"No."

"No . . . of course not. You a junkie trying to get some freebies?"

"No," Michael said.

"Just thought you'd spy on us out here?"

"I didn't even know you were here. I was just walking through. I'd keep walking if you'd just untie me."

"That ain't going to happen."

The door of the trailer slammed open and the skeletal woman Michael had seen before fell out of the inside. She caught herself after one step, found her balance, and proceeded to sit on the top of the metal steps that led to the ground. She looked over at Michael and his captor, but her eyes were vacant. She looked both childlike and grizzled, aged and infantile, as if she had experienced too much of the world in too little time.

"Artie, get in here!" a voice yelled from the darkness of the garage.

Michael's captor slung the gun over his shoulder and walked into the apparent laboratory.

Artie was met outside the stall by the haggard beast of a man in overalls. He was shirtless underneath, and rolls of skin hung from his waist over the denim. He had a gray mop of hair that shot in every direction but up, and on his hands he had thick industrial rubber gloves.

The two men talked at a level that Michael could not hear, but he surmised from the random glances and nods in his direction that the men were talking about him.

It didn't take a rocket scientist to realize what he had stumbled into. The years in prison had brought him in contact with folks like this. Illiterate white trash who somehow possessed the chemistry expertise of Einstein, cooking up lethal concoctions out of household products. The vapor coming out of the garage looked like their business was in full swing and the woman sitting on the trailer steps a waiting and eager customer.

The men talked for a long time and the sun beat down on the spot where Michael sat. The world had stopped and was considering what to do next. As Michael looked on, out of his peripheral vision he saw the woman stand up and approach him.

She was rail thin. Her blonde hair was ratted out and the color was returning to its darker brown in patches across her scalp. Her face contained numerous sores, acne gone too far, and in a couple spots there appeared the faint color of bruises. The way she was walking toward Michael made it appear that the earth below her was in a constant state of flux, her equilibrium vaporized from her possession.

"So who are you?" she asked. Her voice sounded like tires on a gravel road.

"I'm nobody," Michael said.

"Yeah? Me too."

"You live here?"

"No. This place is a dump."

"So why are you here?"

"Why? Because this is heaven," she said. The woman stood uneasily, looking toward the garage, and then to the sky, lost in a daydream creation of a boiled mind. She looked back at Michael and giggled in a childish laugh as she slumped to the ground, ending up a few feet from him. "They make it up extra special here. Plus they give me extras."

Michael stared back at the garage. The men had walked inside and gotten back to their work. He could see their shadows inside working with bottles and canisters, mixing and pouring. The smell emanating from the place was nauseating and vile.

"You use?" she asked.

"No."

"Too bad. It'd be better if you did. It's not like you're ever leaving this place. A hit would just make it not so painful. Artie is a horrible shot."

Michael knew she was right. He knew from the moment he was led out of the woods that they wouldn't let him leave. They had too much at stake. Their small enterprise wouldn't exist with spectators lurking about. He knew this, the inevitability of the future rolled out before him. He knew when harm was coming, he could feel it in his bones like a coiling snake readying itself to strike, but during this whole process of being tied up and held captive, he had done his best to quiet the beast inside him. Now, though, the situation was so obvious it couldn't be ignored.

The wanderer.

The scourge of Coldwater.

He knew when people were contemplating his death. And he knew that they were painfully unaware of what the result would be. Now, sitting in the sunlight next to a riddled-out addict, he could feel the tension stirring that would spell the end of Artie and whoever joined him in his future plan.

"Are you hostage here too?"

"Me? No. I'm here by my own free will," she said, throwing her hands up in the air and smiling to the sky.

Michael watched her with morbid curiosity. "I don't think you'll want to be around here soon," he said. "It's not going to end well."

She giggled as if his words were a joke. "It always ends well. Every day. Ain't no way I'm leaving," she said. Her hands rubbed the grass as if she had never felt such a pure sensation in all her life. She was gone, physically here in this world, but permanently checked into a different plane of existence.

"Cathy! Get away from him!" Artie screamed from the garage and then disappeared back inside.

Cathy managed to get herself upright again, looking around at the world painted new with each breath.

"Bye!" she said seductively as she started to walk away.

He could feel the impending storm forming within himself. The men had made up their mind, in that garage, to kill him. They had set their minds to it, and the protective shade inside him felt the danger and was preparing itself.

"I wouldn't go in there," Michael said to her.

155

Cathy stopped and cocked her head back at him. "But, honey . . . that's where heaven is."

She strolled casually into the bowels of the garage.

The coiling snake tightened in Michael's stomach. He knew it was coming. He knew it was now.

Michael rolled to his side and onto his stomach. He tried to move farther away from the structure, every foot of grass an extra foot of safety. He hadn't moved far when it happened.

The garage exploded in a brilliant fireball of blazing chemicals and flame. The screams of the three people inside mixing with the roaring plasma. Michael buried his face in the ground as he felt the heat singe the back of his legs and his feet. He rolled over and watched as a body ran out of the doorway. He couldn't tell who it was—Cathy, Artie, the man in the overalls—as the person was engulfed in flames. The human torch dropped to the ground after just a few steps and was still, melting out of existence. The heaven that Cathy sought, now an inferno.

Michael's stomach released itself as he continued to crawl away from the burning structure like an inchworm escaping the heat of a magnifying glass.

THIRTY-NINE

HAYWOOD HUNG UP HIS CELL PHONE and put it back in his pocket.

How had this gotten so out of control?

Frank and Earl had just told him how the mystery woman who had showed up in Coldwater had spotted them parked on the side of the road outside Michael's place. They also mentioned how they were in pursuit of her, which he sternly advised them to stop. The last thing he needed was for this woman to go to the police, claiming that she was being stalked and harassed. Anything and everything that brought in the prospect of the cops coming up to town and sniffing around filled him with anxiety.

He couldn't be everywhere at once, and even if he could, that in itself would bring suspicion on him. It was good he was at Jackson's store when the authorities showed up and pronounced a heart attack. It was good to be at the crash scene when the investigators ruled a simple accident. He was worried about Kyle flapping his guilty conscience to the police, and he had worked extra hard to get Tami to go and sit with her on-again, off-again boyfriend at the hospital. As long as Kyle knew he hadn't lost everything, he could be trusted to keep his lips zipped.

Now Frank and Earl were causing new problems.

When he heard that this woman was in town snooping around not long after they had buried Michael at Springer's Grove, a slow, creeping dread had invaded every pore of his body. He felt like he was barely keeping it together, and every time he got one loose end tied down, another one would rise to take its place.

He had told the boys to just keep an eye on what she was up to, not chase her down the roads, putting a scare into her, adding to her curiosity about what could be happening in Coldwater.

This lady's appearance in town, though impossibly ill-timed, was not catastrophic. He could deal with it, as long as the boys stopped acting irrationally. Stupidly.

He hated that his fate was tied to such ignorant people as Kyle, Frank, and Earl.

But he had made that decision without thinking it through.

Haywood had gone to his oldest friends in Coldwater that day when he decided to bury Michael. He went to the familiar, rather than thinking of the aftereffects. The life after the act that would bind them all together for the rest of their days. He didn't think about who could handle the burden, the guilt, the anxiety. He just thought of those available at the time.

Even as they had sat in the back of Gilly's waiting for Michael to come in that evening, Haywood knew it had been a mistake including Kyle and Earl. Their vocal hesitation and backtracking was the only conversation in the bar.

"Are you sure about this?" Kyle had asked.

"Yeah, man, I mean, should we be doing this?" Earl added.

"It needs to be done, for everyone's safety," Haywood said.

"But . . . if what you said about him is true . . ."

"Yeah, how are we not going to bite it . . ."

"Boys, we've already talked about this. We've already de-cided."

Silence would fill the room for a breath, and then they would start again.

"Are you really sure about this?"

And even now, sitting in the passenger seat of Clinton's SUV, bouncing through the rough terrain of the north woods, Haywood could hear Kyle's voice in his head.

"Are you sure about this?"

He had been, hadn't he? Michael was dangerous. Haywood knew, without doubt, the ex-con had killed Morrison. He would be driving east of town and see Michael walking into Coldwater, passing him on the shoulder, and the bile would rise up in his throat at the sight of him, and he wanted nothing more than to swerve the wheel and plow the man over, avenging the murder of his friend.

And if Michael had killed Morrison, why wouldn't he kill again . . . and again . . . and again.

The boys did not see the depth of danger they were in. To entertain the presence of evil was to invite it in and let it fester until it would unleash itself on the world. How could he, an upstanding citizen, a decent man, allow this cancer to reside in his community? The state might have deemed Michael fit for release from prison, but no one had thought to consult with the people who would be forced to live every day of their lives with him as their neighbor.

The state had failed, just as it failed at almost everything it did.

Haywood was not going to leave his fate and the fate of

his town to bureaucrats and lawyers sitting in their offices a hundred miles away. They had done nothing when Morrison was found in the woods last spring. They had written it off as an accident and headed back to the city before his friend's body was cold. They had no interest in the welfare of the people of Coldwater. It was up to Haywood to fill that vacuum. His right. His divine right to protect himself.

Morrison's death in the woods, it was a sign. A sign that the evil in Michael was coming alive again. The boogeyman stories from Michael's past were true. He had come home to Coldwater and planned on continuing his murderous ways.

Then Old Man Jackson and James confirmed the power that was being unleashed on them. Haywood was not about to wait for it to happen to him.

FORTY

THE WOODS BLENDED TOGETHER in a constant cacophony of color as Haywood, Clinton, and Davis crisscrossed the north roads and service trails. They would stop occasionally, get out of the SUV, and fix their eyes on the landscape, looking for movement amongst the sedentary trees. The sun was high in the sky and the day seemed to have no end.

This particular stop placed them on a rise that gave a bird's-eye view of the world south and east. Clinton stood to the right of Haywood and cast a shadow from his giant frame. Davis leaned against the vehicle, his constant stream of nicotine going full bore, tainting the air with a thin tang of bitterness.

"How long we going to be out here?" he asked between puffs.

"Why, you almost out of smokes?" Haywood said, not bothering to look back at the human chimney.

Clinton eyed his friend, who simply shrugged his shoulders and proceeded to ignore his comrades.

"He could be hunkered down anywhere," Clinton said. "Chances of us tripping across him are pretty slim."

"He's out there."

"That he is, but out there's a pretty big place."

"That boy's dugout was almost straight north of where James and Kyle were found."

"That gives him three ways to go. Doubt he'd double back toward town."

"Yeah," Haywood said. "Then how come I got this nagging feeling that is exactly what he is going to do? He ain't going to keep heading north. He wouldn't survive out here very long."

Clinton nodded, his cold stare looking toward where the earth met the sky.

"East. He'd head east. Toward the interstate."

"That's a long walk. Through the woods, take him a week," Clinton said. "Could be taking the long way back to his place."

"Most likely. That's why I told Frank and Earl to stake out the place."

Clinton chuckled. "So that's where you sent them two."

"Couldn't stand Earl's crying no more."

"He's not cut out for this. Frank neither. Should have left them and Kyle out of it," Clinton said. "James too."

"Couldn't keep James away," Haywood said.

"He sure was fired up, wasn't he?"

Haywood nodded. He turned and saw Davis walk over across the dirt two-track and begin to relieve himself on an unsuspecting tree.

"Davis seems not to be bothered."

Clinton smiled. "Not sure he gives two cents either way."

"And what about you?"

"What about me?"

"You wish you had been left out of this?"

"Don't matter anymore. No use regretting it."

"That all you got?"

"I think we should have let Michael be, if that's what you want me to say. I know you're trying to even the score on account of Morrison. But Morse was poking a hornet's nest with Michael from the beginning. Not to say that he had it coming, no way I'm saying that. But ever since Michael came back, you guys been thinking the worst of him. I figured he done his time. Leave him be. But now . . ."

"But now what?"

"Now, whatever I thought before don't matter. We finish what we started." Clinton looked at Haywood, his face fixed with firm determination. "This ain't something you quit halfway through. We've already crossed the line. Ain't no going back as far as I can tell." He returned his gaze to the south. "I'm in this till the end. However it ends."

"Thanks, man," Haywood said.

Davis walked back across the trail, zipping himself up, cigarette hanging out of his mouth. "You boys hear that?"

Haywood looked back.

"That noise," Davis said. "That boom? You hear it? Look! There!"

Clinton and Haywood looked to where Davis was pointing.

About two miles away a puff of black smoke started to spire toward the heavens, snaking its way up and dispersing into the blue sky.

"That's him," Haywood said as he ran back to the truck and jumped into the passenger seat, leaving the others gawking at the site. "Come on, guys! Let's go!"

Davis and Clinton loaded up, and they set off through the forest toward the rising pillar of black.

163

FORTY-ONE

NSIDE THE METH HEADS' TRAILER, Michael found the remnants of white-trash life. Most of the paneling inside had been ripped down, the furniture old and stained, with more cigarette burns than there was fabric. A large screen TV was propped up to one side, set up like an icon, the only thing of value in this hovel of depravity. He stepped into the kitchen and searched the cupboards for any food. Most of the boxes were empty or had been looted by insects boring into their sides. He found a couple canned items and an opener in one of the broken drawers.

He opened one of the cans, fruit cocktail long past expiration, and slurped it down like a savage. The syrup clung to the growing stubble of his chin and he wiped it off with his sleeve. He searched the cupboards again, found a few more items, and put them on the counter.

In the bedroom in back, he found some clothes that were close enough to his size. He grabbed them and headed to the bathroom. The earth and river smell had become so embedded in his senses that he could only guess at how repugnant he had become. He stepped into the shower and found that it worked. Cold water poured out even with the handle turned all the way over, but he scrubbed the past several days' journey off his skin. The bar of soap he found was all but a sliver, but it did its work.

Now clean and dressed in another's clothes, he grabbed his scavenged goods and headed back outside.

The garage was smoldering in a heap of embers, collapsing in on itself and leaving only the foundation to show what it used to be. The burnt body lay blackened on the grass in front of it.

Michael had thought about going over to see who it was. To see if it was Cathy, the addict girl, the one so enamored by the men's manufactured tickets to heaven that left her burnt, but he decided against it. What did it matter? All three were gone. It didn't matter which one ran out. It wouldn't soothe his mind knowing that she had died instantly versus suffering on the run. She had found the ultimate release and where she was now wasn't for him to decide.

He turned and headed east again, the sun at his back and the looming assurance of more death to come. Before long he was deep in the woods again, and the smells of nature returned to their undiminished fullness.

He had to be more careful. Thrice now he had been caught unawares and he knew his luck could only run so far.

He had escaped the grave.

He had escaped the naive friendship of an innocent boy who knew not what he was in the presence of.

And now he had escaped the paranoid jitters of backwoods entrepreneurs.

But he would never escape from himself. The shadow lay dormant, constricted around his spine and ready to protect its host. He would never be free of it. It was his burden to carry, his wages, his judgment.

Michael's thoughts returned to Will. Sitting in the presence of innocence reminded him of a time so long ago when he felt free, when smiles, rather than horror, rained down on him. When companionship wasn't something to be thought about, because it was always there and always would be.

He knew these were dangerous thoughts. He had spent so many years hiding his memories as much as he hid from the world. But now, with the adrenaline leaving his body and the thoughts of the young innocent boy he had left that morning, he couldn't keep his mind in check.

Michael thought of his brother.

FORTY-TWO

THE HANDGUN ALWAYS FELT SEDUCTIVE in his hand whenever he swiped it from his father's dresser drawer. Its black metal appeared to suck in all the light around it. It was too big for him to hold like he saw on TV, but with both hands he was able to lift it and aim it with one eye scrunched closed. It made him feel powerful, which is why he often found himself running to grab it whenever his mom and dad left him alone at the house.

Michael could still remember the day his brother and sister came home. Marcus and Melissa, the twins. What used to be his world had now become someone else's, and his seniority did nothing but let others think that he was in no need of attention. He watched as his mother and father soon enveloped the twins in all their thoughts. Michael would look on from a distance and watch Marcus smiling as his father played with him on the living room floor.

Fewer and fewer were the times when it was Michael who was the one smiling.

When the twins were finally down for the evening, his parents were too exhausted to even look at him. Michael would find that he was drifting further and further out of their orbit. He took to walking in the woods on his own, thinking about running away, and always, always, thinking about his former life when it was just him and his folks who occupied the house.

The handgun brought back control. He loved it. Each time, he would envision himself as the hero of the day, battling enemies, rescuing whole countries just as Rambo did. And killing all those in his path. The righteous maniac, the one-man army. His daydreams drifted to saving the day, winning the girl, how the whole world would love him.

This particular time would change his life forever.

Marcus had been infuriating this day. He had snuck into Michael's room and proceeded to ruin his prized possession of baseball cards. The cards he had spent a long time collecting when his father used to take him to the shop way down in South Falls. It had been forever since he had looked at them, but they were remnants of a cherished and mourned-for past. And Marcus had all but destroyed them. His parents had told him to calm down when he told them what his brother had done.

"He's just a kid, hon," his mother said. "He didn't know what he was doing."

"It's not like you played with them anymore," his father said.

His cards, just like Michael himself, had become disposable to both his mom and dad. They were no longer used, no longer looked at, no longer valuable. Looking back now at the motivation, it wasn't the cards themselves, or the annoyance of a seven-year-old boy, but the pushing away, the growing irrelevance of his own existence in his parents' eyes, that led him down that path. So on that afternoon when his parents went into town and left him in charge of his siblings,

Michael took the handgun, placed it in his waistband next to the small of his back, and took Marcus outside.

The two boys walked into the woods and stopped.

Michael pulled the gun from his belt.

"Look what I have, Marcus."

"Wow."

"Do you want to shoot it?"

"Yeah!"

"Okay."

Michael held the gun out and Marcus grabbed it with both hands. It was too heavy for him to hold, so Michael put his arms around him and helped him aim it at a tree not too far off. They pulled the trigger and watched the bark erupt in splinters. The blast rocked their ears. Marcus was amazed.

"Awesome!" he yelped, his smile beaming from ear to ear.

"One more time," Michael said. He moved to his brother's side, his right hand on top of Marcus's, holding the handle of the pistol, his left on the boy's thin upper arm.

He was so small, so malleable. His brother, relaxed and trusting, excited about this unexpected thrill.

Michael rolled his wrist quickly to the side, the gun suddenly pointed back at his brother, and as he did so, he pulled the trigger.

The blast deafened his left ear as he felt his brother's body go limp in his arms.

The sun in his parents' sky snuffed black with the twitch of a finger.

Michael lowered his brother to the ground and made sure the gun was still firmly placed in his little hands. Blood from the wound seeped into the thirsty earth.

"Goodbye, brother," he said as he walked back to the house.

FORTY-THREE

WHAT CAN A CHILD possibly know of mortality? How can they, so new to life, understand the finality of death? Michael had remedied a season of sadness with an eternal prescription. He had calculated his brother's death that fateful day, but he had not thought of every day after. He had wished only to be wanted again, in the way that he had been accustomed to before the twins came, and so, with a bold stroke, sought to tip the scales back into his favor. His child mind, evaluated now with his adult conscience, appeared as depraved to him as others saw it. But what could that child have known? How could he have possibly evaluated the evil he had unleashed? A single blow bearing eternal consequences.

In court, in prison, in the life since, Michaél wished away his past. He wished that he would have turned the gun on himself instead, and thus his brother would have lived on, enjoying the affection of his parents which Michael had foolishly sought to recapture with a gunshot.

But once done, there was nothing to fix his sin.

He missed Marcus. Every day he missed him. He saw his face in his dreams, not as a reminder of his own action, not with misguided anger for the penalty that he had to endure since killing him. No. He missed him as a brother misses a lost piece of himself.

Michael would replay the scene in his head and will his younger self, the one who knew not the momentous consequence of his actions, to not go outside, to not lead Marcus down the path, to not use his little brother's trust as a trap. And each time, his younger self moved on to the death blow and walked back to the house with the cold calculation of a child oblivious to the immensity of what he had done.

But there would be no reprieve, no pardon in this lifetime.

Michael was forever trapped on the other side of that action. Coldwater's thoughts of him were formed by that action. He could never alter it. No amount of contrition would pay off the world's opinion. He could beg forgiveness again and again until his mouth ran dry, but his words would fall on deaf ears. He knew this now. Knew it all too well. He had been educated to this fact and wished beyond reason that he could go back and instill that knowledge in his younger self.

■ ■ ■

Like a stone dropped in still water, Michael sat in the woods and felt the world retreat from him in concentric circles. He was outside of nature, wandering in a vacuum. The woods went on forever and he thought that he could spend the rest of his life unnoticed by another living creature.

He looked out at the trees ahead, their foliage starting to show the early signs of autumn, the seasonal dying off. But fall was not the end of the world. It would bud and blossom again. The fall would be forgotten. The forest would go on, resurrecting each year.

He would not.

His fall led to a terminal winter, one without thaw. Without the hope of a season of rejuvenation.

Michael would wander, and wherever he would go, the fall would go with him.

What point was there to going on? There would never be an eternally green pasture for him to lie down in. His presence would poison the ground and turn the rolling prairie of life into a wasteland devoid of promise. Devoid of hope.

Hope.

A foolish emotion that was implanted in the genes of men. Michael still felt it as he rested against the trunk of a sycamore tree. His mind knew there was no paradise awaiting him, but somewhere a quiet whisper within him still cast his eyes forward, to keep going, to keep searching for the elusive place where he could find some comfort in a world that dreamed of his absence.

And in that quiet moment he felt something pulling at his soul, a mystic beacon through the trees.

There was something in the woods.

Michael wasn't sure how far away it was, but it was there. He latched on to it and focused his mind, his thoughts, his wishes.

Out beyond the trees there was a place created by one like him. The pressure in his spine tensed, not out of fear, but akin to the anxiety of meeting an old friend and failing to recall their name.

He stood and brushed off the twigs and leaves that had stuck to his clothing. He would keep heading east, and with each step forward he felt the pull of this foreign place.

How long had this invisible pull been calling him? Had it compelled him unknowingly from the beginning of this ordeal, since the river, since Old Man Jackson's? Had Will and Otis just been a distraction on his way to where he was supposed to be?

Michael walked, and as he walked, he became aware that he was not alone. That he was not an anomaly. That there was at least one more like him in the world, and that person was in these woods, and was calling to him like a lighthouse in the fog of a dead winter night.

He walked with purpose.

He walked . . . with hope.

FORTY-FOUR

NO MATTER WHICH WAY THEY TURNED, Haywood and the boys couldn't get within a half mile of the column of smoke. The dirt roads all skirted or wandered off from the direction they tried to go, and all they managed to do was drive in agonizing arcs in the dense forest. The mazes of the Minotaur would have a hard time competing with the two-tracks that meandered through the woods. The smoke signal would be before them, then on the right, then behind them. The SUV kept doubling back, and Haywood's frustration was taken out on the dashboard more than once, Clinton giving him a dirty look each time the man punched the console.

After heading down the same two-track for what must have been the tenth time, Davis saw a small break in the brush and ordered them to halt the vehicle. He jumped out and ran into the woods.

Clinton and Haywood sat silently as they waited for him to return. It wasn't long until he walked out from where he had entered and waved the truck back. Clinton reversed the short distance and put his window down.

"There's a drive right here, past these logs. Looks fairly

well used. Must have wanted to hide it or something," Davis said, putting another cigarette in his mouth.

"Could be where the smoke is coming from," Clinton said. He got out of the SUV and proceeded to move the debris from the hidden lane. Once it was cleared, the two got into the vehicle and Clinton drove them in.

The two-track wound back and forth deeper into the isolated area. The smell of burning material filled the car and overpowered the noxious fumes Davis was producing from the back seat, but the relief of finding the source of the pillar of smoke canceled out the grit that was scratching at their eyes and throats.

They pulled in next to an old trailer. Behind it, a smoldering heap of what looked to have been a garage sent ash and a gray haze into the air where it fell back to earth like a hellish snow. The place was deserted, and the men sat in the car contemplating their next move.

"So what you think?" Clinton asked.

"Don't know," Haywood said. "Doesn't look like anyone is around."

Clinton honked the horn several times, but no one emerged from the trailer.

"Hand me that gun," Haywood said to Davis, who obliged. "I'm sick of waiting."

Haywood stepped out and walked up to the trailer. He knocked on the door and it swung open of its own accord. "Hello?" he said.

Silence.

He looked around. The smell from inside was nauseating. The trash of humanity living in squalor beyond the purview of normal folk. The place was a mess. On several surfaces he saw the remnants of drug use, and every episode of *COPS* he had ever seen validated his suspicions. He stepped back outside and called to the truck.

"Nobody here. Let's look around."

Clinton and Davis got out, their rifles in hand, and the three of them approached the burned-down garage. They didn't get more than five steps when they saw the charred remains of a person on the grass. The smoke obscured what was left of the building and the horrors it might hold inside.

"Is that what I think it is?" Davis asked.

Clinton didn't respond as he approached the corpse and squatted down. The body was burned, the life scorched out of existence.

"A woman," he said.

Haywood dared the smoke and heat and peered through the fog at the remains of the garage. Black soot mixed with white ash. An image of more bodies mixed with charred remnants of various materials.

"What you thinking?" Clinton asked.

"Drug lab maybe? I don't know. You ever seen one up close?" Haywood asked.

"No."

"Me neither."

"Coincidence that this just happened, or you think it was Michael?" Clinton asked.

Haywood turned and walked past Clinton, tapped Davis on the shoulder, and headed back to the truck.

■ ■ ■

Davis stood still. Never much for words, he had none to give. The sight that lay before him left him numb.

Clinton rose. "Awful way to go," he said, staring at the body on the ground. He turned to Davis. "Come on, let's get going."

"How much further? How much further we going with this?" Davis asked. "I'm not sure I want to end up like that."

"We won't."

"You promise?" Davis asked.

Clinton didn't answer. He walked to the truck, got in, and fired it up.

"That's what I thought," Davis whispered to himself, as the smoke floated up to the heavens.

FORTY-FIVE

MICHAEL CAME UPON THE HOUSE from the western side of the property. The trees fell away in a perfect line and circled the house like a noose. Not a thing was growing in its radius. The place felt familiar but different. It was just as his piece of land down in Coldwater, only tended to by a more meticulous hand.

The house was hand built and not of randomly found material but planned, milled. Great care had been used in its construction. The owner must have been a craftsman. To its side and closer to where Michael sat in the woods was a barn with several animals roaming about. He could hear the sound of chickens and the braying of some small beast. There was an old trough and next to it a water pump. At the sight of the pump, Michael's mouth began to water. He had gone through his supply too fast and now his thirst surged to the forefront of his mind. What would it matter if he just walked up and got a drink? Even if the owner came out yelling, he could be off into the tree line before he caused too much of a stir. This property was nothing like the meth addicts' place that now lay in ashes. This was a home tended to by a constant and careful individual.

But what harm could Michael do? That was the thought

that now tormented him. The blood stream from Will's face haunted his thoughts. Even the seductive voice of the meth addict who walked into the furnace bothered him. He was responsible for all the deaths that lay strewn behind him the past couple of days. How many more would go on his record, would be added to his guilt list before this odyssey was over?

But thirst won out over apprehension.

Michael stood and walked toward the barn. The dry earth below him crunched under his feet and the smell of farm life filled his nose. He walked up to the water pump and worked the hand lever until there was a flow of liquid into the trough. It started out rusty but soon became clearer, at least enough to look like water. He stuck his hand in, it was cold and inviting.

"I wouldn't drink that if I were you," a voice from the barn said.

Michael looked up and saw a man leaning against the barn door, cleaning his hands with an old rag. The man was older but not ancient. He wore too much denim for anybody's taste. He looked relaxed, and Michael assumed that he had been standing there watching him the whole time.

"That is, unless you want it coming from both ends for the next week."

"What's that?" Michael asked, his voice low and scratchy.

"That water, it's bad news. Well is poisoned. It will flip your stomach inside out."

Michael stopped pumping and looked at his hand, not knowing whether to trust the stranger or to give in to the coolness.

The man stopped the incessant wiping of his hands and

started walking toward the house. "Follow me, I'll get you something to drink from inside."

Michael watched as the man went into the house and disappeared behind the screen door. He waited, not knowing what course of action to take next. He knew that the man's fate would be sealed when he reappeared. A drink in hand, he'd live . . . a gun in hand and the whole house might collapse on top of him, the bad-luck shadow within Michael taking action to protect itself. Michael didn't want to be too close when fate decided to cast its dice. Thankfully the man returned to the porch with a mason jar filled with what looked like tea. He placed it on the railing and then sat down in a chair and waited for Michael to approach.

Michael walked up the steps and grabbed the drink, chugging most of it down as if he would never get enough inside him. The man motioned to another chair on the porch and Michael had a seat.

"You been wandering out there for long?" the man asked.

"What?"

"The woods, been out there long?"

"Longer than planned."

"You responsible for that explosion I heard earlier?"

Michael didn't say anything but slowly took another sip of the tea. He felt the man's eyes staring at him, but Michael didn't give the satisfaction of eye contact and worked to change the conversation. The man's confidence unnerved Michael. He questioned his easiness, his lack of reserve toward a stranger coming through the woods and, apparently, from the direction of a fireball that would have been heard for miles.

Michael looked down from the porch at the dead grass

encircling the house, the tree line that seemed to noticeably recede inch by inch before him. "Nice place you have here."

"Thanks."

"I'm Michael."

"Nick," the man said. He kept rocking casually but didn't extend his hand.

Michael finished the last of the tea.

"Property has been in the family for a long time. Grandfather built the house and barn."

"Well, he did a nice job."

"He let me come here after I got out. When he died, he passed it on to me."

"Got out?"

"Prison."

Michael's interest grew all at once, and he noticed the man for the first time, as if he had gone from a blurry black-and-white figure to a being illuminated in Technicolor. Nick was big, not heavy, just thick all over. Neck, shoulders. He sat like a rock in his seat and kept his eyes on Michael.

"How long?" Michael asked.

"How long have I been here, or how long was I locked up?"

"Both, I guess."

"Almost twenty."

"Long time."

"Yes it is."

The sound of the rocking chair on porch boards filled the air. Michael put down the empty glass. Nick did not offer to refill it.

"So, where you headed?"

Michael raised his hand slightly to the east. "That way."

"A lot out there."

"It's something."

"You running away or running to something?"

Nick's matter-of-fact questioning was an irritant under Michael's skin. The man was too free with his history, and too free with his questions. Michael didn't need to ask what Nick had done to be locked up, he already knew when he set foot on the property. The dead earth, the pressure he could feel in the base of his skull. It was as if he had stepped into his own presence but was observing it as an out-of-body experience. He could tell in the man's eyes what he was, for he saw those same eyes whenever he looked in the mirror. Michael wondered if Nick could sense the same about him.

The sun began to dip below the tree line.

"It's getting dark," Nick said. "You need me to call to have someone pick you up?"

"No, there's no one."

"I figured as much. Well, you can sleep in the barn for the night if you like."

"I'd appreciate it."

"You say that now. In the morning you'll be cursing me and smelling like chickens."

"Beggars can't be choosers, I guess."

"No . . . no they can't."

Nick got up and showed Michael to the spot in the barn where he could sleep. It wasn't much, but it was out of the elements. There were some blankets and a small space heater. The man then walked to the house and left Michael to his own thoughts.

It gave him a strange feeling, this place. It felt so familiar yet eerily unwelcoming at the same time, like looking into a smoked-glass mirror and recognizing the blurred reflection of his own home. He was thankful to Nick for giving him a place to stay, for the drink. When generosity is shown to those who never receive it, they will rarely forsake gratitude. However, if prison taught him anything, it was that generosity was never freely given. There was always a motive. What could Nick's be?

FORTY-SIX

THE BARN WAS A DARK MENAGERIE—within its walls, nature had been deconstructed and reassembled by a half-mad creator. Above the door hung a web the size of a blanket, spun in chaotic designs by a drunk spider, forgoing its evolutionary bent toward order and spinning a fractal trap in which to catch its dinner. Michael saw a chicken move against the far wall, masked in increasing shadow. Its feathers hung in molt clumps, falling off its body like a leper bird's. The air reeked of decay and the things living there had grown like children raised near a nuclear reactor.

The isolation of the woods now seemed a better option to Michael, but he sat on the old mattress in the corner and tried to not think of the creatures that may reside within its springs.

This place, this whole place, was like a grand palace built for a man like himself. This was his existence writ large. Nick was very much of his own ilk, and as Michael sat here in the dark, he realized for the first time how the world experienced him . . . how it saw him, how it felt his presence. He had observed how the world hated him, how he had sickened it, but here in the barn he could actually feel how he pressed upon its senses. This farm was his own damnation aged and mature, poured in an old cask and fermented to a heightened state.

Nick was what he would become in time, the inevitable outcome of a life lived outside the realm of human fellowship.

Michael took off his shoes and examined his feet. His socks were stiff with sweat and grime, and blisters had sprouted up in abundance up and down his soles. The ground was cool to the touch and he let the air bathe his sores. He removed his garments and lay on the bed.

The chicken clucked in the darkness and scratched the dry earth.

From the bed Michael could see the farmhouse through a crack in the slat wall. The light in the upper window shone through drapes, and behind them a faint shadow moved back and forth. Rocking. It seemed rocking was Nick's sole purpose, like a caged animal at a zoo that goes mad with captivity and paces back and forth at the front of its enclosure.

Michael's eyes grew heavy as he watched the oscillating shadow in the window, slowly being hypnotized into oblivion. The chicken found an opening in the wall and disappeared into the night. The spider in the corner settled down to await what the night would bring her for dinner, and Michael drifted off to dreamless sleep.

■ ■ ■

Nick sat in the chair rocking, his motion a metronome in the dark. He stared across the bedroom and watched the dust float through the single beam of light that came from the lamp in the corner and rested on the baseboard across from him. He felt the message grow heavy in his mind.

The ticking cadence of his chair lulled him to a state between awake and asleep, his feet grinding the floor before him.

He could feel the presence in the barn, the specter that arrived in the human vessel.

He was of two minds.

Nick was filled with the anticipation of what was coming. For far too long he had sat here, isolated from the world with no recourse. Through the woods had come something that could free him from this prison. His rocking quickened with his heartbeat as he thought about it. All these long years living as an outcast of society with no means or method to ever regain acceptance had driven him to the point of madness.

Was he mad?

For too many days he had questioned this. But how could he know? The world is rational even to a madman. It was rational and reasoned and true. But crazy or not, he felt the desperation weighing on him as the years passed until the thought of being done with the seclusion became the sole point of motivation. The one thing his mind, mad as it might be, focused on. He would find himself lying in bed for days at a time, thinking through the puzzle of his own containment, for a way out. Alas, he would never discover one.

Failed attempts at escape scarred his body. From the burns on his neck, the cuts on his wrists, the broken and set bones of countless falls, they were all a testament and reminder that he was here and would be here until nature had run its long, winding course, for even nature would win out eventually.

From the back of his mind, he could feel the scrutiny of his shadowy companion. Sitting there, in the dark, chained to the part of his soul that his mind's eye could never focus on. He could feel the pressure of its grip. It was aware of his anticipation and excitement and threatened to squeeze every last drop of hope from him before it could plant its seed in his heart.

But even this foul beast of shadow could feel the presence in the barn, and in this feeling it could sense its own vulnerability like a walking loophole through the fabric of time.

It did not fear it, but it read Nick's mind, his thoughts, his small realization of a plan, and the shadow beast realized that the man's thoughts were plausible. The end could be possible, and so it coiled around Nick's spine and buried itself deep into the fabric of his consciousness in an attempt to blacken out any thoughts of absolution that Nick could conceive.

The man rocked as the motes drifted in the still air. His knuckles clenched the arms of the chair. He moved deliberately. Stubbornly.

He rocked back and forth, giving rhythm to the coming storm.

FORTY-SEVEN

MELISSA HAD MADE IT BACK to Coldwater without realizing most of the route back. Her eyes were fixed to the rearview mirror, from dirt road, to gravel, to paved . . . retracing the line that she had taken out to her old home. Going too fast for some of the curves and with her pulse racing, she finally saw the truck pull off on a side road. Even when she was sure they were no longer following her, she kept her foot on the gas.

She finally saw the stoplight in Coldwater on the horizon and her nerves began to relax. She was now back to civilization, though *civilization* would be a stretch of the term. She stopped at the red light and weighed her course.

She could turn left and go home to South Falls, chalking this up to a poor time to execute her plan. A plan to be thought out more cautiously. There was no rush. She had waited a lifetime to get her revenge, there was no harm in waiting longer.

To the right was her motel. She could stop in, regroup, and move forward.

Melissa looked in the rearview mirror. The empty road behind her stretching to the east.

There was no sign of her pursuers.

As her mind began to clear, her resolve returned.

She turned right onto Main Street and into the motor lodge parking lot. She parked the car, grabbed her things, went inside her room, and locked the door. The blinds were closed, but she dared to peek out across the parking lot onto the road, expecting to see the truck pull in. It never did.

Over the next hour she moved from the bed to the window and back again, checking the lock on the door. The day crept on.

She had come to Coldwater as the executioner. The predator. Now all of a sudden the script had been flipped and she was the one being pursued. Hunted.

Was it Michael who was behind her in the vehicle?

But there were two people in the truck. From what Lila had told her yesterday, Michael was a loner. He had no accomplices in town.

Then who were they?

Were the people in Coldwater just a brood of vipers, every last one of them?

Melissa thought of her brother.

Where was he?

Was he observing her movements like the men in the truck? The realization that she was being watched the whole time she was at Michael's place knotted her stomach to near nausea. Now, everywhere she looked she expected to find someone's eyes on her.

She stood and went back to the window. Cars were pulling into Gilly's for the evening, but there was no sign of the truck that had followed her. The lights of the parking lot came on as the sun dipped below the horizon. She thought again about heading home to South Falls.

All at once it dawned on her that she might be out of her depths.

The plan had seemed solid. She had thought of herself as operating amongst predictable actors, that she was the sole character with free will, that all others were automatons. But now she realized that there were stories going on all around her. That her plan would have to slip in between the cracks of another narrative. That the means to the end had to be fluid. She would have to find Michael, all the while avoiding those who might be following her.

Another trip to the window.

She checked the lock.

She lay on the bed and watched the blinking red light of the smoke detector on the ceiling. A visible twinkling that matched her pulsating thoughts.

That's when someone knocked on her door.

FORTY-EIGHT

MELISSA CREPT TO THE DOOR, put her hand gently on the handle, and her eye to the peephole. She was expecting to see the pickup in the parking lot and the two shadows standing outside ready to break down the door. But what she saw relaxed her and she unfastened the chain lock. Lila was standing on the other side, cigarette in hand.

"Hey you," she said, "I saw you pull in so I'd thought I'd stop over. You mind if I come in?"

"Well, I'm kinda—"

"Thanks," Lila said as she brushed by Melissa and into the room, a stream of vapor flowing behind her.

"Yeah, please, come in," Melissa said, annoyed at the intrusion.

Lila took the seat next to the dresser in the far corner. The room was small and getting smaller with each exhale that the waitress unleashed. Melissa stood next to the window and tried to get oxygen without appearing rude.

"So, I just got back from talking with Tami. She's the usual waitress over at the diner I was filling in for. She was telling me about her boyfriend Kyle. He's down at the hospital, one of the guys who got in that car accident a couple days ago that I told you about."

Melissa tried to hide her irritation by showing a thin veil of empathy. "Is he okay?"

"No. He's pretty messed up. The doctors think he'll never walk again. As if that's all Tami needed. She can barely keep her own life straight, now she's supposed to take on an invalid?"

It was hard to gauge if Lila truly felt sorry for her friend, or if she was venting about the work that could undoubtedly fall on her lap. She was of the ilk that would get mad at a sick person because it forced her to do more chores.

"She was telling me how Kyle wishes he would have died rather than lose his legs. He was ranting and raving . . . very hysterical . . ." Lila released a slow cloud of smoke and looked for a place to put the butt.

"Lila, I'm sorry. If there is anything I can do . . . ," Melissa said in that way people use that phrase without ever thinking they will be called to task to fulfill it.

"Well, you could start by letting me know about this accident."

"Letting you know?" Melissa asked.

"Yeah. Don't act surprised. You show up in town all of a sudden the same time that all this stuff is happening. You a reporter?"

"No," Melissa said.

"A cop? A PI?"

"No. How could I possibly know anything about this?"

"Why were you asking so many questions about Michael Sullivan?" Lila prodded as she lit up another cigarette.

Melissa sucked her bottom lip, thinking of the next words

192

that would come out of her mouth. She walked away from the window and sat down on the bed.

"I don't understand how my questions yesterday have anything to do with a car accident. It was just small talk, nothing more."

"Because James and Kyle were out looking for Michael when they wiped out."

Lila proceeded to tell Melissa the story as it was told to her by Tami, who in turn had heard it from Kyle. She told of how Haywood had gone to the guys and explained to them how much of a threat Michael was to all those in Coldwater, how the boys had taken him out in the woods, how he got away from them. She told Melissa about Old Man Jackson being found dead at his convenience store and how they were out looking for Michael on the back roads and bridges. She told her how James and Kyle came across Michael on a northern road, the truck crash, James dying, and Kyle ending up paralyzed.

"I told you he was bad news. According to Kyle, Michael caused the accident that killed James and near killed him."

Melissa's head began to swim, not only from the nicotine fog that was filling her room, but also from the realization that she apparently had competition in the retribution game.

Melissa came out of her contemplation when Lila spoke again.

"You know something. I can tell." Lila released another cloud of vapor. She looked intently at Melissa. "I can read people. Call it a gift, and I can tell that your being here in Coldwater isn't a coincidence. You know something, don't you?"

Melissa stood and paced the room. Lila sat toking on

her cigarette and watched her carefully. Melissa admired the steeliness of this woman. She was no-nonsense backwoods-country strong. She was also someone Melissa felt like she could let in. She stopped her pacing and looked at Lila.

"He's my brother."

"Michael?" Lila asked, her eyebrows racing to her hairline. Melissa nodded and sat back down.

"Oh really? You just happen to show up when all this is happening? Do you know where he is? Did he call you to come here and pick him up?"

"No, not at all. I haven't seen him since we were kids."

Lila blew more smoke into the room. The haze drifted through the air like the haze floating through Melissa's mind. Why was she here, at this particular time? Perhaps Lila was right, perhaps Michael was calling her back to Coldwater. But how ridiculous was that notion? Melissa was a realist, but somewhere in the pit of her soul, she could feel this pull back to the broken home of her youth.

Silence stood between them. It was as if both women were processing the story at the same time. Melissa spoke first.

"So what did they do with him? To Michael? You said that Kyle and some others took him out to the woods?"

"I know what Tami told me, but I don't half believe her."

"What?"

"She said that Kyle was doped up on morphine when he talked to her—"

"What did they do?"

Lila took a slow toke for encouragement, and then told Melissa what she had heard.

"Alive? They buried him alive?"

"I told you, he was doped up," Lila said. "I can't imagine

they actually did that. Not Kyle. He's too scared of his own shadow to be involved with something as crazy as that."

Melissa's stomach dropped to the floor. She was here to do the same thing to Michael as this posse had attempted, but her reaction to the news was subconscious and reflexive. Shock, defensiveness, empathy . . . the same empathy that had tried to find a way into her heart when she was at Michael's house, her house. Just like all siblings who fight each other without mercy suddenly come to each other's defense, Melissa felt the encroachment of such sentiments. The method they had used seemed bent on barbarism. Animalistic.

But how was she any different? Was her rage, her quest for punishment, somehow more holy than theirs? Michael was hers—hers to punish, to defend, hers to decide what to do with.

"Who is this Haywood guy?" Melissa asked.

"Local prince of everything. Most of the boys follow his lead, seeing as he is the only one of the group who made it through college. He thinks he's the smartest and they all fall in line."

"Even Kyle?" Melissa asked, still trying to gauge the credibility of the injured man's story.

"Especially Kyle," Lila said.

"Even if Haywood told him to help bury a body?"

Lila sat in silence, pondering the question but not offering an answer.

Melissa straightened in her seat. "How can I meet this Haywood?"

195

FORTY-NINE

TOWARD MIDNIGHT, Haywood and his men stopped at a dirt drive that led to a farmhouse, tucked away on its own plot of ground miles away from civilization. They had come upon it by chance on their way back south to Coldwater.

The afternoon had been spent in silence, each man contemplating in their own way the image of the burnt corpse at the drug trailer. Each left alone in his own thoughts. There was a collective, unspoken agreement that it was time to turn home. The woods would not produce their prey. It was a fool's errand, but one they were all willing to play out.

Clinton got on the next north-south two-track, turned on the headlights, and drove. The beams projecting a small world in front of them as blackness crept in on the edges, trees standing like skeletal guardians on each side of the passing vehicle.

The two-track slowly morphed into a dirt one-lane drive that widened with each passing minute, and eventually Clinton was able to get the truck up to speed. They spotted the house in the woods simply by chance. They stopped and stared at it.

"You know who lives there?" Haywood asked.

"No," Davis said, a crimson ember illuminating his face from the back seat.

Haywood unfolded the map from the glove box and turned on the dome light.

He had marked the spot of the sick boy's home with a black circle. Another mark indicated where the trailer and burned bodies were found. His finger searched for where the possible unmarked road they were on might be until he stopped, grabbed his pen, and X'd a location.

"Pretty sure this is where we are. If so, it's almost a straight course," Haywood said. "Pull in."

Clinton did as he was told, and turned into the drive and brought the SUV up to the house. It was still, as if all sound had been sucked from the earth. The boys looked around from the safety of their seats.

"You see what I'm seeing?" Clinton asked.

"I believe I am," Haywood said.

In the wash of the headlights, circling the house in a concentric circle was nothing but dead earth. Just like the sick boy's dugout, just like Michael's house back in Coldwater.

As they stared, the porch light flickered on and a man came out the screen door and stopped at the top of the steps. He didn't motion to the truck, just stood there watching, like a statue content to watch the ages pass before its granite eyes.

Haywood opened his door and stepped out.

"You guys stay here," he said. "And Clinton, keep your gun handy."

Clinton nodded as he watched Haywood walk forward.

■ ■ ■

Michael heard the slam of a car door, the sound echoing through the dark like a rifle shot. He sat up from the mattress and pressed his face against the slats of the barn. Across the dead space, by the house, an SUV idled with its headlights piercing into the dark woods south of the barn.

He could see Nick standing on the porch as another man walked from the vehicle up to him. They were two gunslingers facing off at high noon, Nick commanding the higher ground of the porch, the other man looking up at him from twenty paces away.

Michael strained his eyes until they felt as if they would pop out of his skull. The gait of the stranger, the way he held himself, the way he walked from the SUV with the air of owning every footstep he took. He knew him. He knew who now stood before Nick.

It was Haywood.

They had found him.

Michael gathered his things and looked for another way out of the barn, but it was already too dark to see. He inched his way to the back wall and groped for a door, a loose board, anything that would allow him to escape into the woods behind the cover of the building. Nothing.

In his blind searching, he tripped over the mutant chicken and fell to the dirt floor. He held his tongue, but the deranged beast cawed at him and then disappeared into the shadows. The only way out was through the front, in perfect view of the house and the waiting vehicle.

He was hopelessly and utterly trapped. The wooden barn a more grandiose version of the coffin box Haywood and his men had put him in just days before.

Michael made his way back to the bed and pressed up against the wall to see what would happen.

■ ■ ■

"Howdy," Haywood said to the man on the porch as his eyes scanned the house, the property, the shrouded barn on the edge of the encroaching forest.

"Can I help you with something?" the man asked.

"Name's Haywood."

"Nick."

"I was wondering if you happened to notice any odd characters in the area lately," Haywood said.

"You mean, other than right now?" Nick said.

Haywood smirked. "Yes, other than right now."

"That seems to be the only type of people I see up here."

"Today. Did you see anyone today?" Haywood's patience was already running thin from the long day in the car, the endless crisscrossing of the north woods. He didn't need lip from a backwoods hick.

The man stood silent, just staring at him.

"We're looking for someone," Haywood added.

"One reason people come up here, they usually don't want to be found," Nick said.

"This one broke out of South Falls jail. Cops said he was sighted up this way. We've been trailing him for hours now."

"And you boys are just doing your civic duty?"

Haywood set his jaw. It was in him to walk up to the porch and punch Nick in the head, but the way the man stood lent an air of toughness to him. The man had a grizzled streak in his manner that made Haywood question his own ability to intimidate him.

He relaxed his shoulders a bit and tried a different course of action. "There was an explosion not too far from here earlier today."

"I heard it."

199

"Know anything about it?"

"No."

"Didn't make you curious at all?"

"The way I see it, ain't none of my business what others do. Probably just one of the things we differ on from what I can tell," Nick said.

Haywood was not used to being blocked at every move he made. He was the boss in the circle he ran in, had always been. Now this man was thwarting him, but for what reason? He was either just a misanthrope living out in the sticks, or he was hiding something.

"You mind if I take a look around?"

"I would mind."

"Well, maybe me and my guys might just look around anyways," Haywood said, pointing to Clinton and Davis sitting in the SUV like the shadows of mob hit men waiting for the cue to practice their trade.

"Then you and your *guys* would be making a bad mistake." Nick seemed to grow in stature as he spoke.

With each passing second, as Haywood's thoughts turned to a rising hatred of the man, a budding pressure started to expand at the base of his skull as if someone had reached into him, grabbed the top of his spine, and started squeezing. He had felt this before . . . this same mystic constriction intermixed with rage and anger.

All at once, Haywood felt the sensation of being entirely outmatched. That if he stayed too much longer, his bones would shatter under his skin. He looked to the barn, to the house.

"Alright," Haywood said quietly. "Alright."

"Probably best if you all just get going."

Haywood turned back to the car and walked deflated to his seat. He got in and told Clinton to head back to Coldwater.

"What was that all about?" Davis asked.

"He's hiding something."

"Michael? You think he's here?" Clinton asked as he turned onto the dirt road and headed south.

"If I was betting on it, I'd say yes."

"Only one of him," Davis said. "Can't be too hard to get around."

Haywood exhaled. The throbbing in his head diminishing with each passing moment down the road. "Something tells me we wouldn't stand a chance."

FIFTY

*T*HE WARDEN STRODE ACROSS THE YARD *of the prison, his hands behind his back, each step echoing on the paved walkway and adding an air of authority to his gait. Michael walked behind him, his bedding stacked in his arms, two strides for the warden's one, just to keep pace. A guard rounded out the informal parade. He was several steps behind the boy and seemed more focused on enjoying the fresh air and sunshine than worrying about the child doing anything foolish. From the windows of the cell blocks, heads looked out and wondered at the small inmate being led away.*

They soon arrived at a small outbuilding that had not been actively used by the prison for some time. It had become a utility shed for the maintenance workers. The building was in its own fenced area, no yard attached to it. A large metal door hung on giant hinges. It was more of a brick hut. The warden opened the door and it squealed like a large beast emerging from the depth of the ocean and sucking in air for the first time in a millennium.

Two barred windows curtained the door, and the warden stepped inside and breathed the stale atmosphere. Michael stood on the step and peered inside.

The warden had the maintenance crew clean out the small enclosure of all their accumulated items. The only thing inside now was two rooms. One had a cell much like that of an old western town. It was an open cage, in it was a wood slat that the boy's curled mattress would go on. A steel toilet, recently scrubbed, still looked as if nature was winning the war to rust it out of existence. Across from the cell stood another locked door with a thin window in it. Through the window Michael could see the remains of a large wooden chair. A throne. A king's chamber that had not been occupied for years.

Michael took his place in the cell, unrolled his bedding, and sat down. The guard closed the cell door behind him and locked it with a key that was as old as the prison. The key was huge and stuck out amidst all the other keys the guard carried with him on the ring.

"You sure about this, Warden?" the guard asked.

"I am."

"Just seems . . . I don't know."

"It's the safest place for him. Safest for him, and safest for everyone else."

"What if his lawyer catches wind of this? Or some bleeding-heart group. Keeping a kid in the old execution cell ain't going to sound good on the news."

"I know. But if the state refuses to provide a solution for him, I am left on my own to improvise. Segregation from the others will keep him out of harm's way, and I can't afford to clear a whole cell block for him."

The guard stepped out of the door and back into the sunshine. He may have felt a twinge of guilt in his belly at leaving the kid out here, but the warden was right. There was no place to put him that would guarantee his safety. And the guard himself had been suffering from an unrelenting headache for months. When he caught wind that the boy had something to do with it, he also felt a sense of relief that this might just cure him. He walked back to his duties and left the warden with the boy.

"Now, you'll be alright here. I have it worked out with the guards for them to swing out here on their rounds and make sure you're doing fine. I'll have some books brought out for you, and I'm working on getting a TV to keep you company."

The warden turned and opened up the door to the king's chamber. Michael watched him as he walked into the room, reached over his head to a pull chain that was next to a light-bulb, and tied a string to it. The warden unraveled the string and brought it back out through the door, tying the end to one of the bars on the cell.

"Now, this is a bit unorthodox, but if you have an emergency or anything, pull this string so the light comes on. I'll be able to see it from my office. I'll have it in mind to keep an eye for it. Other than that, the guards will be around.

"Same routine as usual: Breakfast, lunch, dinner, recreation."

The warden stopped and gazed at the child.

Nothing in this world made sense anymore. During his career he had taken pride in bringing a firm hand to the state's prison population, but being the keeper of this boy had made him feel more like the devil than a man of justice. He turned to leave when he heard the small voice of the boy.

"Warden . . . what's that? In there?"

The warden looked and saw that the boy was pointing at the chair.

"*That's what we used to do to the worst of the worst.*"

"*Am I the worst?*"

The warden thought about it. "You know, son, if you are, I don't see it."

FIFTY-ONE

THE BARN DOOR OPENED and the morning light rushed in, exposing the interior like an otoscope. Michael opened his eyes and saw Nick standing at the door.

"I have some breakfast on if you want some."

"Alright."

Nick led the way back to the house and through the screen door on the porch. Michael followed him, but stopped at the doorstep. Inside he could see a small kitchen that looked as if it had been designed in the '50s, its built-in cabinets with chipping white paint and uneven doors. The table was set for two.

"You can come in," Nick said. "It's just eggs."

Michael opened the screen, walked slowly to the closest chair, and sat down. Nick put a bowl on the table and sat down across from him.

"How'd you sleep?"

"Fine, I suppose."

"Better than outside."

Michael nodded, looking at the bowl of eggs with reservation. He was starving and his stomach was begging him to grab the eggs and devour them all. But if life had taught him anything, it was to not trust the appearance of kindness.

"It's okay. It's just eggs. Ain't put nothing in them. Here, see?" Nick said as he scooped himself a helping and started eating them. "Ain't poisoned."

Michael allowed himself to relax and felt a grin force its way to the corners of his mouth. He grabbed the spoon and served himself. Before long the two had polished off the meal.

His stomach now somewhat full, Michael leaned back in his chair and looked around. He wasn't sure what the next course of action was. Part of him wanted to get moving, to keep heading home. But there was another part that wanted to linger. He wasn't sure of Nick, but at the same time felt like he was in the company of a kindred soul. That feeling, however, also unnerved him.

Michael was fully aware of himself, of *his* sins, of *his* crimes, but since they were *his* sins, he thought of them like they were external baggage. Not entwined with the fabric of his character. When those same sins were in someone else, he didn't trust that person.

We gloss over our own sins, softening their edges, while assuming the sins of others are forever razor sharp and at the ready to slash our throats.

Michael had met several people in prison with lesser crimes to their name, but they were always worse in his eyes than when he reflected on himself.

"So what are your plans?"

Michael came out of his daze and looked across the table. "Keep on moving, I guess."

"Suppose to rain today. You're welcome to hold up till it passes."

Michael nodded.

Nick reached across the table and grabbed the plates. As

he did so, Michael caught a glimpse of his host's wrists. They were scarred up like those of a suicidal teenager who repeatedly tried to slice their veins but could never find them.

Nick put the dishes in the sink and returned to his seat. He looked Michael dead in the eyes and rolled up his sleeves.

"I had a hard time of things once," Nick said, exposing his scars.

They were on both arms. He then unbuttoned his shirt at the collar and exposed his neck. The flesh was scorched, a rope burn that went all the way around to his spine.

"I'm going to assume that you have some marks of your own," Nick continued. "If not, well, you will someday."

"I've never tried . . . tried to . . ."

"Kill yourself? Someday maybe you will. If you're human, that is. I met a lot of guys in the pen who didn't mind the solitary life. They were animals. It's how you know when you've crossed the line. You don't miss being part of the world."

Michael studied Nick, listening intently to each word.

"My first years out, I thought I could manage this here lifestyle. Do my thing, mind my business. But the world cutting you off—and I mean, absolutely cutting you off—doesn't do much for your well-being.

"I tried reintegrating myself back into society, but they won't have it. I often thought how great it would be to be anonymous, to have nobody know me, know my past. The gloriousness of being invisible.

"But I'll never be invisible. I'll never blend in to the background and melt into the fabric of society. No matter where I go . . . where we go . . . we will be marked. Outcasts. We will never be trusted. Never let into the community of civilized men." Nick took a sip of coffee and pressed his lips. "These scars, well, these scars are from times I got tired of the life altogether. I thought I could put an end to it. But that's just one added-on bonus to this judgment that sits upon us. No man can end us, and we can't end ourselves until our time has come."

"You hung yourself?" Michael asked, pointing to the scar on Nick's neck.

"Out there in the barn. Tied up to the beam, put my head in the noose, and kicked over the chair."

Michael looked at him in awe.

"But . . . it didn't work. So I tried, again. And again. And again. Either the rope would break, or the noose would unravel. One time, I just hung there for what seemed like an hour until I got bored and cut myself down."

Outside the rain eased in gently across the yard, and once it had lightly dampened the ground, the clouds unleashed sheets upon sheets of water.

"We ain't immortal. God knows I wish we were. But we are destined to live out the full penalty of our crime unhindered by our fellow men or ourselves."

"Who'd you kill?" Michael asked.

"My brother," Nick said. "Much like what I suspect you have done."

Michael remained silent and cast his gaze at the rain beating against the screen door.

"Nature has a way of preserving its work. I am the fruit of my father, obligated to pass down my nature and so on. My brother carried that same fire. We were born of the same coals, passed on and on through generations. When I killed him, I took away all the future fire he would create. His fire was the same as mine. I killed myself in the doing. I'm all that is left of what my line has produced through eons of struggle and survival. And nature will preserve it until its last possible moment. Perhaps there is a chance to rekindle that flame. To pass it on. But nature doesn't know the world anymore. It ain't the same as when it started."

Nick drifted off into a half-mad philosophical dream and then snapped back to the present moment. He took another sip from his mug.

"Or maybe we're just cursed. Straightforward like."

"Or crazy," Michael said.

"Or that. But who knows. Maybe it will be different for you. Maybe you won't get to this point of desperation. Maybe you'll keep trying to get yourself out of this lot that we've cast for ourselves."

Michael hesitated, then cracked open the door to his soul. "I have hope. Sometimes. I don't know why. But I plan to go on living."

Nick smiled a malevolent grin. "If that's what you want to call it."

"So what are we doing here?" Michael asked.

"We're just having coffee, waiting for the rain to stop."

FIFTY-TWO

MELISSA! YOU IN THERE?"

The pounding on the door woke Melissa from a fitful night's sleep. She rolled over and saw the alarm clock. It was so late, later than she usually slept, but the poor night's rest coupled with the room-darkening blinds of the hotel room had not prompted her inner timer to go off. She sat up in bed and ran her hand through her hair. Her head hurt as if there were too many thoughts crammed into too little a space.

"Melissa?"

The pounding continued.

She walked to the door and peered through the peephole. The fish-eyed lens distorted Lila's face in a grotesque way. She opened the door.

"Good, you're here," Lila said. "I got Haywood over in the diner. He said he'd love to talk with you."

Melissa looked past Lila to the outside world. It was gray and cold, a bitter rain dropping from the skies onto the asphalt parking lot. Her thoughts quickened at hearing the man's name.

"Give me a minute," she said. She walked to the bathroom,

put herself together, and stepped back out. She put her coat on and her hood up and stepped out the door.

Lila walked with Melissa across the parking lot of the motor lodge and through the front door of the diner. The chef called out to her in Chewbacca-like noises, and Lila waved off the words with a discourteous shrug. She pointed toward the back booth to a man sitting by himself. His cell phone rested on the table, along with a plate of burnt eggs and toast. Melissa walked over to the man cautiously, wary that he might turn and attack her at any moment, but he just sat motionless, his eyes ever vigilant on his phone.

"Are you Haywood?" Melissa asked, doing her best to calm the tremble in her voice.

Haywood looked up at her absentmindedly, but his gaze quickly focused when he saw the woman standing before him. He stared at her, looking as if he'd seen a ghost. It occurred to her that she looked a lot like Michael, easily passing as his sister. As nervous as she was, she nearly laughed at the thought of how it must have unnerved the man.

He cleared his throat. "Melissa Sullivan, I assume?"

Melissa nodded.

"Lila told me about you. Please, sit down. Can I get you something? Coffee?"

"No . . . I know what they do to coffee around here."

"Smart choice."

Melissa sat down and the two looked at each other for what seemed like an eternity. Neither one flinched at the other's gaze, sizing the other one up and coming to the quick conclusion that they were of equal fortitude.

"I guess there is no easy way to start this, so I'll just jump right in with both feet," Haywood said as he pushed his plate aside and slipped his phone into his pocket. "Lila said that you were asking after Michael."

Melissa wasn't in the mood for idle talk. "Was that you following me in the truck out at my brother's house?"

Haywood was taken aback. "Me? No."

"Someone you know?"

"Earl and Frank. Yeah. But they were not there to scare you. I asked them to go up to your brother's house to make sure everything was alright. They aren't the brightest of people, and so they probably thought you were up to no good. Dim-witted as they are, they thought they were doing right by following you back to town."

"You expect me to believe that?"

"Believe what you want."

Melissa stared at Haywood, but his steeliness was impenetrable. "Were they part of your group? The group who kidnapped Michael?"

"Now hold on, that's a pretty big accusation."

"One of your lackeys has already been talking. I wouldn't think that the accusation should surprise you."

"You mean Kyle, don't you? Down at South Falls? He's half comatose, drugged up on painkillers. He probably knows who the second gunman was on the grassy knoll. I wouldn't trust his word on anything at the moment."

Lila stepped over with a glass of water and some toast, setting it down in front of Melissa. She appeared to do it more as an opportunity to snoop than to be gracious, but the ice-cold countenance of the two conversationalists had her heading back to the kitchen at a quick pace.

"So, you see anything interesting at Michael's house?" Haywood asked.

"It was practically destroyed. Falling down."

"A house is a reflection of the soul."

"What does that mean?"

"It means that your brother is a lunatic. Now, you might have some romanticized memory of him, but us here in Coldwater, those who have lived with him the past little while, know where he comes from, where he's been, what he's done, well . . . wouldn't expect anything less of him if he chose to live in a junk pile."

"It looks like he lives in the trailer behind it."

Haywood shrugged as if that piece of information had little bearing on his opinion.

"Why do you consider him a lunatic?" Melissa asked.

"Because that's what he is. Tell me, what did you see out there, besides a fallen-down old house? Did you see anything . . . unnatural?"

Melissa thought about the wasted earth around the cabin, the absence of any living thing forming a buffering circle around her brother's house. The retreating nature. The place felt like an open grave and its lingering absence of life still shaded the corner of her heart.

"You did, didn't you? You saw it. You felt it even. Now you are starting to understand, just a little bit. So, before you sit over there and sling any more accusations around, let me tell you some more."

FIFTY-THREE

MELISSA SAT AT THE DINER and listened to Haywood spin a tale of tragedy that would have been ridiculously improbable if Lila had not told a similar tale the night before. She listened to him talk about a friend, of his dying in the woods in a mysterious way, of an old man dying an untimely death in a convenience store, of cars crashing uncontrollably. Of a sick child in the wilderness, burnt bodies at a hidden drug lab . . . the story was as inconceivable as the ramblings of an inmate at a psycho ward. When Haywood finally stopped, he looked exhausted.

"So this is why you buried him alive?" Melissa said, her voice emotionless.

Haywood looked straight at her and his eyes gave no indication of being affected by her words. "This is supposed to be a conversation," he said, his voice steady. "Why don't you tell me why you're here."

"What's to tell? I'm here to see my brother."

"You two must be close."

"What is that supposed to mean?"

"It means that I haven't seen you in Coldwater since he got out of prison and moved back to your parents' plot of dead earth."

"You keep a pretty tight watch on the town?"

"I know everything about this town. And I will know everything about this town after you two are long gone."

"Is that a threat?"

"It's no threat. It's just the simple truth," Haywood said. "I assume you won't have a reason to stay. Michael's gone, he ain't coming back."

"You seem certain of yourself."

"Coldwater is a good town filled with good people. It's going to stay that way."

"Well, if I was Michael, I don't think I would just run and hide. No," Melissa said, "I think I'd be coming back here as soon as I could. You know, to thank all these good people for being so nice."

A smirk slowly spread across Haywood's face, but his eyes stayed set deep in their sockets. "Now, is that a threat?" he asked.

"The universe bends toward justice, does it not? If that is the case," Melissa said, "then Michael's path should lead back here."

"Justice? Is that what you're getting at? Michael's trajectory of justice should have ended with him rotting away in a cell at the state prison. But no, what does the world know about justice? It has no real concept of the idea. Where is *our* justice? Where is the justice for Morrison, and for these poor men who died this week?" Haywood grabbed a napkin, lifted the brim of his hat, and wiped his brow.

"He had no business coming back here," he continued. "And if the world doesn't have the grit to do what needs to be done, then it's left to us to do it."

Melissa sat and let the words pour over her. She was here for the exact same reason. Justice. But Haywood had set himself up too high to presume this was his role to take. It was hers by right.

"You've overstepped your bounds," Melissa said. She was calm and firm. "You might think you're judge and jury in this town. but you're not. You're just a scared little man hiding behind a bluster of words."

"So, you're here to help him then," Haywood said. "He call you? Tell you to pick him up?"

Melissa didn't respond, but Haywood could read her face.

"No? You're here for different reasons, aren't you? Could it be that you are here for the same reason as me? Could it be that you feel the same way I do?"

"We are nothing alike."

"I wouldn't bet on that."

"I'm here because I've been wronged," Melissa said. "You're here because you're a coward. You're afraid. You hide behind the notion of justice, but you don't care about it. Not really. And I bet a guy like you can't handle being afraid. You've never had to deal with it. Never had to learn how to hide it away, to cope. You don't like it. You hate the feeling. So the first chance you got, you buried it . . . but you messed up. You didn't bury it deep enough. Now, it's come back to bite you and it's driving you nuts."

Melissa got up from the table and looked down at Haywood. He was looking where she had been sitting, he didn't move a muscle.

"My advice to you," she said. "Quit. Quit what you're doing. Quit chasing him. Leave him alone."

"And what, may I ask, are you planning to do?"

"My business is my own," Melissa said as she walked toward the door. "It's family business."

FIFTY-FOUR

THE DAY TRUDGED ON and the rain kept falling. Michael had wandered back to the barn after breakfast and sat on the old mattress. Staying in the house with Nick was unnerving, and the conversation had dried up after the breakfast sermon.

The man was crazy. There could be no doubt about that. Years of seclusion had driven him into a delirium that now passed the border of eccentricity to straight-out lunacy. His scars were just physical representations of a lacerated mind.

But what fueled the uncomfortableness of the whole situation for Michael was that he felt as if he was looking at himself several years from now. Nick was what he would become after time had slowly eroded the hope that he managed to cling to, the desire for normalcy. How long could he possibly hold on to such a notion?

Nick's words had stung because they were true. They were outcasts now and forever. Society would never let them forget what they had done. The system might have spit them out and sent them on their way, but mankind had cast them out forever.

What was the point then? Isolation only brought madness. A slow decline into self-destruction. It was inevitable.

The rain kept falling, and Michael watched several times as Nick would walk out onto the porch, look over to the barn, and then step back into the house.

It was an odd arrangement.

Several times Michael thought of gathering his things and getting on his way, but there was an attraction to this place that he could not deny. He was tired of being on his own. Deep down inside, he was sick of it. Here, beyond the ramblings of a twisted mind, was a person who knew how he felt. Who knew of the sad existence and could, at the least, understand. This was not so much an oasis but an asylum for the likes of him.

By midday the rain began to ease and Nick came out on the porch and sat down in his chair and began rocking. The noise floated across the yard and into the barn.

The sound settled on Michael's ears like the slow ripping of paper. A steady timekeeping of the winnowing away of hours.

Michael stepped out onto the wet grass.

"It's almost lunchtime, if you're hungry."

"Sure," Michael said.

Nick got up and went inside, the screen door slamming on the doorframe.

Michael walked up onto the porch and put his hand to the door.

He would not become this. He would not become Nick. But his anxiety rose as he entered the house, each step forward making that future reality all the more certain.

FIFTY-FIVE

THE RAIN WASHED THE DAY AWAY as Melissa sat in the motel room. With the blinds open, she could see the trucks that would occasionally drive into the parking lot of the diner or Gilly's pub. As the afternoon wore on, the dominance of the diner crowd gave way to the desires of the bar patrons. Holed up in this room, Melissa found her mind jumping between two separate but related thoughts.

The conversation between her and Haywood had not settled well. Her impressions of Haywood and what his crew had done were now forcing her to evaluate her own intentions. She had always felt justified in her plans, in her right to seek retribution, but as she observed them played out before her by a different agent, her anger turned from Michael, and she caught herself dwelling on the Coldwater vigilantes.

Haywood disgusted her.

He was the quintessential hick-town mafioso. A self-righteous blowhard who found an abandoned fiefdom and set up residence as the leader of the ignorant. In South Falls he would have been a nobody. A person ignored. Dismissed.

But here in the backwoods of the world, he had convinced the easily swayed that he was the arbiter of right and wrong.

He had no right to stick his nose in this. Michael owed him nothing. Her brother's remorse, his repentance, belonged to her. Haywood had no claim to it.

"We are nothing alike," she whispered to herself. She should be focused on the task at hand, the task that she came to Coldwater to perform. But Haywood's smug face kept popping up in her brain, driving her to the point of distraction.

"We are nothing alike."

She repeated the words over and over until the phrase turned from a rebuke to a questioning plea to convince herself that she wasn't at all like him. She sought closure to pain that had been poured on her, Haywood sought freedom from fear. His was the way of the coward. Hers was the way of the righteous.

Her old bedroom in the abandoned house mixed in with her thoughts as well.

Michael had done the work of restoring it. That could be the only possible conclusion. In his own way he must have been seeking a means to atone for his actions by reconstructing the world that he had destroyed. A replica of memory and happier times. Before the fall.

It was a poor imitation. A place that could never be brought back to life no matter how much paint was splashed on the walls. The soul of the place was gone forever.

Gone.

No action could change that.

No building up could ever fix what was torn down.

Gone.

"We are nothing alike."

What could more destruction do?

Melissa stood and walked over to the mirror. She had come to Coldwater to kill Michael.

"We are nothing alike."

We are everything alike.

FIFTY-SIX

THE SPIDER SAT ON ITS WEB in the corner of the barn, its deformed body all but still, save for its tapping leg on the web like the pendulum of a grandfather clock. Its offspring gathering around, their tiny bodies masking the predators they were about to become. One by one they climbed on their mother's back and sank their fangs into her, devouring her, their instinct and nature kicking in as they consumed where they came from and would become who she was.

Michael watched the matriphagy from the mattress in the corner as moonlight drifted in through the slats, his own past and future days reflected in the scene before him.

He was his past, and his future days would be children always feeding on the event that had set his life in motion. There was no stopping it. It was nature. It was the continual perpetuation of his deed. Generation to generation the spider hatchlings would never spare their life source, in turn themselves becoming the food of their offspring. On and on, never ending, until the end of time.

And so, too, Michael's days would feed on his murderous past, becoming another iteration of himself, but always the same.

There was no escaping it. It was inevitable. The choice he had made as a child was a constant variable in each and every action he would commit. The world would not allow otherwise. He would never be able to wipe the slate clean and start as a new creature untainted by past crimes, just as the spider hatchling would never question the devouring appetite that spurred it on in its feast.

The future was set in stone. Hardwired.

The judgment passed by man was temporal, but as Michael lay in the dark, the eternal curse that weighed down on him was unending. Only death would relieve him of that burden, and death was something that no one else seemed capable of delivering to him. And so he would go on. Tomorrow. The next day.

Michael wondered if the spiders knew what they were doing or if it was pure instinct, free of remorse and empathy, free from regret, as the parent who introduced them to life now coursed through their tiny mouths. He wondered if he would ever get to the point of living his life free of such regret.

It had been over twenty years since he had committed his crime. He had not yet arrived at such a state of being, and as the hatchlings finished their meal and scurried off to begin their own narratives, Michael doubted that he ever would.

FIFTY-SEVEN

MICHAEL WAS AWOKEN by the sound of yelling out in the yard. It was the small hours of the night and it took him a moment to realize where he was. He looked through the slat in the wall and saw Nick halfway between the house and the barn, yesterday's rain turning the yard into a quagmire. He was wobbling in place, an almost empty bottle in his hand. He was yelling for Michael.

"Hey! I know you're awake!" Nick screamed in between sips from the bottle. He bared his teeth after each swallow. "Let's get this over with!"

Michael stood frozen, his eye to the gap in the boards, watching.

"I know why you've come! I've been waiting a long time for you! I'm ready!"

Michael thought about what to do next. He looked around the barn, but the same imprisoned feeling he had when Haywood had driven up now resurfaced. The door was the only way out. He had no doubt he could outrun Nick, but the sight of his host's madness had him second-guessing every action he might take.

"I know you! I could tell from the moment I laid eyes on you! You're my deliverer! My salvation! Come out! Now!"

Nick took another sip, his head flared back. He lost his balance and fell down, his face in the mud, and the bottle went flying. Michael gathered his things and stepped out into the night. He looked east and plotted his route into the dark woods. As soon as he stepped by Nick, he heard him speak.

"Wait . . . please. Don't go. I've waited too long . . ."

Michael stopped and looked down at the man. His face was half obscured by darkness, but it looked tormented, almost as if he was crying.

"What are you talking about?"

"You. I've been waiting for you. You're here to kill me."

"You're insane!"

Nick sat up and started searching for his bottle of moonshine. "No. I could feel it when I saw you. You are marked like me. We are the same. I could feel it. I knew that you would come someday. Someone who knows what it's like. The torment. The isolation. Someone who knows and could look at me not with fear, not with hatred, but with the one thing that can save both of us."

"And what is that?"

"Mercy."

Michael watched as the man located the bottle, put it to his lips, but found nothing left inside. He then threw it at the barn and the sound of its shattering cut the silence.

"This world knows nothing of mercy. It never has. I've paid my dues. I've paid more than they asked for. But do you think for one minute they will ever forgive? Do you think they'll ever let me walk among them again? This world, this whole godforsaken world, knows nothing of mercy. They pay lip service to it. Speak it with their mouths but it's just hollow breaths.

"There are those who dream of living apart, but they've never done it. Felt the real detachment from the world. They don't know what the darkness is like.

"But we do. We do! You and me. We know, don't we. We know what it's like to be ignored, forgotten, invisible. To be despised, hated, feared."

Michael stared at Nick. This was another rehearsed speech, one the man had been crafting for years. Inebriated, Nick's thoughts came pouring out of him without reservation. He was broken, sitting in the mud. Michael saw his future— their future—and understood. He felt what Nick said and he pitied him.

"They fear us, and that is why they need us. Fear is what makes us human. When was the last time you felt fear? Huh? I don't even remember. But I know they fear us. They need us, because without us they have nothing to pin their nightmares on. They fear us because they know—they know!—that with one momentary lapse of reason they could be us. We are the reminders of what they could be if they let themselves slip. Yes, yes, that is why they hate us. Why they do not want us in their company.

"I've killed . . . just like you. Does it matter why or does it matter who? I'm marked forever to be alone. From the time I cracked till my last breath, but my last breath won't come, not until nature stops my heart. I've been waiting all these years, praying that it would stop, but I keep waking each morning to the isolation that is this life we have been given. How I've wished it to end. But I'm not given that satisfaction.

"Tell me, how many times have you tried to end your life? Once, twice, a hundred times? You can't, can you? Not that you can't, but fate won't allow it. I know, I've tried more times than can be counted. It's as if the world knows what we want but won't let us have it until it's good and ready to let us go. It wants us to suffer. It wants us to be tormented till the bitter end.

"Which is why . . . is why you're my salvation. You are here, finally, you are here. You know what I speak is true. We cannot be killed by those who fear us. Those who hate us. You know I'm right, you know what I say is true!"

Michael knew. He thought of the inmate from prison, Old Man Jackson, James, everyone who meant to kill him had ended up dead themselves. The drug runners the day before. All of them. The shadow inside him guarded his life like a force field, kicking back their actions and revisiting it on them.

"But you, you are different. You know what it's like. Your action would not be driven by fear, but mercy. Mercy is the only thing that can save us."

"I'm not going to kill you," Michael said again.

The man crawled over to Michael and grabbed his legs. He was too drunk to stand. "Please! You must! It's why you're here, it's why you've come! I beg you!"

"Get off me!" Michael yelled, kicking Nick in the stomach, sending the man sprawling in the mud. Instantly, Michael felt a sharp pang in his gut—the first time he had experienced the eye-for-an-eye reprisal. This is what people felt who attacked him. They felt everything he did, returned on them with more vengeance. He doubled over and nearly vomited until the pain subsided. He could feel blood in his mouth.

With Nick on the ground, Michael regained control over himself and ran for the woods. When he passed the first tree, he stopped and looked back. Nick was trying to stand but kept falling over, his legs working independently of each other. Michael could hear him yelling into the night.

"Come back! It's why you're here! Come back! I'm begging you!"

Michael ran until he could no longer hear Nick's words.

FIFTY-EIGHT

MICHAEL SPENT THE REST OF THE NIGHT huddled under his coat, his thoughts circling around him. The stars had been out and the trees towered above, scraping the blackness. The woods were quiet. There was no wind, as if the earth had exhaled and was between breaths.

He saw his life laid before him the past couple of days. The naiveté of Will, the coldness of the meth heads, the madness of Nick. He knew where he was headed.

He dwelt on Nick's confession. Michael would never know the comfort of another person. The knowledge of this would push him to the edge of breaking, where only by sheer will would he be able to hold it together. He knew his will would not last forever. He knew there would come a day when he would give over to despair and let go of this thread of hope that kept him in the realm of the sane.

Someday he would be the one begging in the mud.

But why bother? What did he have to hope about?

His hope should have died with Marcus.

His little brother.

But he did hope. Michael still hoped.

Perhaps that was the human element, he thought. Hoping

beyond reason was what made a beast human. It wasn't fear, as Nick said, but the constant striving of hope.

The memory of his mother's touch and his father's pride stung him the most. He thought he had lost all before he led Marcus down that path in the woods, the pistol in hand, but little did he know what real loss would feel like. He not only killed his brother with the pull of the trigger, but he had destroyed all those around him. His mom slipped into madness, his father's heart gave out, his sister was taken to live far away from the destruction he had caused. The day he left for prison was the last time he had seen any of them.

The constant second-guessing of his life weighed on him like a lead blanket that he hauled through the forest toward his home.

But why go home? What was there for him?

The people of Coldwater feared him and wanted him dead. He could not show up and expect anything but another round of their hate. People who went as far as burying him alive would not stop at just one attempt. They had already crossed the Rubicon of timidity and would wade in those waters again without a second thought.

But home is where he was headed, something inside him driving him there.

Coldwater contained a remnant of past happiness for him, and he knew—deep down, he knew—that he could never hope to find happiness any other place in the world.

Michael stopped his walk and turned to look from where he came.

Perhaps Nick had been right. Perhaps Michael had come across his future self in the woods on purpose, perhaps he had been led to that house to bestow mercy on a man who had committed the same sins as he had. Only a fellow traveler down this road would know what a mercy they would be doing by ending his life. There would be no more guilt, no more hollowness, no more loneliness to count the days by.

This curse of the murderer's soul that gripped the spine would never uncoil itself from the fabric of the accused. It sat in constant vigilance, protecting its hoard of regret, annihilating all those who would come to end its life with fear and hatred. But mercy—it knew no defense against such an act, for the world was devoid of such sentiment.

Michael was death personified. Destined to be alone, to be hated, to be feared. The earth wilted at his presence, blood ran in his company, and pain came to those who would do him harm.

The scourge of Coldwater.

Michael turned south again. He would not go back to Nick's farmhouse. He would not be the merciful executioner of the man in the woods.

He had killed once before out of envy. Michael thought there would be no lesser retribution if he killed out of mercy.

FIFTY-NINE

THE NIGHT BORE ON, and in his dreams he was back in the dugout, the tarp flapping gently in the morning light. He rolled over on the dirt and crawled outside. Smoke rose gently all around him as if the whole forest had burned and turned to ash. The sky was gray, the earth parched, the woods stripped of all bark. It was a torched world absent of color. He walked north, away from the ridge. His dream consciousness guiding him farther into the woods. It was all dead.

Up ahead he could see a boy kneeling over something small. He could not see his face or what he was looking at, but he knew it was Will, in the same way that a shadow is known in a dream. The boy was covered in ashes as well, his clothes singed, his hair matted and tousled with debris. His neck was the color of bone with ash marks here and there. Michael stood and watched him. From this distance, he could tell the boy was sobbing.

This place was all too familiar. This burned-out world. This dead world. There was no sound but for the rhythmic crying of the boy.

Slowly Michael approached, curious as to what Will knelt over and apprehensive about what he'd find. Closer and closer he walked, and with each step his heart became heavier and heavier. He was coming to the point of all things. His mind raced to question everything, but his heart knew all the answers.

He now stood directly behind Will.

In front of the boy lay a small creature. Its fur was burned off its body and its remains were scorched and charred. Michael could see what it was. It was the source of a crushed boy's heart. It was Otis. Dead, disfigured beyond all comprehension, but he knew the body was Otis just as he knew the boy was Will.

The boy wept on.

Michael extended his hand to Will's shoulder, but the boy flinched and avoided his touch.

"Stay away from me!"

"Will, are you okay?"

The boy's face was buried into his hands. "How could you! How could you do this?"

"I . . . I . . ."

"How could you destroy all this?"

Michael could feel the pressure building inside him as if his skin were shrinking over his frame.

"We trusted you. How could you?" the boy went on, inconsolable. "We trusted you and you did this. You've ruined everything. Everything!"

Michael's mouth went dry. He could feel the dead air slowly start to suffocate him. The dying wood encroaching from every side, the world closing in around him.

"You said you wouldn't hurt us. You said so! How could you!"

"Will, I . . ." Michael's voice escaped him. He could not

233

speak. His vision began to turn slowly as the trees closed in. He looked down and saw Otis, burnt Otis, who rolled over to his feet, stood, and began barking with a skeletal growl.

"We trusted you!"

The world made no sense and perfect sense.

"How could you!"

The boy turned and looked into Michael's face, but it was not Will. It was another boy. It was Marcus. His brother.

"How could you!"

And with that, Michael awoke.

It was still night, and the wood was still alive, save for the small dead patch of ground upon which he had been sleeping.

Michael adjusted his back and tried to find a position on the ground that would contour to his body in a more comfortable manner. The breeze rocked the top of the trees, and with the rustling of the leaves he could hear another sound entwined. It was a voice, faint but human.

"Michael!"

The voice carried on the wind. Repeated. Laced with exasperation and anger.

"Michael!"

It was Nick.

He was in the woods.

He was coming after him.

SIXTY

MICHAEL COULD HEAR NICK yelling in the woods behind him, calling his name, screaming. His heart raced as quickly as his feet, and the low-hanging branches scratched at his cheeks and his eyes. His sweat mixed with the chill in the air, his skin cold while his muscles burned. But he ran. Ran as if the devil was behind him. For all he knew, it was.

"Michael! Michael!"

The voice sounded more and more angry with each yell.

Michael had left Nick drunken and delirious in the mud. He seemed a madman intoxicated and desperate but harmless, or at the least, not much to worry about. But now the drunken madman had sobered up and had turned into something else. He could tell by the voice echoing through the woods. The tenor of it. It was peppered with rage.

He kept running, high-stepping over fallen logs, ducking under low branches, bobbing and weaving through the forest. He was pushing south toward home, but he had no idea what he would do when he actually arrived. The voice through the trees was unrelenting. The voice would not stop. It would keep pursuing him to the end of the earth if it had to. It was the voice of a man who had waited years to speak and he wasn't going to shut up ever again.

"Michael!"

His own name sent a shiver down his spine. He thought about finding a place to hide, but each tree and stump he hurdled never looked like a secure place to take cover. Michael knew he had to keep running.

Suddenly his foot caught on a line of barbwire covered in the underbrush. Before he could realize what was happening, Michael fell and rolled down an embankment, the roots of the trees exposed in the bank punching at him as he tumbled down. He ultimately came to a stop on a bed of white stones. He looked up and saw railroad tracks. They ran across his path, but he could see that the tracks heading west curved south not too far away. Michael pushed himself up and started moving again, even though his back and legs were screaming from the punishment of the fall.

"Michael!"

The voice wouldn't stop.

He got on the tracks and started a shuffled cadence on the railroad ties. Every few steps he would look back to the point where he had emerged from the woods to see if Nick had caught up with him. With every stride he got closer to the bend in the tracks, and every second his mind told him that he would not make it. His panic was starting to rise.

Almost there.

Almost.

He turned again. Nothing.

Shuffle.

Shuffle.

Turn.

The false safety of the curve in the track was almost in reach. He would be hidden from the point where the forest had spit him out in just a few more steps.

Shuffle.

Shuffle.

Turn.

And there he was, emerging from the tree line. A silhouette in the distance.

"Michael! Stop!"

For some reason, Michael did so. Fear was rising, and even though his mind was commanding every fiber of his being to keep running, his feet remained planted on the railroad tie. He turned around completely to see that Nick had something in his hands. It was a rifle.

Michael watched as Nick raised the gun to his shoulder, and he could feel the burning in his spine. Like a spiderweb cording around his muscles, up his stomach, to his neck. The dark web leeching off every fiber of his body. The shadow was constricting. Michael stared down the tracks as fire erupted from his veins and burned his nerves just as a flash exploded from Nick's gun.

The bullet ricocheted off the rail not more than ten feet from where Michael was standing. He also saw that Nick had trouble of his own. The rifle had malfunctioned, the barrel seeming to have exploded in Nick's hands.

Michael came out of his daze and he turned and started running down the tracks again. Nick had dropped the weapon and was clutching his hands to his chest, but he was also on his feet, running after him.

He was stuck between two bookends of death. The mob in the south and the madman in the north. At some point he knew, Michael knew, that he would have to stop running and confront them, but for now, he kept moving as fast as he could down the tracks.

Shuffle.

Shuffle.

Turn.

Nick was gaining on him.

SIXTY-ONE

THE LANDSCAPE FELL AWAY and Michael could see a bridge up ahead. This was the old stone viaduct that crossed the Coldwater River northeast of town. He had come a long way. He remembered the viaduct from his childhood as a structure that looked like something the Romans had built thousands of years ago, with its arching supports towering over the river below. He approached the bridge knowing he was losing ground with every step. Nick was gaining on him—the madman propelled by wings of a demon.

Michael made it to the viaduct and began crossing. The bridge was massive as it stretched out before him. A low fog covered the river below like dragon breath, the viaduct a drawbridge across the sky leading toward the safety of the southern woods. He was halfway across when he heard his name again and he could feel his body freeze as if by some uncontrollable force of nature.

"Michael! Stop!"

Michael turned and saw Nick standing on the tracks one step from the bridge. "Why are you doing this?"

"Just stop!" Nick yelled.

"Why?"

"Because I need you. And you need me. You know you do!"

Nick took a step forward onto the viaduct and started coming toward Michael with a slow, confident stride. Michael wanted to run, to keep moving, but now he felt himself wanting to hear Nick, to listen to him. Somewhere deep inside, he saw himself across the bridge, his future self, driven mad with the pursuit of release.

"It's not by accident you ended up at my door. We are the same. We are the same, you and me," Nick said, each step getting closer. "We wander this world alone but not alone. We are the storehouses of the fallen. Me and you. You are young, you don't yet realize what the isolation can do to you. You have no idea. You leave now, you keep running, someday it will be *you* chasing someone over a bridge, down a road, through the woods, begging them to put an end to your life."

"We are not the same."

"Oh, but we are. I know what's inside you. I know what is wrapped around your gut and cradles you like a baby swaddled in its mother's arms. I know that feeling, that feeling of constriction, of a beast awakening from its slumber. You know what I am talking about.

"We are symbiotic men with the host of hell living off us like parasites. I felt it, far off, when you were clawing your way out of the grave. I could feel your approach in the woods. This black cloud that lives in me awoke, knowing that the means of its own destruction was near."

"You're crazy!"

"You think so? So tell me, who did you kill?"

Michael's heart skipped several beats as he suddenly felt a spotlight on his soul had instantly been turned on, only to find him naked on the floor.

"Your parents? A sister? Your best friend? I know you killed someone. Someone close, someone who trusted you deeply."

"Shut up!"

"You hollowed yourself out and became the perfect shell. A cell for an outcast of heaven to be chained in. A host. It's why all that surrounds you suffers. Dies."

"Shut up!"

"But we can end this. You and me. We can finally be free. Free of this black hole that we threw ourselves in. We can escape the event horizon of our own curse."

Michael thought back to the night before, to Nick's ranting as he slobbered drunkenly. "I'm not going to kill you."

Nick and Michael were standing face-to-face now in the middle of the viaduct, both between the tracks.

"Last night, I admit, I was weak. I was overcome by the long years of isolation, of desperation. Me, groveling in the mud, that was pathetic. I know. You'll have to forgive an old man some things. But I'm not crazy. Then it dawned on me, this morning, when the haze of the whiskey wore off. I was wrong. I was all wrong.

"It was like in school, when you stare at those sheets of math problems and it looks like it was written in Greek. And then something shifts in your mind and it makes sense. That's what happened."

"What are you talking about?"

"I was wrong to ask you to show me mercy. To kill me. I was wrong to think that was the only way to end my suffering."

Nick slowly put a hand inside his coat. His fingers were singed from the rifle that had exploded in his hands. He grabbed the handle of something and slowly drew it out. It was a knife, a massive one.

"The things inside us, these inmates of the damned. They protect their home. I don't know why. Perhaps we are a better residence than hell. I know I'd prefer to be in here than out in the ether somewhere."

"What are you doing?"

"They will not go gracefully. They will fight to the end. They will destroy anything that comes to expel them."

"Get away from me."

"I was wrong to ask you to kill me. I can end my suffering, just by killing you," Nick said as he lunged at Michael.

SIXTY-TWO

THE WORLD TURNED in slow motion.

Michael saw the blade coming up toward his throat and something inside him took over. Rage moved his body with elegant efficiency as he parried Nick's hand away and delivered a punch to his attacker's stomach. As his fist connected, Michael felt a bomb go off in his head that stunned him and made him stumble back, almost tripping on the railroad ties that were under his feet. Nick doubled over at the waist. One hand still held the knife, his other went to his head as well. He felt the same sensation with his own offensive move. He looked up at Michael with a sick grin.

"You feel that? It's them. They will die defending their hosts. That is how we get free of them once and for all!"

Nick raised himself up and threw the knife. It spun faster than seemed possible and found its mark just above Michael's right knee. The pain was excruciating as the blade sunk into Michael's thigh, causing him to drop. His back hit one of the rails and sent another jolt up his spine.

Blood erupted from Nick's mouth the instant the knife struck Michael. It ran down his shirt and he looked like a fighter who just said goodbye to all his front teeth. Nick wiped his face with his sleeve and stared at it.

"You see? You see this? It's working!" Nick cackled. He

was in a full-blown psychotic state of madness and ecstasy—a homicidal maniac overjoyed to finally see the electric chair.

He walked over to Michael, reached down and grabbed his hair, lifted his head, and punched him. He swung again and again. With each hit Nick's own face started showing the effects as well. Both men were taking a beating, even though Michael was doing all he could do to shield himself from the blows. He could feel Nick grab the hilt of the knife and pull it out of his leg.

The dark tension in Michael's soul deepened to the point that he thought he would erupt from the pressure. He could feel it build and build while the punches rained down on him. He was in the ultimate no-win situation. He was fighting himself. They both would die on this viaduct. Nick would never let him go, and the only way to stop him would be to kill him, but in so doing, the curse within his adversary would end his life too.

It was what happened to James and Kyle.

It was what happened to anyone who tried to harm him.

He was death incarnate. But so was Nick.

They were two men playing poker, each with a dead man's hand.

The punches stopped and Nick stood and staggered back a step or two. Michael looked up and saw the toll on Nick's face. It was as if he had been hit by a cement truck. Michael could only imagine his own visage.

The curse of reciprocity.

A demonic justice dealing out an eye for an eye.

Nick was to the point of delirium and exhaustion. He stood to his full height but was swaying back and forth, about to tumble over at any moment.

"Almost there, Michael. Almost," he said between shallow breaths. "You have no idea how I've dreamed of this day. To finally be rid of this pain. To be free of this . . . weight. This burden. I don't blame you. You don't fully understand yet. You think there's hope for you. For people like us. But I know. Yes. I know all too well that there isn't."

Michael stared at his attacker with fear and trembling but also with wonder and sadness. If by some miracle he survived this battle on the viaduct, would he someday come to the point where he was clawing at his own skin, pining away for death to release him from this life? Nick was right. He didn't understand. For all the guilt he carried with him, for all the darkness that haunted his mind and soul and cursed his steps, he still clung to the desire to live.

"Now," Nick said, "let's send these beasts home and see what's on the other side."

Nick raised the knife and went to bring it down on Michael's chest, but the fight had taken too much of a toll on his body. He tripped over the railroad tie and tumbled with his full momentum toward the edge of the viaduct. His knee cracked against the rail, his hands flew out in front of him to catch his fall, sending the knife down into the mist. And Nick's momentum sent him rolling, somersaulting over the edge.

Michael instinctively reached out, grabbing onto Nick's coat, a handful of fabric on the back and arm. But he was too spent himself.

Nick dangled over the drop and looked up. Michael was hanging on but his grip was slipping. He made an effort to pull the madman up, but it was pointless. He had no strength left. The powers that rested in them were violent and punitive. They did not come to the aid of others. Michael looked into his attacker's black eyes. They were the eyes of a demon frantically thrashing about in the dark who becomes aware that its cell walls are closing in. And then the eyes cleared, as if the man had come back to the forefront. A sense of peace washed over Nick's face as Michael's grip slipped a little more every second.

"I think, my brother, we found another solution," Nick whispered as Michael's hold failed.

Down toward the river Nick fell, until his body was engulfed in mist. No sound could be heard above the faint roar of moving water, Nick's body washing downstream like a warrior drifting toward Valhalla.

Michael waited for the vengeful retribution to hit him, but it never came. Nick's own curse was gone with him. He didn't know why he had tried to save him, why his inner rage hadn't taken over and pushed the psychopath over the edge, but somehow his desire to do no more harm was stronger. Nick would not have stopped, and there was no way Michael could have ever stopped him without destroying himself. Now Nick was gone, free from the prison of his own making, drifting on to whatever waited for him in the next life.

Michael managed to get to his feet. The wound in his leg burned with fire and the bruises on his body started to swell and multiply with each passing second.

The mob beating, the burial, the exposure in the woods, and now the attack from Nick—Michael was a walking collection of abused muscle and tendons.

He turned south again. The tracks ran into the woods on the south side of the river and disappeared into the distance. Home could not be too far, but with the bleeding leg and slowly swelling eyes that threatened to black out his sight, home might as well have been a million miles away. As he walked the final steps over the viaduct, the earth began to take on an imbalance, the tracks in front of him started to morph and twist, and the sky turned dim as it rotated in his eyes. He made it across when it all went dark and he could feel himself fall onto the cold stones and slide down the raised rail bed, drifting on a wave of rock, dreaming the visions of damned men.

SIXTY-THREE

MICHAEL WALKED IN A CAVE carved by winds of a thousand years, swept clean of any pebble or debris. The walls dripped of water that had seeped up from the bowels of the earth and had never seen the light of day for a millennium, water that had sunk during the primordial oozing of the planet and had bathed Leviathan in the deep. He walked on, not wanting to, but forced by his dream state ever forward, his legs automatons carrying his body farther and farther into the dark. The light behind him diminished into a grayish haze of unfocused glimmer. The cave was level, but he could feel the pressure of the deep pushing on his body with every step, as if he were sinking into the depths of the ocean. He walked and walked.

He thought he saw faces in the wall, but he could not tell if they were carved into the rock or were fossils of men cemented into the foundation of the earth. He walked up close to one and examined it. The face had no eyes, its mouth and nose protruding from the rock as if the sculptor had abandoned the project midway through. The mouth was parted and hollowed out. Michael peered closer and he could feel warmth coming from the lips. Air. Breath. From deep in the wall. A whisper.

Suddenly Michael could hear a multitude of sighing all around him as the walls exposed hundreds of faces, all in different levels of completion, exhaling and whispering. He knew he should leave, but his feet carried him deeper into the cavern. Away from the entrance. Down he went, ever deeper.

He wanted to turn back, but he couldn't. There was something pulling him, latched on to a morbid thread buried beneath his consciousness, reeling him in like a fish on a line. Deeper into the blackness he went, with the breath of the wall faces blowing on his neck.

The cave came to a vault that was illuminated by a hidden source, the stone walls shooting up out of sight into blackness. The room glowed with a crimson hue, an image of hell fashioned by his memory of old Sunday school stories meant to scare kids into doing what was right. In the middle of the room was a man sitting in a chair, staring at him, his eyes all white, as if in a trance. The man did not notice him. At his feet lay another, contorted on the floor. The prostrate man had been cut, his blood seeped from his body and the rock floor drank him in. He was dead and the seated man was his killer. Michael knew this, though this was not a place of reason.

From the back of the cave walked a shadow as old as the rocks and the water and the air. The shadow was mist and flesh at the same time, its limbs disjointed and broken and of unequal size, a beast that had been put together by spare parts of a variety of species. The creature walked up behind the man in the chair and put its paws on the man's shoulders.

Michael could see the face of the shadow. It was the same as the face in the rock. Unfinished above the nose. It exhaled and poured itself like liquid over the seated man, who tensed and straightened as the shadow melted into him. His body began to writhe and shake like a man punching at an old suit that had become a size too small.

Then the eyes closed and opened, and Michael could see the man was staring at him. Looking through him, examining a part of his soul that was not Michael but something locked away beyond his knowing.

The man stood, and Michael wanted to run, but his feet had become one with the stone.

The man began to whisper, but the words were nonsense. The inaudible tones of an infant. But soon a sound began to form, and as recognition began to take hold in Michael's mind, the ground began to shake. The walls slowly started trembling and breaking apart. And still the whisper could be heard. The quaking of the rock grew and grew and the cave was coming apart. The glow went supernova and the man whispered on. As the walls came down, Michael could hear the word finally with all its soul-shattering horror.

"Brother . . . Brother."

Michael jolted awake to feel the thunderous roar of a train rolling by. He had fallen off the tracks and wondered just how close he came to residing in the cave forever, had he passed out in the locomotive's path.

The cars rolled by and soon it was quiet again, save for the whisper in his head from a haunted sleep.

Brother.

SIXTY-FOUR

HAYWOOD MADE HIS WAY through another morning, gearing up for one more day of searching the wilds for Michael.

A wise man once said, "All that is necessary for the triumph of evil is that good men do nothing," and Haywood was nothing if not a good man. He was utterly and thoroughly convinced that he was good, and it was his duty not to let evil triumph.

Nothing reinforced his resolve more than when Earl had called him and told him of the body in the river.

Some of the local kids had been fishing off the banks of the Coldwater River just north of town when one of them saw a man lying on the far bank. His legs were in the water and he was facedown in the dirt. The boys didn't know if it was a corpse or a zombie, and neither of them had the guts to find out, no matter how many double-dog dares were heaped up on each other. They had run back to the road and flagged down the first passing motorist. It had been Frank and Earl on their way into town. In this coincidence, Haywood felt the gods smiling on him.

Haywood arrived to find an almost carnival atmosphere. The group of boys were toeing the water of the south bank,

251

gawking at the sight of the comatose body. One managed the courage to whip a rock at the body and missed wide. Haywood's booming voice caused the other kids to drop their stones and part like the Red Sea as he moved in to have a look.

Frank had crossed the river and was down on the bank, trying to snag the body, while trying not to at the same time. He wanted to look useful but didn't want to be the one who actually had to touch the man in the river, if it turned out he was dead. Earl was holding on to Frank's shirttails, trying his best to keep his friend from sliding into the water.

"Who is it?" Haywood yelled, his voice carrying over the river like a thundercloud.

"Don't know," Earl said. "We haven't been able to get a good look at the face."

"Is it Michael?"

Earl didn't respond. He kept his concentration on Frank, who was just a couple inches shy of reaching the body with his hand.

"Got him!" Frank yelled from the river side. He was pulling the body onto shore, trying his best not to touch the stranger, as if he was afraid death would be transferred to him. "And he ain't dead!"

Just then, the man in the water opened his eyes. Frank shot back, and it was all he and Earl could do to keep from tumbling head over heels into the Coldwater. The man's eyes focused and then he pushed himself up and over until he was sitting on the bank. There was a wound on his leg that started to seep as soon as it was above the waterline.

Haywood strained his eyes and recognized the man. It was the man from the cabin. Nick fixed Haywood with a strong glare. It was a stare that pierced to the bone, even across the flowing water. Haywood could feel pressure building in the base of his skull like a thumb pressed to the top of his spine. He watched as Nick got to his feet and took a couple steps up the embankment, then sat down again.

"You want to tell us what happened?" Haywood shouted.

"Ain't your concern," Nick said.

"Something tells me that's not the case. You look like you could use some help."

Nick took his shirt off and wrapped it around his damaged leg. He cinched it tight and then stood upright. There were bruises over his body, and he looked like he'd played chicken with a train and came up on the losing side.

"I know who did that to you," Haywood said, doing his best to keep the uncertainty out of his voice. "I knew he was probably out your way too. You should have let us know the other night."

Nick stood motionless. His body language gave no indication that he felt like talking to Haywood, which riled Haywood up even more. The man turned and walked north into the woods, one leg dragging behind him, and disappeared from sight.

"I don't know why you'd be protecting him. We're on the same side!" Haywood yelled, his voice echoing back to him from the other shore.

■ ■ ■

Frank and Earl made their way back to the south shore to join Haywood. Most of the kids had run off now that the excitement was over, and the three men stood on the riverbank.

In the distance a siren could be heard approaching their location.

253

"You called the cops?" Haywood asked with more irritation than he had intended.

"Of course we did. There was a possible dead body floating into town. What did you think we were going to do?" Earl said, exasperation tainting his voice.

"Alright. Alright. Calm down."

"No, I will not calm down!" Earl responded, summoning the strength to talk back to Haywood for the first time in his life. Glancing around at a few kids still lingering around him, he reduced the volume but spoke in a strong whisper. "I will not calm down. This is completely out of control. This is beyond anyone's control. We have dead men in stores, on roads, and now we got people floating in the river. It's like the whole area has turned into a slaughterhouse. And it all started with you."

"Me?" Haywood said.

"You got us all worked up, telling us some story about how Michael was a danger to us all, and now all this is happening."

"What more proof do you need that I was right?"

"Right? No, no no. You are dead wrong," Earl said. "We were all doing fine until you got us caught up in your . . . your . . . insanity."

"Insanity? You better watch yourself, Earl. You just better—"

"Or what? Huh? You going to put me six feet under too? If you haven't noticed, there's not going to be too much of us left to help you do that. And for the life of me, I ain't going to go quiet."

Haywood looked at Earl. The man was scared out of his mind. He couldn't fault him for that, but his patience with Earl's inability to see Michael as the real root of all evil was starting to drive him to the brink of hysteria. He grabbed Earl's arm and shook him with an iron grip.

"Don't threaten me, Earl. Don't you dare. Just because you're blind to the real threat that is hanging over our heads. Has been hanging over our heads since that cretin moved back here. The only guilt you should feel is the guilt of not having the courage to wipe Michael out of existence. And we share in that. You, me, Frank . . . all of us."

A steely silence filled the space between the three men. The siren in the distance was getting closer. Haywood turned and walked back up toward the road, readying himself to send the policemen back to South Falls again. Frank and Earl caught up to him.

"What do you think happened to that guy?" Frank asked, trying to defuse the already tense situation.

"Don't know, but we'd be foolish to think it wasn't Michael."

"How long you think he was lying in the river?" Frank said.

"Not long," said Haywood. "A couple hours, a day maybe."

"If it's Michael, then that means . . . ," Earl whispered.

Frank and Earl looked at each other.

"It means . . . Michael's coming back toward town," Haywood said. "First, we have to get rid of these cops you called. After that, I'm going to make sure he's got nothing to come back to."

255

SIXTY-FIVE

THERE WAS ALWAYS A SADNESS that accompanied any thought Melissa had of her twin brother. It was a darkness that pressed down on the pit of her stomach and gave the faint feeling of nausea. This sadness, this empathy of pain, was slowly becoming more and more pronounced the longer she stayed in Coldwater. She could feel the isolation following her like a shadow, barely perceptible until she quieted herself. The loneliness always took the form of Marcus standing as a little child on the porch of their family home. Now, old memories and new memories intermixed and blended into one. In her mind's eyes she could see Michael standing on the steps, the broken and battered door behind him, and the barren ground encircling the cabin.

It was anger that brought her back to Coldwater, but it was sadness that was the foundation of the rage.

She had tried throughout her life not to think about Marcus. Sometimes it had come naturally; the years as a teenager, off to college, the self-absorbed times. She would feel guilty when things went especially well for her, as if she had an obligation to perpetually mourn her lost brother.

As she grew older, though, her thoughts turned more and more to that childhood scene and the desire to go back. A longing to go home. To put to rest that image of the boy on the steps with his hand outstretched.

But that boy was gone.

Gone to the hazy recollection of a seven-year-old girl.

Melissa could not remember Marcus's face, and the harder she tried in her mind's eye to focus on his features, the more impenetrable in shadow his aspect became. He was a van Gogh painted in black. But she could feel the memory, and the memory was cold and lonely.

That's who Marcus was. Marcus was the center of sadness.

And the wantonness in her heart to soothe this hurt is what compelled her. Had driven her to Coldwater to pursue the guilty brother who had killed the innocent.

That's who Michael was. Michael was the first mover in catastrophe.

But he was also a lost brother, was he not? He had disappeared from her past at the same time as Marcus. But was he not in some way salvageable from the wreck of history? Marcus was dead, but was Michael dead to everything as well?

Melissa felt a tear form in the corner of her eye.

No. No. She could not entertain this thought. Justice for Marcus was what mattered most, and empathy for his killer, even though it was her own kin, would sacrifice that goal. Composing herself, she opened the door and stepped outside.

She left the motor lodge and drove east of town, down several dirt roads, frustrated by the lack of road signs. She backtracked and drove on, over and over, back and forth, until she was sure she had gone in circles multiple times. Finally, she saw it. A rusted road marker that said "Old State." Turning south, she followed the road until it went deep into the woods, turning gently as it meandered through the trees. Up ahead, on the right, the trees cleared and she saw the brick posts that held the edges of an old gate.

Behind the gate was the cemetery.

The grave markers looked old, older than the trees, but the grounds were well manicured. Either the county mowed the property, or a good Samaritan did, but in the end it really didn't matter. Someone cared for the property, and that simple act took the mystery out of the place.

Melissa got out of the car and walked in. The gate wasn't locked and it squealed on its hinges when she pushed it open. She walked into the center of the plots and read the names on the headstones. In the middle of the property, there was a cinder-block outbuilding used for storage. The shed stood out as a snapshot in her mind. She remembered standing near it when she was seven. They had all gathered there at one point in time.

She started making ever larger circles around the building, peering on the ground to read the markers as she passed. Some were worn almost too smooth to be recognizable; some, glistening marble; others, a fieldstone sticking out of the grass. North of the shed sat an angel kneeling on a white slab, its eyes pointed down. The shade of a nearby tree darkened its wings. It looked to be relaxing from an arduous flight.

Melissa followed the eyes of the statue toward the ground and saw a small placard nestled in the lawn. She walked over to it and knelt down. Her hand came to her mouth and the sadness that had enveloped every memory of her childhood in Coldwater wrapped around her like her own set of wings.

The marker had just a name and age on it. A small stone for a small life.

MARCUS SULLIVAN. AGE 7.

SIXTY-SIX

MICHAEL STAGGERED SOUTH down the train tracks. His stab wound had festered into a burning numbness, and he dragged the leg behind him more than used it to walk. With each step he felt the wound open and close, blood rolling down his leg into his shoe and leaving a trail of gore on the rocks behind him.

His head was in a daze. The beatings, the wandering, the dehydration, the lack of sleep had all wound together in a cocktail of agony that clouded his consciousness and left him in a state of delirium. The train that had awoken him was gone and the forest echoed with birds gathering around to witness this new creature invading their woods. If the train had returned, or if one had followed up behind, it would have rolled right into Michael and he would not have noticed it, would not have cared, would have embraced the mountain of moving steel as the natural evolution of all that he endured. But a train never came, and Michael trudged on in a slowly decaying ambulation that brought him ever closer to home.

His head would swim and he would stumble, his arms at his side not breaking his fall against the stone and timber ties of the tracks. By some feat of will he would force himself up again, forever south.

The tracks soon crossed Countyline Road, and he had no perception as to how long he had been walking since the viaduct. Michael stood at the crossing and gazed out with vacant eyes into the distance. He looked but did not see, his body working on automatic pilot and running a self-preserving program but not taking in any data. He staggered across the road.

Several days earlier, many miles to the west, he had calculated his crossing with as much reservation as a soldier charging across no-man's-land. Down that road was where the truck had rolled, where James and Kyle lay broken and bloody. He had been running away, but now he was dragging himself back to the community that had tried and failed to bury him from their sight.

His fear was gone. The pain had sapped all energy from him and there was no more to spare for that emotion. Just the steady stepping of a blackened soul.

There was no more thought.

No thinking of what he would do when he arrived home.

He walked down the tracks, and in his mind, walked out of the cave he had dreamed about. Both were equally real and Michael cared not which world he was in.

He fell, banging his head on the track, and the shock echoed through his skull like a miner's hammer sounding in the caverns of the earth.

With his strength diminishing, Michael still managed to get back on his feet.

Forever south.

The sun moved overhead. He had no idea what time of day it was.

He kept moving, a frame of skin and muscle with no conscious mind, swaying in an endless painful journey.

The hours passed and soon Michael could see another crossing in the distance. It was a road he knew. It was the road into Coldwater, the one he had walked down many times before. He had come full circle.

Michael stepped off the tracks and headed west through the woods, his muscles relying on memory to take him home. His feet sank into the soft earth, the shaded wood cooling the air around him as he felt for familiar ground.

SIXTY-SEVEN

HAYWOOD, FRANK, AND EARL ARRIVED at Michael's house in the woods. They had made a stop at Haywood's on the way, and the two men watched as Haywood went into the garage, grabbed two large gasoline cans, and put them in the back of the truck. Frank and Earl remained quiet on the drive out to Michael's place, but in their minds they had guessed at what Haywood was cooking up.

The woods looked especially ominous on this trip, as if nature knew what Haywood had come to do and had donned mourning attire in anticipation. The limbs of the overhanging branches drooped low over the road.

They arrived at Michael's, and Haywood parked the truck, got out, and retrieved the gas cans. The two men remained in the truck. Silent.

"Well, come on, guys!" he snapped at them, and with reluctance the two lackeys got out of the vehicle.

"Haywood, what are you doing?" Frank asked.

"He's come back. Or he's on his way back. This will let him know there is no reason to stay."

"You can't do this, Haywood. This has gone too far. We can't burn his house down."

"We can and we will, Earl. We are going to wipe him from

Coldwater once and for all. If he's got no place to go, he might just keep on moving."

"No."

"What's that?"

"No. I'm done, Haywood. I'm done. I ain't doing this no more," Earl said. "I can't go back and change what we did, but I can make sure I don't make it worse."

"He's right," Frank added. "This is where we stop. We ain't killers, we never were, and we sure ain't arsonists."

"So you boys are just going to sit by and wait for Michael to come for you? Wait in your house, hiding in your closet, and when he pounds down the door, you going to apologize for burying him in the hopes he'll be merciful?"

"If that is what it comes down to, yeah. That's what I'm going to do," Earl said. There was a tremolo in his voice. The fear of Michael mixing with his fear of standing up for himself.

"You get this straight, Earl. That's not what's going to happen. He is going to find you, find all of us, and it isn't going to be pretty. It's going to end in the worst possible way."

"It already has, Haywood," Frank said.

"Cowards!"

"No. We were cowards ever listening to you," Earl replied. "Cowards for following you on this . . . this . . . vendetta of yours. But I'm done. I'm done with this. I ain't doing this no more. You want to burn down his house? Chase him down and kill him? You're doing it without me."

Frank nodded in agreement.

"Fools!" Haywood yelled.

He picked up the cans and stomped toward the house and up onto the porch. He walked through the door, splashing the gasoline as he went inside. Before long he was back outside with the empty cans. He pulled a book of matches from his back pocket and prepared to light a flame.

"Stop, Haywood! Just stop!" Frank yelled.

"I'm never going to stop. Not ever!"

He lit the match and tossed it on the porch. He walked back to the truck as the house was engulfed in flames, burning high into the darkening sky. Haywood put the empty cans back into the bed of the truck and climbed into the driver's seat. He started it up and yelled at the two men standing before the burning wreckage.

"Don't come begging for help when Michael comes banging down your doors. Maybe the long walk back to town will clear your heads and get you both thinking straight!"

And with that he drove off, leaving Frank and Earl stranded in the dead woods.

■ ■ ■

The two men stood in silent repose as flames licked the sky.

"So what are we going to do now?" Earl asked.

"Walk home, I guess," Frank said.

"That's not what I mean."

"I know."

"You think he's going to kill us?"

"Michael?"

"Yeah."

"Wouldn't you?"

"Maybe I would be forgiving."

"You wouldn't be."

"I know."

"We'll stick together. Me and you."

"Thanks."

"We'll stay at my place. In town. Be as close to other people as we can."

"Sounds good," Earl said.

They turned from the fire and stared down the dirt road.

"We might as well start walking."

"Okay."

"We'll stick together."

"Okay."

The two men started on their way back to Coldwater, their hearts jumping at every sound that the forest produced, as if judgment would come with each noise of the dying woods.

SIXTY-EIGHT

SMOKE DRIFTED THROUGH THE FOREST like the tentacles of a prehistoric beast reaching up from the depths looking blindly for prey. Michael, half conscious from the beating and blood loss, limped through the woods. He was walking on instinct, his compass directing him home. The haze from the far-distant fire blurred his vision. The wound in his leg reopening with each step.

Soon he came to the dirt road that ran across his path. His road. Without thinking, he stepped onto it and turned south. He took no care into looking for cars, or people, or life. Driven on by the idea of home, his gait out of sync, he stumbled down the road, his leg dragging a groove in the dirt behind him. He came to his place.

His home.

His inferno.

The fire consumed every part of the house. Flames shot out of the roof, the windows, and smoke rose to the sky. Michael walked forward until the smoke choked his throat and the heat scorched his skin.

It was gone. It was all gone.

The last place he could escape to was no more, engulfed in a blazing fury and falling to ash. He was an orphan of the earth. There would be no place to call home. The north woods had cast him out into a scorched world that burned away every memory of him.

The men of Coldwater had erased him.

Michael's legs gave out and he collapsed to the ground. The wind blew, sending soot and smoke pouring over his body as he breathed in the dirt from the dead ground. His hands scratched at the soil until he could feel the pressure beneath his fingernails.

Why had he dug himself up from the grave?

Why had he not just lain down in the deep and awaited the forever night to carry him off to the other side of his last breath?

He had been a fool to hope. He had no right to hope for anything in this life. That right had died when he shot and killed his brother.

Michael coughed to clear his lungs of the pungent stench of the burning house. The timbers collapsed on themselves, bringing down the roof, sending another large plume into the sky. His eyes burned as the world around him burned.

Every step along this journey he had fought to live. From the grave, to the north woods, down the tracks, until his body screamed in agony. But here on the bonfire of his life, he had no more strength. This is where it would end. It would end where it all started. The home he destroyed in spirit, so many years ago, now crumbling under its own burning weight.

Maybe at last, justice was served.

The dirt was his bed, the smoke his blanket. He wished for sleep. He wished for eternal sleep.

SIXTY-NINE

MELISSA WALKED BACK TO HER CAR, leaving the grave-stone of Marcus Sullivan to lie lonely in a field of green. And though the memory of her brother was more of a data point than a living, breathing emotion, what she felt was the anger of a lost lifeline. The grave marker was the pivot point in history that changed everything her life was meant to be. She was supposed to have her mother, her father, a normal life filling photo albums with birthday parties and graduations, weddings and holidays.

The aunt who had taken her in was not a mother. Her childhood in South Falls was robotic, automated. She was looked after but not cared for. Life had been hollowed out, and all that she was given was a shell of an existence.

Marcus, in death, was luckier than she had been. He had missed out on the tragedy that his death, his murder, had unleashed.

And it was murder.

That was one point that she always, always, took to heart.

And Michael was the one who had done it all.

Now, in this corner of the world where nobody bothered to look, after years of brewing the resentment in her heart and the resolve to finally bring justice—complete justice—for

Marcus, the board had been set so incredibly in her favor that all Melissa had to do was follow through. The town had tried to kill Michael. They had failed. She could prevail, all while having no fear of anyone ever linking her to the deed. She was absolved ahead of time. All accusers complicit in what would be the perfect cover.

Melissa could walk right up Main Street, shoot Michael in the head at high noon, and no one in town would dare say a thing, lest their own guilt be brought out into the light. Their own hearts would stand convicted should they even dare to speak.

All she had to do was wait. Wait for Michael to show himself.

But where was he?

Melissa pulled the car to the main road and sat thinking.

To the left was Coldwater, to the right was the old cabin. Her old home. Michael's home. The faint smell of burning graced her nostrils as she saw a truck approach from the east. It sped past her, and in the driver's seat she saw Haywood. He was alone, his face determined. Her gut told her to go to Michael's—something, some reason, that was the place to go.

She turned right and headed for the cabin.

A mile from the turnoff, she saw two men walking, headed back to town. As she drove past, she eyed them and she could feel their eyes upon her. The interaction was in slow motion, but she recognized them as part of Haywood's posse. She had seen them before, masked by the windshield of a pursuing truck. Two more accomplices.

The men slowly grew smaller in her rearview mirror. Melissa noticed, before she turned onto the dirt road and into the cover of the forest, that they had stopped walking and were watching the car as it veered off toward Michael's.

The woods were awash in a gray smoke that hung heavy in the trees. The smell of fire came through the vents on the dashboard, and even with the windows rolled up, the fumes were becoming almost unbearable.

Melissa drove up to the cabin and saw hellfire leaping into the sky, burning the house down to its foundation. The only thing saving the forest from incinerating was the dead ring around the cabin, which kept the flames contained like a giant fire pit.

Whatever memory she had of the place was now ash and charcoal.

The smoke blew in scattered gusts, the heat hitting her in waves.

Before her was hell on earth.

But there was more.

Through the haze she could see a body lying on the ground. Blood pooled in the dirt around one of the legs.

Melissa pulled the collar of her shirt up over her nose and mouth, jumped out of the car, and ran to the body. She grabbed the man's legs and dragged him toward her car. Her breath pushed against the fabric that covered her face as the heat and suffocating stench of the fire forced its way into her mouth. She pulled and pulled until the vehicle blocked the heat from the fire. She rolled the man over and looked down on him.

There before her, unconscious, beaten and bloody, was the murderer of the life she should have known. The destroyer of everything she ever wanted. There, lying in the dirt, was her brother Michael.

Her heart leapt in her chest. He was here. The time was right now.

She went around the car to the driver's door, opened it, and pulled the gun from its hiding place. Without thought, without hesitation, Melissa walked back to where Michael was comatose on the ground. She aimed the pistol at his head and committed herself to finally bringing justice into the world.

SEVENTY

HATE IN THEORY is worlds apart from hate in practice. Every armchair general watching the war on television is a different man than if he was placed on the other side of the camera. As Melissa stood over Michael, this realization slowly filled her body, starting with the trigger finger that felt like a lead weight with each passing breath, moving up her arm, and into her chest. She swallowed, but the saliva hung in her throat and felt jammed in like cement.

The culmination of all the planning, the scheming, the endless days of focusing on the man-child who selfishly murdered Marcus, was laid out before her. All she had to do was squeeze the trigger. She had done it on the firing range many times—it was easy, the gun so smooth that it took little effort. She had wanted this moment. Dreamed of it. Coveted it as the moment in time that would set all things right.

And yet, she doubted herself.

There would be no great resolve in shooting an unconscious man. Michael would never know. Would never see the look in her eyes when she blew a hole in his head. Would never beg for his life. He would never see in her eyes the pain he inflicted morph into righteous action.

Whatever guilt he carried in him, if he had any at all, was tucked away in his blacked-out soul. She would not see the guilt manifest itself in his face, his body. She would not see him suffer.

Was that what she wanted? Was that what all people who sought revenge wanted? To see contrition present itself in the contorted flesh of the accused? Remorse only being counted as real if the body presented itself with regret?

Regret is not believed if it is not visible. Is not physical. Michael could be filled with it, but Melissa could not see it. Before her, he slumbered on the ground, bleeding out from his leg, covered in bruises from beatings or thrashings, she could not tell. He had run a gauntlet. But it was not one that she had set up.

She sensed that even if she put a bullet in his head, she would get no relief. No victory. The boogeyman she had created in her mind over twenty years of anger lay before her like an etherized patient, calm, tranquil.

She lowered the weapon, wiped the smoke from her eyes, and looked at the burning house. Her past, any monument to where she came from, was now cinders. She stood on the brink of the abyss, the precipice of a new world. There was only one thing left tethering her to that old life.

She raised the gun again at Michael's head, and breathed.

His unconscious face, illuminated by the dying embers, became clear through a break in the smoke. It was a familiar face, it was her face. Michael had the same jawline, the same cheekbones. His hairline matched that of her father's, what she could remember from old photographs. His body was carried to birth by the same body that had produced her. Her mother at some point rocking him to sleep, singing the

273

same songs that she could faintly recall when the nights were quiet and she listened to her memories.

This killer, this murderer, this destroyer of all things good, was not some mythical beast. He was flesh and bone. He was real.

He was her brother.

She lowered the gun.

Of all things she had considered in plotting Michael's death, there was one thing that she had overlooked. Coming face-to-face with him. She had not entertained, not once in all her laid-out plans, that she would actually feel . . . empathy.

The feeling startled her as if she had jumped into a cold bath.

In his limp countenance he seemed, to her shock, human. Redeemable. A being that eats and breathes and thinks like all others of the species. He was not something apart, different. He was her, and as he lay there in the dirt, she imagined herself in his place.

Melissa walked slowly around the car, opened the driver's door, and placed the gun back under the seat. She went to the trunk and retrieved a bag of supplies.

She walked back to Michael and bound his hands and ankles with rope. Once he was secure, she put a tourniquet on the wound. The blood had stopped flowing and his skin felt cool to the touch as she dragged him to the back door of the car. He was thin and the weight of his body felt skeletal. She loaded him into the back seat, closed the door, and walked to the driver's side.

Melissa took one last look at the cabin. It was all but gone, and the heat began to diminish as the flames had nothing left to burn. It was dead. All dead. Her childhood home torched to dust. And with it, everything that said she had come from this godforsaken town.

She got in the car and headed back to Coldwater, Michael unconscious in the back seat, and the course of action she was going to take still undecided. She had no script for this. When he awoke, if he ever did, perhaps the story that she had written would unfold like she had planned. Perhaps he was the beast she envisioned.

Perhaps all she needed was the stimulus of watching him suffer.

Or perhaps—and this was the scariest scenario of all—she needed him to keep her from crossing over to the land of the murderous, needed him to be worth redeeming.

Perhaps, after all, she still needed family.

SEVENTY-ONE

FRANK AND EARL WERE BEYOND RELIEVED when Clinton's truck was the first vehicle that came into view. They double-stepped toward it and jumped in, looking back to where they had come from every five seconds, expecting to see a car come barreling after them.

"Get us out of here," Frank said.

"What's going on?" Clinton said, turning the truck back toward town and hitting the gas.

"Haywood's lost it," Earl said, his legs stuffed to his chin in the middle of the bench seat. "We went out to Michael's, and he set the place on fire."

"He did what?"

"No lie," Frank said. "He set that place off without flinching. He left us out there because we told him we were done. Ain't doing this no more. We're already up to our necks. I ain't digging no deeper."

"Why did he torch the place?" Clinton asked.

"He's convinced Michael's on his way back. He thought that if he had no home to go to . . . I don't know . . . that he would move on? Stay out of Coldwater? Who knows? The only thing I'm sure of is Haywood's gone and lost it. He's completely off the reservation now."

"There's more," Earl said. "That woman Lila was telling us about . . . she just headed out to Michael's. She saw us plain as day on the road when she passed us. She's going to be calling the cops for sure, man."

"That same woman you saw snooping out there before?" Clinton asked.

Frank grunted an assent.

"Haywood tell you who she was?"

"No," Earl said.

"That's Michael's sister," Clinton said.

Frank and Earl looked at each other and cringed.

Clinton took his trucker cap off and wiped the grease from his brow. The sun was setting and the cool night air was sweeping through the street when they pulled into town. He parked the truck in front of Gilly's and turned off the engine.

"What are we going to do?" Earl asked.

"I'm going in to get a drink," Clinton said. "You boys can do what you want. If Haywood is going nuclear, then so be it. But you should think about where you stand, and where you'll be standing when this is all said and done. Haywood ain't never done us wrong. He's one of us. We stick together around here. You guys should know that by now. If he's got it in his mind that this needs being done, then let's get it done and over with."

Clinton got out and shut the door, then looked in through the open window at his two comrades sitting spooked in the cab.

"We've already come this far. I'm with you in that we never should have started this, but we did. Ain't no changing that. But to leave it like it is, that ain't good for anyone. We need to ride this through. If you guys can't handle that, then go home. I won't think any less of you. I can't speak for Haywood, but we're good no matter what."

Clinton walked away from the truck, offered a tip of the head and a barely audible grunt to the shadows by the building, and went into Gilly's. At the side of the building, an ember glowed and then fell to the concrete. Davis emerged from the dark and followed Clinton inside.

Frank and Earl sat in silence.

"What we do, Frank?"

"We stick together. Clinton's right. Haywood's going to do what he's going to do. A year from now, when this is all behind us, we still have to live here. Don't think we'd be welcome in Coldwater much if we bail now."

"So we just go along. That's the right thing to do?"

Frank opened the door of the truck and stepped out. "Don't know if it's the right thing. But it sure feels like the only thing to do."

He left the door open, leaving Earl sitting in the vehicle by himself, contemplating if this was another pivot point of his life, or if he had already passed all points of change.

SEVENTY-TWO

THE FIRST STARS IN THE EAST hung like fireflies pinned to black felt, the creeping night engulfing the forest. Brake lights illuminated the smoke from the fire. When Melissa turned onto the road to Coldwater, the sun was below the horizon. The eerie orange glow that stretched out across the sky made Melissa think of a demon's hand clawing its way out of the pit. She shook off the thought.

In the back seat, Michael lay motionless. She kept one eye on the road and one to the rearview mirror, having seen too many low-budget horror films to trust the ropes that bound his bloodied limbs.

Her mind was still a wave of confusion.

Driving back to Coldwater was at least action. Movement. Progress.

She was doing something.

The town came into view, and she turned onto Main Street, past Gilly's, and into the parking lot of the motel. The lights from the diner shone out into the dark several feet from the building. The motor lodge, tucked in the back of the parking lot, was dark, save for the thin neon glow of the vacancy sign in the office window.

Melissa pulled the car in sideways right in front of her

door. She got out, opened her room, came back to the car, and when she was assured she was the only living thing in the parking lot, save for the body in the back seat, dragged Michael into the room.

She closed the door behind her, parked her car in a more conventional manner, and grabbed the gun case from under the seat. She looked at it, took a deep breath, and stepped out of the car.

Melissa then went back to her room, opened the door, and went inside.

■ ■ ■

Across the parking lot, on the side of Gilly's, an orange glow fizzled into existence and then diminished. A puff of smoke, an extinguishing flash of a cigarette snuffed out on the side of the building, and Davis, who had observed the goings-on, went into the bar.

He entered the back room where Haywood held court. Clinton sat to his left, looking up at the television suspended in the corner of the room. Frank and Earl sat sheepishly to the right, their drinks on the table but every aspect of their bodies withdrawn in on themselves as if showing the world that they were not really part of the entourage. Davis stood, grabbed his bottle from the table, and took a swig. Then he set it down.

"I think I just saw Michael," he said.

■ ■ ■

The air in the room was suddenly sucked out and all the men stared at Davis as if his next word would stab them all in the heart. Clinton clicked off the television with the remote on the table.

"Where? Outside?" Haywood asked.

"Yeah," Davis said. "Could have been him. I saw that woman you said was his sister pull into the motel. She parked in front of her room, then dragged in a body from the back seat."

"A body?"

"Pretty sure."

Clinton looked over at Frank and Earl. "Tell 'em," he said.

"Tell me what?" Haywood said.

"We saw her, driving out to Michael's house," Earl said. "On the way back to town, when you left us out there."

"Did she stop and talk to you?"

"No," Frank said.

"And you saw clearly, it was a body?" Haywood asked, turning his question back to Davis.

Davis nodded while taking another sip.

"Has to be him, then," Clinton said.

"Has to," Davis said.

Haywood stood and walked around the room. His mind was racing, trying to calculate his next move in this grand chess match. He knew where his adversary was, and quite possibly, he was incapacitated, maybe already dead. Yet Melissa had inserted herself right in the middle of the game. How was he going to get around her? If he barged in there, she would be a liability that he would have to take care of.

His determination and anger got the best of any rational thought. Michael was just across the parking lot. The end was in sight. He merely had to go over and get him, take him back up to Springer's Grove, and do things the right way this time. If Melissa got in the way, then so be it.

"Let's go get him," Haywood said.

"We just going to bust in there?" Frank asked.

"Might as well add B&E on to everything else," Earl said.

"If that really is Michael she dragged into that room," Clinton said, "it might be best not to underestimate her. She could be on the other side of that door with a shotgun or something."

"Or something," Davis echoed.

"And she ain't going to quietly open the door if we all barge over there," Clinton said.

From the bar, Lila walked into the room with a serving tray and picked up some of the empty bottles. She looked casually at the motley crew around the table.

"You boys need anything else?"

Haywood looked at her with slow revelation.

"Actually, there is one thing," he said.

SEVENTY-THREE

THE WARDEN LOOKED OUT THE WINDOW of his office. He was going to miss the place. The scene of the yard below, the cell blocks in winter, the expanse of cornfields before harvest time. He had managed the place for many years, and now it was time to move south to the mandatory retirement condos of Florida. He had always planned on retiring at sixty-five. That was the plan. But then Michael came to his prison. The young boy.

He felt obligated to stay, at least until the boy turned eighteen, and then he would just be like every other eighteen-year-old boy who came to prison and he could go off to retirement without any pangs of guilt.

That day had come and his wife enforced her will on his career, and he submitted his resignation that morning.

As he stood looking out over his kingdom he had a different feeling creep over him. One of almost sadness. The boy would no longer be his responsibility, and even though Michael was now a man, the warden felt somewhat like a father to him. He had in fact raised him, albeit in a nonfatherly way. He had clothed him, fed him, kept him safe. It had seemed an impossible task all those years ago, but he met the challenge, had grown to thrive on the challenge like a protector beating back the most vicious of savages. Now his time was done.

There was a knock on the door, and a guard entered with Michael. The guard ushered the prisoner to the chair in front of the warden's desk and then assumed a granite posture next to the door. The warden remained looking out the window.

"I'm going to miss this place. Seems absurd. Every man in here wants to get out, and now that it's my chance, I feel it almost impossible to leave."

Michael sat stoically in the chair. He had had many conversations such as this with the warden, almost all one-sided. The warden would talk, Michael would listen, the conversation would end, and the guard would take him back to his cell.

"It's not the prison I'm going to miss," the warden continued as he removed himself from the window and took a seat in his own chair. "It's the challenge. The challenge of taming barbarians. I don't think I'll get that same type of challenge down in Florida.

"I have to say, Michael, I think I'm going to miss you most of all. You've become more than an inmate to me. I know that sounds wrong. Sappy. I remember your first year here. I had no idea how you would survive. I had no idea how I would keep you alive, to be honest. But we did it. And here you are."

"Here I am," Michael whispered.

"You'll be up for parole someday. I've written up my recommendation. It is my hope that if that day ever comes for you, that you take advantage of it. The new warden won't see you the way I do. He won't see you as the boy who grew up here. Just keep yourself out of trouble, keep your head down, and you might walk out of here."

Michael thought for a minute. "But where would I go?"

"Anywhere you'd want, I guess. I imagine this is what a father would feel like when his kid is going off to college. The worst thing you could do is think of this place as home. You don't want to spend the rest of your life here, do you? I hope not."

"I don't remember much of anything else."

"All you'd have to do is conduct yourself out there as you do in here."

"By staying away from everyone?"

The warden nodded to the guard, who left the room and shut the door behind him. The warden stood and moved his chair around the desk and sat facing Michael.

"That might be the best course of action."

The warden gathered up his thoughts and spoke slowly.

"Michael, I've seen things these past eight years that I can't explain. You know the things I'm talking about. Now, I don't think you actively . . . that you intentionally . . . did these things. I can see it in your eyes. Always have. You were just as scared of these things as anyone else in this prison. But it follows you, boy. It follows you wherever you go. I don't know why, but it does.

"I believe that you are a decent kid . . . man. You're a man, now. What you did, way back when, whoever that was, you're not him anymore. I believe that. And so, my last piece of advice to you is to live apart. Don't hurt anyone, either by action or . . . by just being."

The warden stood and called for the guard. Michael was led out the door and the warden returned to his window. The *wave of nausea he always felt in Michael's presence soon passed and he was now resolved to go off into the sunset to the condo on the coast.*

He had done his duty. He had kept the boy convict safe. His part in the story was done.

SEVENTY-FOUR

MICHAEL LOOKED DECIMATED as he lay on the bed in Melissa's motel room. He was a full-grown man, but Melissa had been able to drag him into her car and into the room without too much effort. He was a stick. Though taller than her, his body felt like a child's. The smell emanating from him was almost unbearable. She didn't know if it was his usual lot in life to be so disgusting, or if it was the days of hiding out in the woods, the added stench of the house fire. Soon the room was thick with the repugnant odor.

He lay on the bed like a corpse in the county morgue. He was hot to the touch, a fever keeping its hold on him. A few times on the drive over from his burned-down house Michael had mumbled incoherently, but he never gained consciousness. This was for the best, according to Melissa. She didn't know what would happen if he woke up and started fighting her.

His leg was bloodied. When she examined it closer, she saw what appeared to be a puncture wound above his knee. Though his pants were covered with blood, it appeared that the wound was healing itself. She could feel heat rising from the scar, as if it was being cauterized by an unseen force. She was not a doctor, but what she saw didn't seem natural.

She kept him tied up. Despite having years to contemplate the idea of exacting revenge on her brother, she soon found herself woefully underprepared. Now, after all these years, here he was. The boogeyman who had killed Marcus.

Her resolve had strengthened again on the drive back.

She walked over and pulled the drapes shut again, not sure if the small crack in between them left an outsider with a full view inside. She walked over to the box, pulled out the gun, and held it in her hand. From across the room she pointed it at Michael.

Melissa's hands had a slight shake to them. She tried and tried, but she couldn't seem to hold the weapon steady. She lowered it, walked up to the bed, and placed the barrel against his forehead. He didn't move, just the slow rise and fall of his rib cage gave proof that he hadn't already expired. She held the gun, her eyes starting to water, and her anger started to rise. She was angry at this stranger in the bed. She was angry at herself. Coming to the brink a second time and finding herself unable to kill him. Her heart raced and her head pounded with trepidation.

From the bed she grabbed a pillow, placed it over his head, and drove the gun into it. She didn't want to look at him when she pulled the trigger. She didn't know if she could live with the image of the violence to be unleashed on his skull. She held the gun in trembling hands.

Her anger quickly turned to shame, shame at herself. Her weakness in not being able to follow through with what she had mentally rehearsed for many years.

She lowered the weapon, dropped it to the floor, and felt the emotional turmoil of all the years flow up inside her and come crashing through. She raised her hands and all the anguish of a lost childhood, a broken family, came pouring out of her and she wept. Her body shook, and as she cried, a feeling in the pit of her stomach began to form. It started as a faint groan and then stirred to a deep nauseous void, threatening to send her heaving to the bathroom.

Melissa reached out her hand and removed the pillow from Michael's face, and flinched when she saw him.

One eye was partially opened and it looked as if he was staring at her. Sizing her up.

She stared back, shell shocked to finally make connection with her brother.

His face was a tapestry of deep colors. Bruising, both old and more recent, covered his face. Healed scars and fresh cuts. As he lay there, his face looked both villainous and peaceful. Melissa stood, frozen, examining every beaten-down pore of his skin. To her utmost surprise, she felt a feeling creep up inside her that she had never before thought to contemplate.

Here was her brother. Her kin. Her childhood companion. A person who had done things and suffered things that she could not possibly fathom. Her anger, her animosity, slowly seeped out of her veins, and what she felt shocked her. She felt sympathy.

She gazed on her brother, actually looked at him in his most vulnerable state, and saw him as he was before he had murdered Marcus. She had not seen him since he was taken out of the courtroom and sent to prison.

She did not know him anymore. The kid she raged against was no longer there. She had no idea who this man was. Was he the same person? Was he different?

"I know you," Michael whispered with the labored pains of a broken man, his voice as one from the grave.

She clasped the pillow to her chest as a shield, and simply nodded.

"I . . . I'm . . ." Michael was moving back to the brink of unconsciousness.

"What?" Melissa asked. The pit in her stomach began to fade.

"I'm . . . sorry." And with that, he was gone again.

Melissa stared at him. She felt empty, hollowed out, as if the burden that had weighed on her heart for as long as she could remember had been lifted off her. Two words breathed into existence a simple thread, a lifeline to guide her back from deep water. To raise her from the pit of sorrow that she had sunk into deeper and deeper since she was a little girl.

She slowly reached down and grabbed the pistol from the floor. The tool suddenly felt foreign to her. Her resolve was shaken. Her determination wiped out. She had lost, and in losing, had freed herself from the bonds of revenge.

Confusion came pouring over her, clouding her mind, and she looked around the room, disoriented, not knowing what to think. This plan had been the guiding star on which she had plotted her course. What now? What was life without this?

Melissa slowly walked across the room and placed the gun back into the box. As she did so, she heard a knock. She turned quickly, expecting to see Michael up and poised to attack her, but he still lay unconscious.

Another knock. It came from the door.

Melissa walked over, composed herself, and with one hand holding the doorknob, she spoke.

"Who is it?"

"It's me, Lila. Can I come in?"

Melissa unfastened the chain lock and cracked the door to shoo Lila away. What she saw wasn't the chain-smoking waitress standing outside but a large, hulking figure filling her line of sight. She stood, frozen, as her mind tried to make sense of what she saw. The door came smashing against her face as the shadow kicked it in. Melissa went crashing to the floor in a daze. She had never been hit before and her body was slow to process the sensation.

"Sorry about that," Haywood said as he stomped into the room.

He grabbed Michael from the bed and dragged him out through the door. Lila came rushing in, yelling at Haywood in some trailer-park dialect of words and phrases that weren't part of Melissa's vocabulary. Lila knelt down beside her.

"Are you okay? I had no idea he was going to do that. No idea. He asked me to come with him to talk to you, that's it. I'm so sorry."

"It's alright," Melissa said as she tried to get to her feet.

"No idea. He's gone crazy. I'm sorry . . ."

"Lila, it's okay."

"Who was that? Who did he drag out of here?"

"Michael."

"Michael? That was Michael?"

"Yes."

The sounds of squealing tires were heard as Haywood's truck pulled out of the parking lot and headed off into the night, with another vehicle close behind.

"I need to know where he is going!" Melissa screamed.

Lila stepped back and held her tongue, an act that seemed both foreign and awkward on her.

"Lila, if you know, tell me. Where are they taking him?"

"Same place. Springer's Grove. I heard Haywood say it again. They're taking him back up to Springer's Grove."

291

SEVENTY-FIVE

HAYWOOD AND THE BOYS, the remaining ones, got out of their vehicles. Springer's Grove was dark, the headlights shone forward like the beam of a grind-house movie theater. Haywood walked to the passenger side and dragged Michael out.

Michael's head was hooded with a black sack, his hands and legs still bound from when his sister had tied him up. Haywood pulled him out of the vehicle and he fell limp to the ground.

Frank and Earl, Clinton and Davis stood back and watched the scene. None of them attempted to help Haywood pull Michael away from the vehicles and down the path to the burial site. They watched him disappear into the dark and then looked at each other, none of them wanting to take the first step down the trail. Eventually it was Clinton who led, and all the men slowly caught up with Haywood.

They arrived at the spot. The hole in the ground.

Haywood dropped Michael next to it and stretched his back.

"Where's the shovel?" Haywood said as he looked at the men. "Where is it?"

None of them responded.

"Forget it," he said, and marched back to the trucks alone.

Four reluctant men, a comatose hostage, a hole in the ground, all left alone waiting for the judge and executioner to come back with a shovel.

"I can't . . . I can't do this again," Earl said.

"He's gone crazy. Absolutely crazy."

"What do we do? He's intent on doing this on his own. He's far past us now."

They all knew the score without saying it. If Michael lived, they all would either go to prison if he chose to talk, or they would live in fear of retribution all their lives. If they went against Haywood, who knew what would happen? He was no longer rational. He was borderline insane, driven to the point of obsession. He would not stop until Michael was dead. He would not allow anyone else to get in his way. Over the course of several days they had watched him take one step over the line, then another, and another, until he was at a point where none of them wanted to be.

"This is a chance," Earl whispered. "This is a chance to do what we should have done the first time. We stop it. We stop this madness. I ain't blaming anyone for dragging me out here the first time. It was on me. It was on us. We weren't thinking. But now, now we are. We know full well what we are doing. We do nothing now . . . then we deserve so much more than what we feel right now."

"Earl's right," Frank offered. "This ain't us. This ain't never been us."

Clinton and Davis looked at each other. "Yeah . . . it ain't."

"Ain't what?" Haywood asked. No one had heard him reappear from the trail, and his presence was masked by the darkness. A voice coming out of the deep dark places of the woods. He was answered by silence.

293

Haywood walked next to the hole in the ground and then handed the shovel to Earl. "Here, start digging."

"No."

"What's that?"

"I said, no. I ain't doing this."

"No? You think you have a choice in this? You think you all aren't up to your necks in this? Here! Dig!"

Earl tried his best not to flinch when Haywood pushed the shovel into him. The tool dropped to the ground in slow motion, a gavel slowly falling in judgment of the group. Earl could feel the nerves firing up inside him, but he held himself together. He wasn't sure if Frank would follow his lead, he was even less sure of Clinton and Davis. But he was sure he was done. His fear filled him to the brim, but he knew that fear would never leave him if he kept following Haywood. He turned and slowly started walking back to the vehicles.

"Hey!" Haywood yelled. "Where do you think you're going?"

Earl took another step.

"I said, where do you think you're going?"

Another gut-wrenching step.

The first blow came as a shock, but his body was trembling so much that it didn't feel like pain but a blunt force pushing into his back. The second one he was more alert for . . . the punch against the side of his head. Haywood was on him in an instant, and Earl tried his best to protect his face with his arms as the punches rained down on him. He could hear Haywood yelling incoherent insults between each strike. The beating seemed to stretch on in time for Earl, the shock wearing off, replaced by pain. The others joined the scrum and managed to pull Haywood off, but he was an enraged bull, kicking and flailing at Earl.

"You're not leaving!" he kept screaming.

The boys could not contain Haywood. They were in disbelief themselves, and the rage coursing through Haywood's body had transformed him into a beast. He was soon out of the grasp of the boys and was heading back to Earl, who lay on the trail trying to get up.

"You are going to finish this, Earl. You going to finish this or I'm going to put you in that grave with him!"

It was then that the dark woods and the sounds of night were pierced by the lightning-bolt crack of a gun. The scene froze. Earl on the ground. Clinton, Davis, and Frank scattered around the clearing, Michael tossed into the leaves and brush, and Haywood's manic form standing in the middle of it all, his chest heaving with deep breaths of fury. The woods fell silent again.

Melissa stepped down the trail, the lantern catching her eyes like a cat's in the dark. In her hand was her Glock, and it was pointed straight at Haywood.

"No," she said calmly. "I'm going to finish this. I'm going to finish this right now."

SEVENTY-SIX

WHAT ARE YOU GOING TO DO? Shoot me? Going to shoot us all?" Haywood asked, his fury not subsiding even with a gun pointed at him.

The rest of the men moved slowly. Frank moved toward Earl and helped him to his feet. The man wobbled and relied on his friend for support. Everyone but Haywood soon found themselves positioned behind Melissa as if she had the sole means of stopping a charging rhino.

The smell of tobacco drifted through the woods and caught Haywood's nose. His eyes narrowed.

"Lila. You brought her out here? Lila!"

"Yeah, I did," Lila said, stepping into the dim light.

"You have no idea. None!" Haywood said. "Do you know what this monster has done? You heard about Kyle. About James. And yet here you bring her out here. You come out here to stop me?"

"The only monster I see out here is standing right in front of me," Lila said as she took another toke, no doubt to calm her nerves. She stepped beside Melissa, who still had the gun outstretched.

Haywood smirked, a sarcastic evil smirk. "You know, boys. We are all in this together. You walk down that trail, you all will have to answer for this. Not just me. All of you. Every single one of you. But right here, we can bury this. We can wipe this stain away."

"No, Haywood. We can't," Frank said. "Ain't nothing we can do but stop. Stop what we're doing and go no further."

The woods fell silent.

"Lila, can you untie Michael?" Melissa said, keeping the weapon trained on Haywood.

The waitress walked over and did as she was asked, wary still of the ex-con comatose in the dirt.

One by one the boys started up the trail. When Lila was done, she turned and helped Frank walk Earl back to the trucks. Clinton and Davis followed until there was just Melissa and Haywood. Michael's slack body gave no evidence that he was aware of the battle that was waging around him. Melissa stepped aside and, with a wave of the gun, ushered Haywood up the trail.

The light from the lantern over the grave soon dimmed behind them as they walked through the woods until the headlights of the vehicles parked in the clearing took over. Haywood and Melissa emerged from the path to find the company standing facing the lights, all lined up, silent. Melissa squinted her eyes and she could see another vehicle had joined the party. Its driver stood in front of the truck, leaning back against the grill.

As she stepped into the clearing, Melissa could feel her stomach flip over and she felt as if at any moment she could bend over and vomit. A throbbing like a low bass sound began quietly in her head and started to increase in pressure at the base of her skull. She looked at the others and could see that they were feeling the same effects, as if they all had just walked into ground zero of a radioactive blast site.

"By my counting, there is someone missing," the man said. "The one I'm here for. Don't tell me he's run off on you again."

The man stepped forward, and when he did, the pressure in Melissa's head deepened.

The man, his face bruised and gashed, took another step and looked over the crowd.

"Now, where's Michael?"

SEVENTY-SEVEN

THIS IS NONE OF YOUR BUSINESS," Haywood said.

Melissa could see he was feeling the same odd physical effects that she was—they all were—but his bluster was not diminished in the least.

"No. I suppose not. Point is, I'm here for Michael. You all are of no interest to me. Feel free to get in your trucks and go, just tell me where he's at and we can all part on good terms."

"And why would we do that?" Haywood asked.

"Just be thankful I'm not looking for you. I don't think you'd want that. Now, no more questions. Where is Michael?"

"He's gone," Melissa spoke up, gritting her teeth as her head throbbed. "Took off. He's never coming back."

"I doubt that, very much."

"Believe what you want."

"I don't need to believe. I know it. I can feel it. Much like you can feel it right now, I suppose," Nick said as he took another step.

He was toying with her, letting Melissa stew in the growing cancer that was his presence. Melissa raised the pistol, this time with absolute certainty. She had pointed the gun at too many people without the grit to do the deed. Now she felt like a caged animal taunted by an aggressor, the only option but to lash out. As soon as her mind was made up, however, her eyes exploded with a flash of pain and she dropped the gun. Falling to her knees she yelled in pain, blood coming from her nose, the pressure in her face feeling like a mask being pulled too tight.

■ ■ ■

Haywood saw his chance, picked up the gun, and positioned himself away from the group, equidistant from his ex-accomplices and Nick. With the headlights behind him, he had a clear view of the scene. Clinton and Davis to the left, Frank and Lila were holding up Earl in the middle. Melissa was on her knees blocking the path into the woods. And Nick, the stranger, was standing aside, staring him down with an iron gaze.

"So what is Michael to you, then?" Haywood asked. "He kill a friend of yours too? You and him partners? An old friend from prison?"

"He's my exit out of this world. I sure hope that you haven't done anything to him."

"Not yet, I haven't. And neither you nor anyone else is going to get in my way again."

Nick held up his hands in a mock gesture of surrender. He gave a soft grin that Haywood could only see half of in the amber beam of the truck light. "Mister, you have no idea what you're messing with. I think this is well beyond your understanding. It would be best if you left. Ain't no telling what strange things might come out tonight."

■ ■ ■

Melissa lifted her head to see Haywood raise the Glock and train it on her. The gun looked so much larger from

300

the other end, as if it held the entirety of her life in its steel frame. She could taste the blood in her mouth as it dripped down her chin onto the dirt. She never imagined this. That she would die in the woods, surrounded by strangers, having tried to protect a brother she did not know but had hated most of her life. Then she felt a hand on her shoulder and the throbbing in her head ceased. She felt it roll back like the outgoing wave at low tide. It was a hand that felt both strange and familiar. A hand reaching out from the past and grabbing her from behind.

Michael.

■ ■ ■

He stepped to his sister's side and helped her to stand. He was wobbly himself, the abuse he had suffered showing in every aspect of his being. He looked across and saw Nick standing in the clearing. He paid no notice to Haywood, even though the gun was trained in his direction.

Nick looked different from the last time he'd seen him on the railroad bridge. Not just beat up from the fight, or whatever damage from the fall, but the bloodlust in his eyes was gone. He looked calm. Collected. Michael felt confused, staring at the man who had tried to kill him. There was something in his eyes, as if he was hiding an ace up his sleeve at the most important poker game of his life.

"I see that you're still alive, Michael. That's good. For a minute I thought my hope was gone. Why don't you come with me and we'll sort this out."

"He ain't going anywhere!" Haywood yelled.

"It's not for you to decide. What are you going to do, shoot him? In cold blood?"

"Haywood," Michael said, exhaustion weakening his voice, "put the gun down. Your friend tried it once . . . Didn't turn out too good for him."

"Morrison . . . ," Haywood said as he waved the gun around. "See, boys, I told you. I told you it was Michael who killed Morrison! I told you all that what we were doing was in the right."

"Come on. Let's go," Nick said quietly as he stepped closer to Michael and grabbed his arm.

"I told you that he would be the death of us all!" Haywood continued.

Michael could feel the darkness in Nick's hands latch on to that part of his soul that had been clouded since he was ten. The part that had been invaded when he took Marcus into the woods and left him lying there dead. His head swam in the darkness and focused solely on Nick, whose eyes shone differently than at any time before. They weren't filled with rage or hopelessness. They weren't the eyes of the killer who had attacked him on the bridge. They were the eyes of an executioner who had suddenly recanted his profession and showered mercy on the headless victims of his work.

"And now we have him here again! Again! This time we owe it to Morrison to not screw it up again!"

Michael and Nick were so focused on each other that neither man, and neither man's dark inhabitor, noticed Haywood raise the pistol at them. They did not even hear the sound when Haywood pulled the trigger and the blast of the gun echoed through the woods.

SEVENTY-EIGHT

THE SHOT RANG OUT and time stood still. Michael was unaware of anyone else in the clearing but Nick, who had ahold of the deepest recesses of his being. He felt Nick move in front of him, felt the thump in his dark adversary's back, the bullet crashing into his spine. Nick fell against him, his weight heavy and sagging, forcing him to the earth, Michael's legs buckling under the unexpected weight. Nick's eyes widened as if realizing some glorious truth and reveling in the experience.

"Mercy. We have found mercy . . . ," Nick whispered, the blood bubbling up in his throat, ". . . in the most unlikely of places . . . I am free. I am finally free."

His eyes rolled back and Nick breathed his last.

Haywood dropped the gun from his hands, the shock and horror on his face spoke louder than words: He had killed a man. Shot him in the back. He had meant to kill Michael, but Nick, this stranger in the woods, had stepped in front of the shot.

He stumbled back, gasping for breath.

Nick's body slid to the ground, and from his skin began to seep a black mist, rising up to the treetops and coalescing above the clearing. Michael could feel a pull in the depths of his soul, as if his body were suddenly turning inside out, the fog releasing from Nick's body sucking the same ghostly ether from him as well. Spiraling upward, the mists took form above their heads. Earl, Frank, Lila, Melissa, Davis, and Clinton—they watched in wonder and terror as the storm cloud, absolute blackness against the night sky, took two distinct shapes, warring above them. The two entities battled for dominance of the sky until one succeeded in swallowing the other. It then hovered there, a being made of dark matter and emanating the absence of all things pure down on the people below. But its black heart was set on one man. Haywood.

■ ■ ■

Haywood looked up and saw with fresh eyes what he had done. Nick had been right. What he was gazing up into right now was beyond his understanding. This demon vapor looked down and came spiraling toward him, relentlessly swarming in an ever-increasing sea of darkness, the mirage pounding into Haywood's flesh, melting into his body, coiling itself around his spine, inhabiting the far reaches of his soul and humanity that Haywood had emptied out in his increasingly vengeful pursuit of Michael. The shot that he had fired, the fatal shot that had struck Nick in the back during his act of selfless sacrifice, carved out a new home for the exiled ghoul and it took up residence in its new home: Haywood.

He screamed.

After all that had happened, he saw the world as Michael had seen it. He felt the guilt, the madness, the total annihilation of his relationship to all those around him. The people standing in front of him were but strangers, never to be

304

friends again. They abhorred him, stood in shock of him, wanted him removed from their sight.

Haywood could feel the protective coils of the cursed angel squeezing at his mind. He hadn't wanted this, none of it, and now he had become that which he had worked so hard to eradicate from Coldwater. He was now a killer, an outcast. He had rushed in madly to that room with no exit and found that he would be forever alone. The overwhelming sensation threw him into the pit of despair, and all he could see was the spiraling black hole where no hope could escape. He was damned, and he had damned himself.

There was no going back. He realized this and raged against it. The gun in his hand, Haywood lifted it to his head. All he wanted was to be set free. To return to a time when he was not alone, but the demon wind told him it would never be. This was now his curse. His new self. Haywood pulled the trigger.

It did not fire.

He pulled again.

And again.

His new inhabitant knew what it was doing. It had lived through this part countless times before. It pressed Haywood's mind into a dark singularity until the blackness overcame him and he collapsed to the ground.

SEVENTY-NINE

SILENCE CREPT IN FROM THE CORNERS of the clearing like floodwaters spilling into a sinkhole. A ring of participants around an open space, in front of them lay the bodies of Haywood and Nick, Haywood unconscious but still breathing, Nick dead to this world but with a serene look on his face, the weight of the years lifted from his shoulders.

The Coldwater people—Clinton, Davis, Frank, Earl, and Lila—looked at Haywood and then at each other and back again in an endless stream of bewilderment. Their eyes had seen what their brains could not process. A vision of hell swirling above their heads and then absorbed by the man they had blindly followed down this demon path. Every horror story they had ever been told manifested in the woods before them.

Clinton looked over at Michael. The man they had pursued, had made the scapegoat for every fear they had, stood near the encroaching forest, his face illuminated by the headlight of one of the trucks. In some subtle way Michael appeared different. His battered and bloody face still showed the evidence of the past several days, and in all likelihood it would for the rest of his life, but something in his eyes shone different.

The boys stood still. They had no idea what was to come next.

Was Haywood just the first to get what was coming to him?

Davis reached into his pocket for his cigarettes. His hands were shaking uncontrollably and it took several attempts to land one in his mouth and get it lit.

Clinton kept staring at Michael.

"Anybody going to say anything?" Earl said, breaking the silence.

Davis looked at him and held up his hands.

Melissa walked over to Haywood and cautiously picked up her pistol.

■ ■ ■

She turned toward Michael.

Any hint of rage was gone from her bearing, evaporated into the night like the satanic mists that had floated before their faces. She moved in the headlights to her car, opened the door, and placed the gun under her seat. She looked at Michael.

"Come on," she whispered, "I'll take you home."

Michael looked down at Nick. His once-future self. The man who had chased him through the north woods and came close to killing him on the viaduct. The man who wrestled with the same demons he had fought with and who had begged him to take them away.

Nick, the man who saved him.

Michael had no idea where the dark companion that had been dragged out of the corner of his soul had gone, but he felt in his heart that it would not be back. It had been evicted. Nick had done that for him—by taking the bullet in the back, by sacrificing himself, by showing that Michael was worth mercy in his last noble action. As he was unable to ask forgiveness of his dead brother, so he was unable to express his gratefulness to Nick for releasing him back into life by his martyrdom.

Then he looked at Haywood, whose prone body lay on the forest floor.

Michael knew what now resided there.

The shadow that had coiled itself around Nick's soul was now setting up house in the vacant spaces that Haywood's anger had cleared out. The demon finding a new home, a new cell, a new place to live out its days in the hollow thoughts of men.

Michael limped to Melissa's car, opened the passenger's door, and slid inside.

He knew the woman sitting next to him.

He knew her when he had walked up behind her in the forest and had placed his hand on her shoulder, as if the cells in his body warmed to the sensation of a similar strain.

They didn't say a word as Melissa backed out of Springer's Grove, the headlights illuminating the faces of the defanged Coldwater vigilantes. They turned around and headed back to Coldwater.

He waited for her to say something.

He waited for her to pull the gun out and place a bullet in his skull.

But she just drove on. Down the two-track, onto the main road.

The silence echoed through the car.

The lights of Gilly's and the diner appeared in the darkness. Melissa brought the car to the stoplight and turned east. She drove past the road to the cemetery. Their brother Marcus, lying quietly now in their taillights.

She turned down the dirt road toward the ashen remains of their childhood home, the embers cooling and giving a soft glow to the dead circle like a scorched bomb blast. She stopped the car in the drive.

And she remained silent.

Michael got out. The heat from the fire now subsided, he could see the trailer in the back, still standing.

The wind through the woods blew the smoke to the heavens, purging the earth of sins gone by. Michael looked back into the car.

Melissa was crying softly.

"I'm sorry. I'm sorry for everything," Michael said.

She nodded but kept her eyes down. Silent.

It would take a while. A lifetime of anger and resentment quickly washed away could not be instantly replaced with a lesser sentiment. The vacuum in his sister's heart would take some time to fill with new feelings, but perhaps this would be the first step to start again.

He closed the door and stood, watching, as she eased the car onto the road and headed south toward a life yet unplanned.

EIGHTY

WHEN THE BOYS WOULD GATHER as elderly men and sip beers at Gilly's like old-timers do at every pub in America, they would tell stories of their grandkids or stories of which new ache and pain they might have been suffering from. They told stories of old jobs, of trips they had taken, of times gone past.

But one story they never told by silent consensus was the story of what happened in the woods that night up by Springer's Grove. Even after years of living and seeing just a sliver of what the world had in it, nothing offered anything close to an explanation of what they saw that night. The gunshot that blasted through the wilderness had opened up the gates of hell and each man had borne witness.

When Kyle returned to their company, wheeled into his spot, they never talked about it.

When Lila and Earl finally got hitched, even they would not talk about it in the confines of their home, their kids none the wiser.

Occasionally they would see a car arrive from South Falls, the woman who appeared that unmentionable weekend. They would see her turn east at the stoplight and disappear into the woods to where a fire once burned an old house to the ground.

But they let the thoughts and memories reside unspoken in their minds.

And when they would see the man walking into town, a hitch in his step from a wound suffered in a story now past, they would hold their tongues and divert their eyes, as if acknowledging what had happened would open up old wounds, old guilt, and old horrors.

EPILOGUE

THE DAY WAS BORN IN DARKNESS.

Haywood opened his eyes and saw nothing.

Blackness.

The motes in his eyes drifted across the void.

He lifted himself from the bed and placed his feet on the concrete slab below him. He stood and walked over to the bars and felt their cold radiance in his palms. Across the space beyond the cage he could see, through the open door, a chair. Its wood withering from age and the memory of electricity scorching the occupants it had held.

The darkness enveloped him.

It resided in him.

The warden had brought Haywood here, to the shed on the edge of the yard. He said it had been used before to hold a special inmate. An inmate that his predecessor had said needed unique accommodations.

To protect himself.

To protect everyone.

Haywood turned and walked over to the bed. Day would come.

Then night.

The cycle would go on, and on, till the end of days.

He lay down, curling on his side as a child had done years before.

Alone. But never alone.

ACKNOWLEDGMENTS

MANY THANKS TO ANDREA, for taking a chance on something different. To the most incredible editor, Barb. To Michele and Hannah, thanks for putting up with me and getting the book into as many people's hands as possible.

To all the family, friends, and old schoolmates who have supported me over the past several years. I could never show enough appreciation for the encouragement you have shown.

And lastly, to Liz. You are always a constant source of support and laughter. Thank you for an incredible life.

Samuel Parker was born in the Michigan boondocks but was raised on a never-ending road trip through the US. Besides writing, he is a process junkie and the ex-guitarist for several metal bands you've never heard of. He lives in West Michigan with his wife and twin sons.

MEET SAMUEL PARKER

SAMUELPARKERBOOKS.COM

 SamuelParkerAuthor   @ParkerSuspense

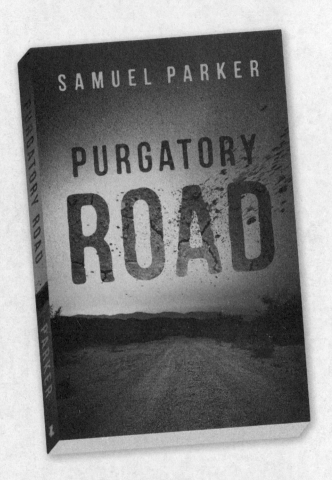